MW01172688

RHONDA BREWER

This book is dedicated to my Mom, who I lost this past year suddenly. She was always my biggest cheerleader and gave me all the love and strength that any daughter could ask for. I miss her with all my heart but know she is always watching over me.

I'd also like to dedicate to my Dad. We both had a great loss this year, but he cheers me on and encourages me to keep following my dream of being an author. I love you with all my heart.

Acknowledgements

There are so many people who made publishing this book possible and saying thank you just doesn't seem enough. First, I want to thank my critique partner Amabel Daniels. As a new author, she supported me and shared her experiences and ideas with me. Next, thank you to fellow author Zoe York for creating the beautiful cover for this book.

I also want to thank the many authors who helped me along the way with advice, experiences and the pep talks to make this possible. Abbie Zanders, Em Petrova, Susan Stoker, Kathleen Brooks, Rhonda Carver, Cynthia D'Alba, and all my fellow Newfoundland Authors from Romancing the Rock, They're amazing authors and amazing people.

To my beta readers, thank you for their time and input. Especially, Jackie Dawe, Michelle Eriksen and Mayas Sanders who have become great friends and are incredible ladies.

Last but certainly not least, thanks to my husband who's encouraged me every day. My children who love and support me every day. Also thank you to my Aunt Gertrude Holwell, who throughout my life has been there for me anytime I need her and has always been like a big sister to me.

Chapter 1

Ian O'Connor let out the huge breath he'd been holding as she popped up on his phone with the word he'd hoped. It was hard for him to build up the confidence he needed to ask her out over the last four years. Although doing it through a text was still cowardly, at least he finally had done it. He'd been called a wimp, a chicken shit, and a bunch of other names by his brothers, names that made him want to throat punch them but they didn't understand how hard it was to trust his heart with another woman. Not that he'd been living like a monk all these years. He just didn't date, but he did have a one night stand now and then. After all, a man had needs, and self-satisfaction didn't always scratch the itch.

The slam of the front door made him jump off the sofa, and hurry to see what was wrong. His brother, James, had left to check on Marina Kelly, their sister-in-law's younger sister. She lived a couple of houses away, and James was head over heels in love with the woman. It was probably the reason he jumped when her young son called saying his mother was screaming.

"God damn it," James growled.

"Whoa there, bro. Are you trying to wake Mason?" James' five-year-old son was asleep, and it would probably take a lot more than a slamming door to wake the kid. James was raising the little boy on his own now since his wife had passed away.

"No." James snapped, as he yanked open the fridge. Ian glanced down at his phone as another text popped up.

Oh, and there will be no dressing up. I only do dresses for weddings. You got that, doc?

Ian chuckled.

"What's so funny?"

"Sandy." Ian shoved his phone into his back pocket because from the look on James' face his brother needed to talk.

"Why the hell don't you just ask her out?" James asked.

"I could ask you the same question." Ian wasn't about to tell anyone he'd taken that big scary step. At least not yet.

"Sandy isn't my type." James pushed at his shoulder, as stomped out of the kitchen. The frustration of being around a woman he was extremely attracted to was hell. Nobody understood that more than Ian.

"Very funny." Ian followed him. "I'm talking about Sandy's cute neighbor, or we could call her John's sister-in-law, or Stephanie's sister, or the woman you've been drooling over for the last four years."

"One, I don't drool over anyone, and two.... well, there's no two, but I don't drool." Ian had meant it figuratively of course.

"Bro, you may not drool, but you do look and who could blame you? Marina Kelly's cute." Ian dropped next to him on the couch. "I'm not the only one who notices. A.J. and Nick couldn't keep their eyes off her at John and Stephanie's anniversary party." He knew that would piss James off. Their two younger brothers wouldn't make a play for Marina since they both knew as well as he did that James was in love with her. Even if James wouldn't admit it.

"They better keep their fucking eyes and hands to themselves. Marina doesn't need their kind of shit." James grumbled.

"Maybe she does." Ian nudged him and was a little shocked when James turned and grabbed him by the shirt.

“I swear to God, Ian if you don’t shut it now I’m gonna pound the piss out of you,” he snapped.

“I’d like to see you try, bro.” Ian narrowed his eyes. He wasn’t worried about it because fist fighting wasn’t something he and his brothers had done since they were teenagers. Well except the fight he had with Nick when Colleen first left, and that was because she’d just about ripped out his heart.

“Go text Sandy,” James mumbled, and Ian chuckled not only to break the tension but to help him cover the pain that still hit him whenever he thought about Colleen Morgan. It wasn’t because he was still in love with her, he wasn’t, but she’d been his best friend before they started dating. When she ran off to Manitoba suddenly with her brother without a reasonable explanation, it almost killed him.

“I’m hitting the hay for the night.” Ian stood up and stretched.

“Yeah... Ok…. Night.” James muttered.

“Ask the woman out, for the love of God.” Ian shook his head as he headed out of the room.

“I could say the same to you, bro.” James glared at him, and Ian had to bite his tongue because he was tempted to tell his older brother that he already had.

After a restless night, he finally gave up trying to sleep. He'd been tossing and turning because it had finally hit him, that he was going to go out with the one woman who made his heart pound and had him tripping over his own feet. She was beautiful, sexy and sassy, but she was also intelligent, and when they talked he could have a real conversation or at least that's the way it seemed by the texts and phone calls. Hopefully, he wouldn't act like a complete moron on their date.

Once he pulled his ass up and out of bed, he yanked on his running gear and headed downstairs. James was slouched over on the couch, and Ian shook his head. He was starting to wonder if James ever slept in his bed. The last couple of nights he'd been staying there, it seemed his brother spent his nights on the couch.

He was thankful that there wasn't a lot of snow yet as he started to run up toward Main road. Hopedale wasn't a big town, and it typically only took him a little over an hour to run all the way around it, but with the hills and valleys it was a good workout, and nothing could beat the scenery.

As he ran by Sandy's house, he slowed but a light over her door flicked on, and he picked up his pace to get out of sight. He was starting to act like a stalker.

By the time, he got back to James' house, his lungs burned from the cold, but he did feel great after a good run. It was a routine he wasn't going to change. Working out had become an obsession since Colleen had left, and even if it did sound shallow, he knew he looked damned good. He'd also put a lot of training in at the dojo in St. John's. His Uncle Kurt had introduced he and his brothers to Karate when they were younger and except for Kurt's daughter Jess only he and his brother Keith had stuck with it.

"Coffee, lots and lots of coffee." Ian entered James's kitchen.

"Good run?" James handed him a cup.

"It's fucking freezing out." Ian sipped from the cup as he pulled off his jacket.

"Nanny's gonna put pepper on your tongue for saying bad words, Unca Ian." His nephew reminded him of his mother threating them for using foul language as kids. Kathleen O'Connor must have kept the same rule with Mason. If any of them cursed, she put pepper on their tongues, but the youngest of the brothers got the most. Apparently, Aaron or A.J. as everyone called him, didn't learn from his mistakes.

"Yeah, Uncle Ian." James chuckled.

"I'm sorry." Ian exaggerated a sigh and tried not to laugh.

“I won’t tell, but don’t say it no more.” Mason stood on the chair next to his father stirring something in a bowl. Ian managed to keep from laughing, but James had to turn away.

“I won’t, buddy,” he put the cup in front of his lips so his nephew wouldn’t see him smiling.

“Daddy, when are you going on a date with Danny’s mommy?” Ian spewed coffee across the table, and James had to catch the bowl from tipping over. Ian kept his head down to hide the smile as he used a paper towel to clean up coffee from the table

“Why would I go on a date with Danny’s mommy?” Probably because he was madly in love with the woman, but Ian kept that little thought to himself.

“Auntie Cora said you and Auntie Marina were gonna go on a date.” Good old Aunt Cora, the family Cupid. Cora was supposed to know when people should be together and she was apparently never wrong. So far, she seemed to be zeroed in on James and Marina even though at John’s wedding she’d told Ian to look for the love of his life a little closer to home.

“You know if Aunt Cora said it then it’s true.” Ian chuckled when James narrowed his eyes at him.

“Maybe we should ask Aunt Cora about Sandy.” James glared, and Ian figured that was his warning to shut up.

“So, where are you goin’ on the date?” Mason asked again.

“I don’t know if we are, buddy. We’ll see.” James looked uncomfortable.

“Nanny Betty says you’re jus’ gun shy.” Mason climbed on his chair. “But you’re not ‘fraid a guns.”

Ian kept his head down to hide his laughing, but his stomach hurt from holding it in. Kids said the funniest things sometimes.

“No Mason, I’m not afraid of guns.” James laughed.

“Nanny’s so silly.” When Mason started eating, he stopped the harassment of his father, and James looked relieved.

Ian finished his coffee and was headed upstairs to shower when his phone vibrated in his pocket. Thinking it was Sandy he pulled it out, but the number appearing on the screen didn’t look familiar.

“Dr. Ian O’Connor.” He received calls frequently from the hospital or the office with questions or requests. When he didn’t recognize the number, he answered it as he always did.

“Hi, Ian.” Something about the female voice was familiar, but he couldn’t place who it was, but it gave him a sinking feeling.

"Hi." He didn't want to be rude so he hoped the caller would give him a hint.

"How've you been?" The caller asked.

"I'm fine thanks. How are you?" He still couldn't figure out who was on the phone.

"You don't know who this is, do you?" The caller asked.

"I'm sorry. No." Ian admitted.

"I guess Jess didn't tell you I was back. It's Colleen." All the air around him seemed to disappear, and he found it hard to catch his breath. "Please don't hang up. I know I'm probably the last person you want to speak to, but I really need to talk to you."

"Go ahead." Ian snapped, as he entered the guest bedroom. He hadn't meant to sound angry, but it was hard to breathe.

"I'd like to meet with you if that's ok." She sounded nervous which wasn't a bit like the Colleen he knew. He didn't want to meet with her since the last time they were face to face she shattered his heart.

"I don't know if I've got time," Ian said.

“Please, Ian. It’s important.” The desperation in her voice was something he really couldn’t ignore, and no matter what happened between them romantically, she was once his best friend.

“Alright.” Ian sighed and flopped down on the bed.

“I’m staying at the Capital Hotel in St. John’s. Room 124. Can you be here around five this evening?” He’d planned on taking Sandy out at seven-thirty, so he could leave the hospital at four, meet with Colleen, and probably be home in time to get ready for his date with Sandy.

“Okay. I’ll be there.” There was a bad feeling in the pit of his stomach, but no matter what had happened this seemed important, and he’d always had trouble saying no to her.

“Thanks, Ian.” She ended the call, and he was left wondering what was so important.

His heart raced as he knocked on the hotel room door later that afternoon. The last thing he wanted to do right now was to see the woman who’d torn out his heart. He was worried how this would affect his budding relationship with Sandy. If he was honest, it terrified him that seeing Colleen would bring back old feelings, and Sandy would get hurt. The click of the lock made his heart thunder in his chest.

"Hi, Ian." She smiled when the door opened, but there was no doubt that she was nervous as well. The worst thing was, she still looked amazing, although he really hadn't wanted her to.

"Hey," was all he could get out. He was pissed with himself because he was still attracted to her.

"Come in." She stepped back, and he reluctantly stepped inside. His eyes zoomed in on the huge bed in the middle of the room, and all he wanted to do was turn tail and run. She wasn't part of his life anymore, and he'd finally taken steps to move on. Now the past was hurling him back where he really didn't want to be.

"Nice room." He looked for someplace to sit that wasn't near the bed.

"Look, Ian, I can see you're uncomfortable, and you have no reason to be. So how about we have a drink and just catch up before we get down to any serious talk." She pulled two beers from the fridge and held one out for him. He wasn't sure he wanted to take it, but the hopeful look in her eyes had him thanking her and twisting the cap off the bottle.

Eight beers later he was still in the room with her and sat on the huge bed propped against the headboard. They'd talked about old times, and he'd filled her in on how his family was doing. She told him about her brother Luke and how his substance abuse issues had probably caused his death. They talked about her other brother Gerry and how she was worried about the group of people he'd become involved with. She talked about being engaged to a great man, and it did sting a little when she told him. Ian didn't mention Sandy, and he'd been ignoring the vibrations on his phone. It was an asshole move, but what was he supposed to say? There was no way he was making his date at that point.

Ian made a quick call to James to let him know he wouldn't be staying there that night. Unfortunately, Colleen started giggling when Ian tripped over her purse and fell on the bed. Ian ended the call and grabbed Colleen to tickle her for laughing at him. He didn't know how it happened, but the next thing he knew was they were kissing, and their clothes had disappeared. He was aware that it was a mistake, but he couldn't help himself. For a second he almost regained his senses and started to pull away but he met her eyes, and she said the words he'd longed to hear from her, so long ago.

"I missed you, Ian. I'm sorry I left." He'd waited for those words for six years, and it was his undoing. Then he was inside her, but he'd be lying if he said it was better than ever before, because it wasn't, and she wasn't Sandy. It was all he needed to prove Colleen was only his past.

His head throbbed, and his stomach was rolling. He grabbed his phone from the bedside table and felt like a complete asshole.

There were eight texts from Sandy. He sat up and read through them and as he got to the last one his heart fell.

I don't know what happened to you last night, but I guess you must've realized we shouldn't do the date thing. It's okay, but you could at least have had the balls to call me and tell me so. You hurt me Ian, and I don't know if I can ever forgive you for this. I know I'll have to see you because of my friendship with your family. All I can ask is that you just not make things harder or uncomfortable. Take care, Ian.

"What the fuck did I do?" Ian pinched the bridge of his nose and sighed. He'd screwed up big time, and he had to make it right. He turned to the other side of the bed but it was empty, and it wasn't until he scanned the room that he realized Colleen wasn't there. Her suitcase and all her things were gone. He jumped out of bed, searched the room for his clothes, and found them folded neatly on the armchair next to the window with a folded piece of paper on top. He snatched it up and began to read.

Ian

I'm so sorry that I didn't have the guts to do this to your face, but I realized after I woke up what a huge mistake we made last night. I'm engaged to a wonderful man, and I love him. We just got carried away, and it was amazing, but it was so wrong. Goodbye,

Ian, I hope you can forgive me, and I hope you have a wonderful life. You deserve it.

Colleen

"You've got to be fucking kidding me!" He balled up the piece of paper and threw it.

He struggled into his clothes, grabbed his keys and then stormed out of the hotel. He needed to get to the gym, and luckily, he always kept his workout gear in the trunk of his car. Pounding on a heavy bag was going to help get these feelings under control.

He'd fucked things up with Sandy now, and for what? A roll in the hay with a woman who broke his heart once before, and left him so broken that it took him six years to move on. Not only had he probably lost the chance for a future with Sandy he'd probably ruined his friendship with her too. Now, what was he going to do?

Chapter 2

Sandy Churchill lay in her bed and wondered why she was disappointed that Ian hadn't shown up for their date. Did she really expect it to happen? Sure, he'd asked her out and deemed it their first date, but something deep down told her it wasn't going to happen. Men like Ian O'Connor had girlfriends that didn't keep secrets, and she'd spent the last four years pining after the sexy doctor. Her friends constantly told her Ian was interested, but it was hard to believe it.

She'd gotten to the point where she could be in the same room with him and talk without her tripping over her words. Over the last few months, they'd texted each other for hours and even flirted, but nothing ever went beyond that. At least not until the other night when he'd said he wanted to take her on a date. She was so excited she jumped up from her chair and almost knocked one of her laptops to the floor.

The previous day she'd spent the whole day picking out the perfect outfit with the help of her sister Kim and best friend,

Stephanie. She'd told Ian she wasn't wearing a dress, but Stephanie had hounded her to wear the tight black dress that Kim had brought for her. She had to admit it looked good on her, and it made her feel powerful and sexy. He said he didn't mind that she didn't want to dress up but she was going to surprise him and blow his mind.

"Guess he wasn't as okay as he said." She wiped away a tear that had slipped from her burning eyes. What the hell was wrong with her? She didn't cry over a man, and she certainly wasn't going to stay in bed and be all depressed over one. Yet, here she was still curled up in the middle of her bed hugging her pillow.

The light from the rising sun began to move across the floor letting her know it was time to get her pathetic ass out of bed and do some work. As a computer analyst for Newfoundland Security Services she got to work from home most of the time, but as a freelance analyst for various police departments in the province, she'd also spend some time working outside of her home. Now the most difficult part of her job was working for someone that happened to be Ian's brother.

Keith was a great boss, and even though most people found him intimidating, she knew the real Keith. He was calm, quiet, and yes, he could be overly serious, but he had a dry sense of humor which he didn't let a lot of people see. There was also sadness in his eyes, but she knew why it was there. For some reason, he hadn't made his family aware of the heartache he'd been through all those years ago. It was heartache for her as well but for different reasons.

She sat on the side of the bed and gazed over the ocean. Her bedroom was her favorite room in the house. Not only was it the biggest, but it had the best view. It was the main reason she'd divided it into her bedroom and home office. She had an incredible view of the Atlantic Ocean no matter where she sat in the room. During late spring and early summer, she'd spend hours watching the whales jumping or enjoy the majestic icebergs that would appear almost every year. They were beautiful, but they certainly put a chill in the air.

The worst thing was, it made it easy to be depressed and work without ever leaving her bedroom. She even kept a mini fridge stocked with drinks and snacks for those days she didn't have time to eat or when she just felt like locking herself away. That was the way she felt, she didn't want to leave the safety of her room.

The first thing she did was check her personal email out of habit. There was an email from her father, and once again it was the only way Stewart Michaels knew how to communicate with any of his kids. Her sister Kim and brother Brad received weekly emails from the man as well, and it was basically the same email addressed to each of them. Even though Kim, Brad, and Sandy had the same father, they had different mothers. Apparently, in his younger years, Stew was a bit of a womanizer and considering he had three children with three different women in less than two years it wouldn't surprise her if there were more siblings they didn't even know.

Sure, he was trying, which was more than he did when her mother was alive. Evelyn Churchill worked two jobs to make sure her daughter had everything she needed. When Sandy was eight, the school told her mother Sandy should be in a school for gifted kids. There was a school in Ontario, but it was expensive, and her mom couldn't pay for it. It ripped her mother apart to contact Stew, but she did to see if he'd be willing to help. The response she got was a letter telling her to take him to court.

Her mother never contacted him again and worked herself into an early grave trying to ensure Sandy got the education she needed. Individual teachers were hired and by the time Sandy was fourteen she'd completed the high school curriculum and started university through correspondence. It was lonely, and she didn't have a lot of friends, but she had her mom, and that was all she thought she ever needed.

Sandy had completed her masters in computer science by the time she was twenty-one, and although she loved working with computers, she also wanted to help people. She'd entered the police academy and graduated at the top of her class. When her superiors found out her background, she was recruited to be an analyst for the department. Then she was offered freelance work from other government departments.

When her mother passed away, she went a little wild and moved to Yellowknife. It was when she met Keith, and her life changed.

Sandy spent most of the morning researching some potential clients for Keith. She'd just completed a search as she sat back in her chair and stretched her arms over her head. The shrill ringing of her cell phone startled her making her almost tip over in her chair. Once she steadied herself, she pushed over next to her bed and snatched the phone off her nightstand.

Fuck!

Ian's picture flashed on the screen. She wanted to answer it and give him a piece of her mind, but she knew the minute she heard his voice she'd melt. She held the phone against her chest until it stopped ringing. She closed her eyes to ease the burning of the tears and swallowed the lump forming in her throat. She took a couple of deep breaths to compose herself. Then her phone beeped telling her a text had just come in. It was from Ian.

Sandy, I'm so fucking sorry about last night. I know there's nothing I can say that will make standing you up alright but I fucked up, and I want to make it up to you. Please call me or text me. The only excuse I have is I'm a stupid ass who needs to learn how to say no. I'll be waiting to hear from you.

What was she going to do? The voice in her head was telling her to forget about him because he was way out of her league, but her heart was telling her to text him. She tossed her phone on the bed and headed to the ensuite off of her room. Maybe after a hot shower, she'd be able to work out her confusion.

The hot water running over her tense muscles felt like heaven, and she almost didn't want to get out from under the spray. She finally turned off the water as it started to cool and opened the shower door. As she grabbed the towel from the rack, she caught a glimpse of herself in the full-length mirror on the back of the bathroom door.

Her hand smoothed across her lower abdomen and the tattoo that covered it from one hip to the other. Three large black butterflies with two roses next to each one. It wasn't only a tribute to three people she loved and lost, but it covered physical scars and emotional ones as well. She turned around and saw the three small butterflies on her lower back that also covered physical scars. Very few people knew about those scars.

She walked out of her bathroom to the sound of her phone ringing again. She wasn't sure if it was Ian, or if she should ignore his call again. Her curiosity got the best of her. She flopped on the bed, and the picture on the screen made her heart hurt. It wasn't him.

"Hey, Steph." Stephanie was one of her best friends, and as luck would have it, she was also married to one of Ian's older brothers, John. No matter what she just couldn't get out of the circle of the O'Connor family.

"Are you okay?" Stephanie sounded panicked.

"I'm fine. Why?" Sandy tapped the speaker on her phone while she got dressed.

"Ian's been trying to get in touch with you, and he called me to see if I'd heard from you." Her friend was checking up on the pathetic woman who'd been stood up.

"I've been working, and I just got out of the shower." It wasn't a lie because she had been working but she'd just been ignoring his calls and texts.

"He said you were probably pissed at him." Stephanie sighed. "What did he do?"

"It's nothing Steph. Something came up last night, and he had to cancel." She wasn't admitting he stood her up.

"And let me guess, the arse didn't call and tell you." By the tone of Stephanie's voice, Ian was probably going to be getting an angry call from his sister-in-law.

“It’s fine Steph. Let’s just leave it at that.” Sandy pulled her still damp hair into a messy bun on top of her head. “Listen, I don’t mean to cut you off, but I’ve got some more work to get done, and you’re supposed to be enjoying your vacation. Aren’t you in Hawaii right now?” Stephanie and John had been trying to have a baby and weren’t having any luck. The doctors had told them that stress could make getting pregnant difficult sometimes. That was when they planned a three-week vacation to Hawaii to relax. She couldn’t believe Ian would call them while they were on holidays.

“Yes, and John is in the shower that’s why I called. I also wanted to thank you for calling the police when you saw Marina’s door open last night.” Stephanie’s sister Marina lived in the house next door, and when Sandy arrived home last night, she’d noticed Marina’s front door open, and Marina’s car wasn’t in the driveway. It turned out that someone had broken in and destroyed everything. Luckily James, another of the O’Connor brothers, had given her a place to stay while the police looked into the crime.

“I’m glad she didn’t come home to face that alone,” Sandy admitted.

“Me too. Well, I’m going to run but if you need to talk, call Marina or me. I’m sure she could use a distraction now.” Stephanie said.

"Don't worry about me. You go get pregnant." Sandy chuckled.

"I'm trying, damn it." Stephanie laughed. "Love you. I'll talk to you soon."

"Love you too." Sandy ended the call and sighed.

The only thing that was going to make her feel better was immersing herself in work, and that wasn't going to be a problem because she'd received several requests for freelance research, plus her work with Keith. She'd also been asked by the local division of the Newfoundland Police Department if she'd be willing to work in the field a couple of nights if they were short staffed. Since the local unit just dealt mostly with the small town of Hopedale, she didn't see it being a problem, and it would be good to get out working in the field again. Since everyone had discovered her aptitude for computers, she spent most of her time behind a desk. She'd give Kurt a call and let him know it would be a go.

Kurt O'Connor was the superintendent of the Hopedale unit of Newfoundland Police Department. He was also Ian's Uncle, and he wasn't the only O'Connor to work with the department. Ian's two older brothers John and James were police officers as well as his youngest brother Aaron. There were seven brothers in all. Mike and Nick were both lawyers. It seemed like the town of Hopedale was overrun with O'Connors, but the truth was she liked the whole bunch of them.

So even though she'd probably end up running into Ian from time to time, the thought of leaving the small town never entered her mind. She'd miss it terribly, and no matter how painful it might be to run into him she couldn't see herself living anywhere else. Besides, before she knew it, the pain would lessen because her heart felt ripped from her chest. Time always cured a broken heart. Right?

Chapter 3

Eighteen months later....

Thank fuck the twelve-hour shift was almost over with only three more hours to go. Ian loved being a doctor, but on nights like this, throwing in the towel and joining his father's private practice full time was looking better and better. It would be dull, though because he craved the rush of the emergency department, but if he heard one more person ask if his diagnosis was correct, he'd probably have to punch someone.

"Another day in a lousy life." Ian yanked open the door of his jeep and pulled his tired body inside. He dropped his head back against the rest, closed his eyes and growled. "What the fuck is wrong with me?" Even as he mumbled the question, he knew the answer. Hangover. Too much drinking at Aaron's birthday party the previous night and of course knowing the issue and fixing it were two different things. "Why the hell didn't I listen to Sandy?"

He smiled as he said her name because they'd finally got back where they were before he fucked up everything. Since he'd bought the house next door to her from his sister-in-law, he and Sandy spent warm evenings on his back deck talking and enjoying each other's company or on colder nights in her sunroom at the back of her house.

She'd declined the invite to the party because she was working, even though Keith was her boss and told her to go. She didn't. She did catch him as he was leaving and told him not to drink too much.

"Ian O'Connor, don't you let those younger brothers of yours get you plastered." She called out from her front door as he was heading out to Aaron's car. "You know those three are nothing but trouble." She shook her finger at him, and her beautiful mouth turned up into a smile.

"Hey now! That's not nice." Aaron shouted back at her and gave her the pout that got him into more women's panties than Ian could count. "I thought you loved me, sexy." Aaron continued.

"A.J. when are you gonna learn that little pout only works on girls with big boobs and no brains?" Sandy chuckled, and Ian rolled his eyes when Aaron slapped his hand over his chest and grunted as if she punched him.

"Sandy, baby, that really hurt," Aaron called back to her.

Ian's jaw clenched. It shouldn't bother him Aaron flirted with Sandy because it was like a sickness with the asshole. Most of the time it meant nothing.

Ian wanted to ask her out again, but the fear of screwing up again kept him from asking. He hated himself for standing her up but mostly for being so stupid. He hadn't told Sandy what happened, but he had a feeling she knew.

The timer on his watch buzzed letting him know his fifteen-minute break was over. Not that doctors ever got full breaks, but when the emergency room slowed down, it was the best time to take a breather. As he was shoving his phone back into his pocket, it began to play the song 'Bad to the Bone.' It was the ring tone he set for Aaron. He didn't need his brother's annoying teasing over how drunk Ian had gotten at the party. So drunk, their oldest brother, John had to carry Ian into the house practically. His finger hovered over the ignore button, but if he did that Aaron would keep calling until he answered.

"I'm not in the fucking mood for your shit A.J. so…."

"Ian, thank God you answered. I needed to give you a heads up." Aaron sounded panicked, and that wasn't like him at all.

"Heads up on what? What's wrong?" Ian sat straight up in the seat.

“Don’t panic, but we were on duty tonight, and well to make a long story short the suspect tried to take off but….”

“For fuck sake, A. J. spit it out.” Ian’s heart pounded because, including Aaron, four of his brothers were police officers. John and James were inspectors, Aaron was a sergeant and Nick had just graduated from the academy. Then there was his Uncle Kurt who was the superintendent.

“Ian, Sandy was struck by the guy’s car, and the ambulance has her on the way to the emerg,” Aaron explained. It was as if someone punched him straight in the gut. “Bro, I know how you feel about her, so I wanted to warn you before the ambulance just showed up with her.”

“What the hell was she doing out there?” Ian snapped as he jumped out of his jeep and jogged toward the emergency doors. “She’s supposed to be behind a desk not out chasing fucking assholes. She’s the computer guru.”

“She’s also a cop, Ian and she fills in from time to time,” Aaron said. “Look, bro, I know you’re working, and you’re not supposed to give out info but come on this is Sandy. She’s like part of the family. Anyway, we’re on the way back to the station to put out an All Points for the dick head, and then we’re heading to the hospital. Just keep us up to date.” Ian grunted a response and ended the call.

He was halfway across the parking lot when he heard the ambulance coming around to the entrance. His legs felt like jelly as he ran toward the door. He wanted to know just how bad this one was. He made it to the door just as they paramedics were jumping out.

"What have you got?" Ian tried to sound like he always did but his hands were shaking.

"Sandy Churchill, thirty-year-old police officer. Hit and run. Unconscious and non-responsive. Pupils are dilating, but she's not responding to any painful stimulant." Ian didn't want to hear any more. They pulled the gurney out of the back, and he saw her face. Dried blood covered her forehead, her right eye was swollen shut, and there was dried blood around her nose and mouth. He gasped and stepped back from the gurney.

"Dr. O'Connor, are you okay?" Ian turned at the sound of the voice. One of the nurses stood behind him as Sandy was wheeled in through the doors.

"Fine. Get this woman to triage." Ian snapped, but as he was about to follow his stomach lurched and he ran for the garbage can next to the entrance. He heaved up everything in his stomach, and he knew why he was sick. It had nothing to do with the hangover, but it probably wasn't helping. This happened every time someone he cared about was hurt or worse. It happened when his grandfather passed, when John almost died in a car accident, when James' first wife lost her battle with cancer, and when Colleen left. Seeing Sandy in such bad shape was all he needed for it to happen again.

"Don't you fucking take her before I get the chance to tell her how I feel," Ian mumbled, as he wiped his mouth with his sleeve. He wasn't speaking to anyone or at least not anyone visible. He'd never survive if she didn't make it.

Chapter 4

"I've got every right to be in this room." A familiar male voice bellowed, but she couldn't quite figure out who it was.

"Look, old man, she may be your daughter but when have you ever given a shit about anyone but yourself?" Another male voice but she knew that voice.

"Dad, please just leave." She knew that voice too because she'd heard that voice for a lot longer than the other two.

"I'm not moving from this room until I know exactly how my daughter is." Now she knew who it was. Stewart Michaels, her father or as her brother referred to him, the sperm donor.

The arguing continued, but she didn't pay attention to it since she was concentrating on getting her eyes to open. It was hard, but as the first flicker of light entered, she slammed them shut again. The brightness was painful, and she groaned.

"She's waking up," Kim said. "Brad, go get the nurse."

Her brother was the one yelling at her father, but that wasn't anything new. She opened her eyes again, and at first, everything was fuzzy. It wasn't as bright either. It looked like Kim had turned down the lights.

"Sandy, it's ok. You're gonna be fine." Several blinks and her sister started to come into focus. Her eyes were red making it obvious she'd been crying.

"Of course, she's going to be fine." Sandy turned her head slowly toward her father's voice. What the hell was he doing here anyway? "She's from good stock or at least on my side." Really? He was going to downgrade her mother. Now.

"Dad, please stop." Kim sighed. He always did this.

Ian's grandmother once told her that her father did it because deep down he knew he wasn't half the parent Evelyn was, and it was his way of trying to build up his ego. Even if it was true, Sandy didn't like it.

"Kimberly, don't tell me what to do. I'm just saying my genes gave you kids the strength to get through tough times."

"Old man, if I hear you say one more word against Sandy's mother or ours for that matter the only thing you're gonna find out is how hard my fist feels against your face." Brad hated their father and made no bones about how much. Brad stood next to the bed and took Sandy's hand.

"See there's your mother's side." Stewart spat.

"You fucking asshole. My mother worked two fucking jobs to support me and put me through school with no fucking help from you." Brad's face was blood red, and Sandy squeezed his hand. When it came to their father, he could never control his temper.

"I offered your mother money and a house, but she didn't want it unless I married her." Stewart's face was as red as Brad's was. It seemed her brother had inherited their father's temper.

"Imagine that. Wanting the father of her child to marry her." Brad growled through his teeth. "I know it's not a fucking concept you'd understand, but some men do step up to the plate with the mothers of their children instead of going right out and knocking up another woman."

"Stop!" Sandy tried to yell, but it came out more of a raspy whisper. They didn't hear her because they were yelling. Kim had moved in front of Brad to stop him from lunging at Stewart. She cleared her throat and before she had a chance to open her mouth the door to her room slammed open.

"What the hell is going on in here?" The deep soothing voice made her heart thud against her chest. "You do realize you're in a hospital? This may be a private room but it isn't sound proof, and people can hear you through the entire floor."

Ian.

"I'm sorry, Ian." Kim kept her position between Stewart and Brad.

"You don't have to apologize, Kim. It wasn't your voice I heard coming down the hall." Ian's voice was firm and sexy as hell. "You do realize Sandy was hurt last night and the last thing she needs is this racket?"

"Young man, I don't know who you think you are, but this is none of your business. Do you have any idea who I am?" It was the tone Stewart used when he was trying to intimidate people, and Sandy couldn't help but smile because her father was about to get an earful.

"First of all, Mr. Michaels, it is my business when people are disturbing my patients. Also, it is my business when you're also disturbing my dearest and closest friend." Sandy could finally see him as he walked between her brother and father. He was beautiful stood over her father like an avenging angel, and all she could do was stare. "Oh, and I'm aware of who you are Mr. Michaels, and with all due respect I don't give a flying fuck." She stifled a laugh when her father's jaw dropped open. "Now visiting hours are over, and if you would like I can have you escorted, I suggest you leave and don't return until you've learned how to control your behavior." Her father didn't move, but she wasn't sure if it was because of defiance or if he was just in a state of shock that someone would dare speak to him the way Ian had.

"What about them?" Stewart finally spoke, and it was the first time she'd heard a quiver in his voice.

"We're leaving too, Ian, but I'm just going to say bye to Sandy." Kim smiled and walked next to her bed. She leaned down and whispered in Sandy's ear. "That man is so damn hot." She giggled, as she kissed Sandy's cheek.

"I'll see you tomorrow." Sandy smiled.

"Ian, I'm sorry. I didn't mean to disturb anyone. It's just when I'm around him…." Brad stopped.

"I know, Brad, but in the future, if both of you can't be in the same room together then you should probably wait until he isn't here." Ian squeezed Brad's shoulder. Ian was aware of the tension between Brad and her father. Sandy had told Ian all about the strained relationship.

"I'll see you later, honey. Get better." Brad walked next to the bed and kissed her cheek and then followed Kim out of the room without a glance back at Stewart.

"Good night, Mr. Michaels." Ian held open the door, and her father actually took the hint. He nodded toward Sandy and sauntered out of the room.

"Are you okay?" Ian pulled a chair next to her bed.

"Well my head hurts, I can't see out of one eye, and I feel like a truck hit me." She smiled when Ian laughed at her comment. "Okay, so it was a car, but it still hurt and other than being utterly humiliated that you had to come in to tell my father and brother to be quiet, I'd say I'm on top of the world."

"I hope you didn't mind me kicking them out?" Ian took her hand, and the warmth radiated up her arm and through her entire aching body.

"Hell no. I was trying to get someone's attention, but my throat feels like I swallowed a knife. Which reminds me, I'd be your best friend if you'd get me a glass of water." She smiled but winced, when pain jolted through her cheek.

"That's gonna be a little tender for a while." Ian gave Sandy a small paper cup filled with cold water.

"I guess I shouldn't be trying to stop cars with my face, huh?" She joked and after she gulped down the water.

“If you’d stayed behind the computers like you’re supposed to, that wouldn’t have happened.” He crossed his arms over his massive chest and glared at her.

“You know computers are dangerous too. Just the other day I tripped over a cord and almost went face first into the wall.” Sandy waved the cup in front of him, and he filled it again.

“It’s not funny, Sandy. You scared the shit out of my family and me.” He sat on the edge of her bed and took her hand in both of his. Why couldn’t she tell him how she felt? How the best part of her day was spending time with him? She’d forgiven him a long time ago for standing her up because since he moved next door to her, they’d spent almost every evening together.

“I’m sorry.” She slid her hand out of his because it felt too good.

“Stephanie and Marina said they want Uncle Kurt to suspend all the officers that allowed the guy to escape and hit you.” Ian shoved his hands into his front pockets. “They also gave A.J. an earful because apparently, he shouldn’t have let you get hurt.” Ian chuckled.

“Poor A.J. It really wasn’t his fault.” She felt sorry Aaron was getting shit because of her error in judgment. She’d jumped out of the car before the other cruiser had been in place in front of the guy's car and he took off clipping her with the corner of the front bumper. Most of the injuries were from her hitting the ground.

"I'm sure A.J. is taking it all in stride. Nothing bothers him." Ian smiled, and it was an amazing smile. He was different than any other guy she dated because of his mild and even temperament. Ian was a wall of solid muscle, but that was because he worked out at least a couple of hours a day. From the bits and pieces, she got from his family, he'd thrown himself into working out when his ex-girlfriend left him. It was his way of dealing with the pain, and he'd said once it was better than drowning himself in a bottle.

"I guess you're right." She met his bright blue eyes, and it became hard to breathe. It happened every time she stared into blue pools. There'd been a few times where she thought he'd kiss her, but he always backed away. Sandy knew she was in love with him, but couldn't tell him, and it scared her to death that maybe someday he'd find someone else, and she'd lose him forever.

She closed her eyes to keep the hot tears from falling. Just the thought of Ian with someone else was heartbreaking to her.

"Whoa." He cupped her face in his hands. "What's with the tears?" She opened her eyes and covered his hands with hers. His eyes searched hers, and for a second she thought about telling him exactly what was wrong.

"It's just been a long couple of days and the fight with Brad and my father, it's just getting to me." She lied because she couldn't make herself tell him the truth.

"Are you sure, because if you're in pain, I can get the nurse to give you something?" He stood up and pulled his hands away from her.

"No. I hate that stuff. It makes me feel all loopy." She moaned, and Ian chuckled as he sat back down next to her.

"It's pretty potent." He pushed one of her stray curls behind her ear. "Last night was one of the most frightening nights I spent in the ER." He ran his thumb down her cheek, and she held her breath. "When A.J. called and said you were hurt…." He cupped her cheek and leaned toward her. "Don't ever do that to me again." He whispered as he moved closer and her eyes closed. The slight brush of his lips against hers had her heart beating a mile a minute.

"Ian." She breathed.

"I can't take this anymore, Sandy," Ian whispered. His hand slid behind her head, and his mouth covered hers. Dear God, he was kissing her or was she dreaming?

Chapter 5

What the hell was he doing? The woman was recovering from being hit by a car, and here he was devouring her mouth, but damn, she tasted good. He needed to stop before he lost his mind completely, but when he pulled away, she grabbed the front of his shirt and held him close, so their faces were only inches apart. Her eyes were still closed, and he ran his thumb across her bottom lip.

“Sandy, look at me.” He whispered. Her eyes opened, and he smiled. “Say something.” She stared into his eyes.

“You waited until I look like I went a couple of rounds with Mike Tyson, to kiss me.” She sighed.

“You’re still the most beautiful woman in the world to me.” He brushed his knuckle against her cheek.

“You really need to get those eyes checked, doc.” She smiled.

“No, I don’t, but I do want to ask you something.”

"What's that?" She ran her hand across his cheek.

"How do you feel about me, Sandy?" He needed to know that it wasn't just him and kissing her only made him fall even deeper in love with her.

"I'm scared to say it out loud. I don't want to lose you as a friend. Next to Stephanie, you're the best friend I've ever had."

"Don't be scared, Churchie." He called her by the nickname he gave her when she started calling him Doc. "No matter what you say to me, I'll never let anything ruin our friendship. I'll tell you a little secret. My brothers think they're my best friends, but the truth is you took that spot a long time ago." She smiled. "But the feelings I have for you are much deeper than friendship." Her sweet little mouth dropped open, and he chuckled as he put his finger under her chin and closed it. "I've been in love with you for so long that it feels like forever."

"You love me?" She squeaked.

"I should've told you long ago, but when things got fucked up with that date, I thought I'd lost my chance."

"You love me?" She said again, and this time a tear ran down her cheek.

“Yes, I love you, Sandy Churchill and I swear if you give us a chance I won’t fuck it up this time.” Ian cupped her face in his hands and brushed his lips against hers.

“I love you, too.” She sobbed as he stared into her glistening eyes.

“When you get out of here we’re going to take a second stab at that first date.” Ian smiled.

“It shouldn’t be too awkward since we already got the first kiss out of the way.” She giggled.

“You’re right, but right now you need to get some rest.” He kissed her cheek, and she lay back on the bed. Ian pulled the blanket up over her and stood up next to the bed. “Close your eyes, beautiful, and sleep. If all your tests are okay, you should be able to go home tomorrow.”

“You think so?” She covered her mouth to hide a yawn.

“I know so. I got an inside scoop with your doctor.” Ian winked, and she smiled.

“You know I’ve got a really sexy doctor.” She turned on her side and tucked her hands under her cheek.

"Is that so? Well, your doctor has a very sexy patient." Ian crouched down, crossed his hands on the bed and rested his chin on his hands, so his eyes were level with hers.

"You do love me?" Her eyes fluttered closed.

"Yes, sweetheart. I do love you. Now sleep." Ian watched her for a few minutes until her breathing became deep and even. Even with the swollen eye and the scratches on her face, she was still the most beautiful woman he'd ever seen and finally telling her how he felt was like he'd lifted the weight of the world off his shoulders. Of course, knowing she felt the same way made things a whole lot better.

The next morning, Ian won the argument with Stephanie over who was bringing Sandy home from the hospital. His sister-in-law gave him hell about waiting so long to open up to Sandy, but she was excited that he'd finally told her.

"You better not screw this up this time." Stephanie followed him to his car with her eight-month-old baby girl on her hip. Olivia was the spitting image of her mother, but of course, she had the O'Connor blue eyes and dimples. She giggled at Ian when he tickled her.

"I'm not going to make that mistake again." Ian kissed Stephanie's cheek. "What the hell are you feeding this kid. She's growing like a weed."

"I know, but she's isn't as big as her cousin." Stephanie chuckled referring to James and Marina's baby boy. He was two weeks older than Olivia, but baby Colin was the size of a two-year-old.

"I don't know how Marina carries that kid around." Ian chuckled.

"Wait a minute! Don't change the subject, Ian O'Connor. I mean it, if you hurt Sandy again, I don't care what type of belt you have in Karate I'll beat you to death with it. Got me?" Stephanie poked him in the chest once for every word. If she weren't such a tiny little thing, he'd be a little scared.

"I won't hurt her, Steph. I love her." Ian met her eyes, and she stared at him for a moment, but she must have seen something because she smiled.

"Well, don't make her wait any longer go get her and bring her home." Stephanie motioned to the jeep.

The whole drive back from the hospital Sandy was quiet, and it made him a little uneasy. She'd seemed happy to see him when he picked her up, but once they were on the road back to Hopedale, her expression changed. Maybe she was having doubts, but he hoped not because it would gut him.

“Are you okay?” He broke the silence as they reached the halfway point back home.

“I'm fine.” She sighed, and she turned to look at him.

“You’ve been quiet.” Ian glanced at her.

“Sorry. My father called just before you got there and wanted me to.... No demanded that I stay with him until I was well. I told him I was going back home, and he proceeded to do what he always does and make fun of people who live in small communities, and how a daughter of his shouldn’t be living around such common people.” She took a deep breath. “I’ve been dealing with that type of attitude from him since I finally gave in and agreed to a relationship with him.”

“Don’t let him get to you, sweetheart.” He’d heard stories of Stewart Michaels. He was one of the best lawyers in the province, and for the most part, he gave the appearance of being a nice person, but he did have a reputation of looking down on blue collar people.

“I know it just pisses me off because he downgrades people like me, Brad and Kim.” She sighed. “It’s like he’s looking down on us and it pisses me off.”

“Well, how about we get you home and I’ll cook supper, and we can forget all about him for tonight.” Ian turned off the highway onto the road leading to Hopedale.

“Sounds like heaven.” She smiled as he took her hand and brought it to his lips.

It took a little convincing, but he did convince her to stay with him for a couple of days because of the concussion. Once he’d brought her into her house to get a few things she needed they had a heated discussion over her sleeping in his bed. She didn’t want to kick him out of his own bed and have him sleep on the couch. He didn’t want to sleep there either, but he couldn’t sleep in the same bed with her and not want to make up for lost time.

As he was getting ready to start supper, his front door opened, and he groaned. He really should have expected it because it never failed, when someone was sick or hurt his grandmother was the first one to show up with food. Nanny Betty was his father’s mother, and although she wasn’t quite five feet tall, everyone in the family knew better than to get in her way.

“Inky, come take dees containers so I can see how our girl is doin’.” Nanny Betty stood inside the door holding two bags. It wasn’t the fact that she was there, it was the fact she used his nickname. He hated it, and no matter how much he complained to his family, his grandmother still called him Inky.

“Nan, you didn’t have to do this. I was about to cook supper.” Ian grabbed the two bags and brought them into the kitchen.

“Ya need ta be concentratin’ on takin’ care of our lass here not in da kitchen cookin’.” She pulled off her coat and hung it on the hook. Ian inwardly cringed because that meant Nanny Betty wasn’t leaving anytime soon.

“Hi, Mrs. O’Connor.” Sandy was obviously trying to stifle a giggle.

“Mrs. O’Connor was me mudder-in-law, and she was a cranky old witch. Ya, call me Nan.” Nanny Betty bent over and tucked the small throw blanket around Sandy’s legs. “How are ya feelin’, dear?”

Sandy glanced at Ian as he braced his shoulder against the door jam. He shrugged his shoulders because he was no longer in control while Nanny Betty was in the house.

“I’m a little sore, but I’ll be fine.” Sandy smiled at his grandmother, and his heart melted.

“Well, a course ya will because ya’ve got one a da best doctors in da world lookin’ after ya.” Nanny Betty sat next to her on the couch, and her small hand felt Sandy’s forehead. “I brought enough food fer a couple a’ days fer both of ye so Inky can concentrate on ya." Ian closed his eyes and shook his head. The woman was never going to stop using that name.

"Oh, I'm sure Inky will take good care of me, Nan." Sandy chuckled, and Ian narrowed his eyes at her. If she thought she was going to get away with calling him that she had another thing coming.

After a discussion on why Nanny Betty was quite capable of walking home on her own, he walked his grandmother to the door. She'd given him specific instructions on how the food in the containers needed to be stored and heated, he walked back into the living room and caught Sandy with her hand over her mouth laughing.

"Don't even think about it." Ian pointed his finger at her. "It's not funny."

"I'm sorry." She said, trying to hold back a giggle.

"I've been trying to get the family to forget that stupid nickname." Ian groaned.

"I think it's cute, Inky." Sandy giggled again.

"Keep it up, woman, and I'll take you over my knee," Ian warned.

"Promises, promises." She teased, and it went right to his dick.

"Don't tempt me." Ian stalked over to where she sat on the couch and brought his face inches from hers. "Because, baby, I've been waiting a long time and my willpower is at its breaking point." When she gasped, he knew she got his meaning. He brushed his lips against her slightly open mouth and ran his tongue across her lower lip. "I hope you heal fast." He winked as he stood up.

"I think I may be feeling a lot better." She smiled making him laugh. She may be feeling better, but she certainly wasn't well enough for what he had in mind.

"I'm going to get some supper for us." He pressed the remote control into her hand. "Find something for us to watch."

"You know that you can be really bossy." Sandy rolled her eyes and flicked on the television.

He'd figured out a long time ago she always had to have the last word. If they were texting, he'd always end the conversation with the phrase *'in the am'* and she would text back the letter *k*. He tested her a couple of times and would text a k back to her and sure enough, she'd text another back. It always made him chuckle to see the k.

When he returned to the living room, she was curled up on the couch with her hands under her cheek and her eyes closed. He stood watching her while holding two plates with turkey, ham and a couple of different salads in one hand and two bottles of water in the other.

The swelling in her eye was gone down a lot, but it could have been so much worse. Her brown curly hair hung over her shoulder tied with one of those stretchy elastic things women always had. When he'd first met her, she had her hair a lot shorter, but he really liked it longer.

"Are you just going to stand there and stare or are you going to feed me?" She said without moving or opening her eyes.

"I thought you'd fallen asleep on me." He placed the bottles and the plates on the coffee table and pulled it closer to the couch.

"No, I was just weak with hunger." She slowly sat up and flinched. She was obviously still stiff and sore, but she was a stubborn one and wouldn't take anything for it.

"You're not going to be a good patient, are you?" Ian put a pillow behind her back so she'd be more comfortable.

"Nope." She grabbed a piece of turkey off the plate and took a bite, and all he could do was shake his head.

Chapter 6

Sandy stepped out of the shower and wrapped herself in the big fluffy towel that hung on the door. The car hit her eight days ago, and she was finally able to move around without everything hurting. The bruises on her body were fading and turning yellow as they healed.

She leaned over the bathroom vanity and checked her reflection in the mirror. The faded bruise on her face could cover with a bit of concealer and foundation. Not that she wore a lot of makeup, but she knew if she had to cover it she could.

She was glad to be back in her own house, but she missed Ian because the six days she'd spent at his house had been both enjoyable and frustrating. Wonderful, because he treated her like a princess and waited on her hand and foot. The last day it was starting to get on her nerves, but she was still grateful that he'd helped her. The frustrating part was that he'd kiss her but kept her at a distance because of her injuries. He was weary of her going back home. Ian worried she'd over do it, but Sandy knew she fine.

She walked into her room and pulled on her favorite jeans and tank top. It was her usual attire when she was working from home. As she started up her computers to check her email and see if she'd gotten any her phone beeped with a message. She grabbed the phone from the desk and chuckled as she read the text from Ian.

I'm here at the hospital. I don't have any patients that are as cute as the one I've been caring for the last few days, but regretfully she's left and has gone back to her home. It makes me sad that I don't get to see her beautiful face in the morning.

She held the phone away from her and smiled as she took a picture.

Here you go. Now all you need to do is look at your phone in the morning.

Thanks, I have it as the wallpaper on my phone.

You're crazy.

About you. I'll see you in a couple of hours. I'm only on eight hours today. So how about I pick up supper on the way back?

I can cook something for both of us.

No, you're still recovering.

Ian! I'm fine, and I'm cooking.

I know from the last few days that it's no use arguing with you but just cook something simple.

Kraft dinner it is!

LOL sounds good to me. Love you.

Love you too.

She held the phone against her chest like a silly school girl because she was still giddy he felt the same way she did. Loving him for as long as she did it was something she'd dreamed of but when he hadn't shown up for that date, she'd been sure he didn't feel the same. Even with the apologies from him for missing it, she couldn't let go of the hurt, and it still stung when she let her mind go there. It was stupid because it was only a date and it wasn't like they'd been together or anything. The thing that hurt the most was he never said why he'd stood her up. The only thing she knew was his ex-girlfriend called to talk to him about something important, and that was information she got second hand. It made her stomach churn to think of why he had been with Colleen all night.

She shook her head because if she let her thoughts go there now, it would ruin her day, and she was feeling too good to let that happen. She pulled out her chair and sat in front of her bank of computers. She needed to get some work done so she'd have time to cook supper for herself and Ian.

A knock had her bringing up the surveillance for her front door. It was too early for Ian, her sister and brother were both working, and Stephanie had gone into town with her sister.

The screen popped up showing a man in a suit and holding a briefcase in his hand. He looked relatively harmless, but Sandy learned a long time ago never let your guard down with people. She pulled her revolver from the safe next to her desk and shoved it into the back of her jeans. She grabbed her phone and shoved it into the front pocket of her jeans as she made her way downstairs to the front door.

When she pulled open the front, door the man standing on her step jumped back and then nervously raked his hand through his hair. His eyes moved up and down her then he met her eyes. He was older and balding but probably quite handsome in his younger years.

"Can I help you?" Sandy asked because the staring contest they were having was getting a little annoying.

"I'm looking for Dr. O'Connor. I was told he lives here." The man stood a little straighter.

"That depends on which Dr. O'Connor you're looking for," Sandy watched as the man pulled a piece of paper out of his pocket and read it.

"Dr. Ian O'Connor. I have the address of 2 Hart Road." He handed the paper to Sandy.

"That is the correct address but the house next door is two." Sandy handed the man back the paper. "I'm his umm... friend. Maybe I can take a message for him. He's not home at the moment." She wasn't sure how to refer to herself because they hadn't really put a label on what they were to each other.

"My name is Leonard Anderson, and I have some legal business with Dr. O'Connor." He said, but something about the way he spoke gave her a sick feeling in the pit of her stomach.

"I'm not sure what time he'll be home but if you give me your number I can have him call you." Over Leonard's shoulder, Sandy saw movement. James and Keith were heading up her driveway talking to each other in hushed tones.

"Sandy, everything okay?" Keith asked as both he and James approached the steps. Leonard turned and took a step back since both James and Keith towered over him. It was almost comical the way he tripped over himself to put some distance between him and the brothers.

"Everything is good. Mr. Anderson was just looking for Ian." Sandy explained. Keith's expression had her raising an eyebrow. He wasn't someone that showed a lot of emotion, but she'd known him long enough to see the concern on his face. It was the way he furrowed his eyebrows and clenched his jaw.

"I'm his brother. What do you need to see him about, Mr. Anderson?" Keith sounded ominous.

"It's.... ummm.... legal business for Dr. O'Connor.... I'll come back later." Leonard started to back down the steps and stopped at the bottom. "Good day gentlemen." If it weren't so strange Sandy would probably be laughing at the way, the man hurried toward the black BMW at the end of her driveway. He jumped into the car and sped away.

"You know maybe if you smiled more you wouldn't scare people, Keith." Sandy chuckled but stopped when she noticed James was also stone-faced. "Okay, what's going on?"

"We're here to meet Ian." James began. "We have something he needs to know."

"Who died?" She knew they didn't miss the sarcasm but something in the way James glanced at Keith and then out over her front yard. "My god someone did die. Who is it?" The first one Sandy could think of was their grandmother since she was in her late seventies. "Is Nanny Betty okay?" James continued to look out over the lawn and Keith was reading something on his phone. "Oh, for fuck sake, are either of you going to tell me what's going on or do I need to call Stephanie?" She placed her hands on her hips.

"Nan is fine, and this is something we need to speak with Ian about first. If he wants to tell you, that's his business." Keith didn't look up from his phone.

"You know, Keith, if it's bad news I hope you let James tell him because you're heartless." Sandy turned back into the house and slammed the front door. Keith may be her boss, but she didn't walk on eggshells around anyone, and if he fired her over this she didn't care because she would have no trouble finding other employment.

She stomped upstairs to her office ready to scream, but halfway up her front door opened, and Keith called out to her. She stopped and debated whether she should just ignore him or answer him. She decided if she ignored him he would just follow her because you didn't ignore Keith.

"What do you want?" Sandy turned and leaned her hip against the rail.

"Don't get pissy with me, woman. I'll tell you this. Ian's going to need some time to digest this, but if by some chance, he contacts you to talk, try to be understanding." With those words, Keith turned walked out the door without waiting for her to respond. The man was so mysterious about things sometimes, but he was a great boss, and she knew his family was the most important aspect of his life. Whatever was going on with Ian, she knew Keith wasn't taking it lightly. She just wished she knew what the hell was going on.

Chapter 7

Ian pulled into his driveway and hopped out of his car humming to himself. After grabbing a laptop and briefcase out of the trunk, he headed toward the front door. A quick shower, a bottle of wine and then over to Sandy's to spend the evening together. He'd been looking forward to it all day.

He got to the door and pulled his key out to unlock the door, but it opened startling him. He stepped back with his fist ready to strike until he saw James standing inside the door.

"Jesus Christ, bro. Warn a man you're gonna be in his house when he gets home." Ian chuckled as he stepped in and placed his things on the chair next to the front door. James didn't speak, and when Ian turned, he saw Keith walking out of the kitchen.

"Ian. we need to talk to you." Keith's voice was calm, but something in his tone told Ian his night just went to hell.

"What's wrong?" Ian glanced back and forth between his brothers.

"I think you should probably sit down." James motioned toward the living room.

"Just spit it out." He was getting that stomach flutter that told him whatever his brothers were about to say was going to make him need a bucket handy.

"Ian, it's about Colleen," Keith said.

"What about her?" He hadn't heard from her in eighteen months, and since the last time ended with her disappearing, he didn't really want to hear anything about the woman.

"Ian, maybe you should sit down before we tell you." James lay a hand on Ian's shoulder, and he pulled away.

"Just fucking tell me." Ian snapped.

"Ian, she's dead." Keith blurted out.

"Christ Keith, couldn't you be a little more sensitive." James sighed.

"What? Dead?" Ian stepped back and fell into the chair behind him, but the familiar lurch of his stomach had him jumping to his feet and running to the bathroom.

He didn't know how long he'd been in the bathroom heaving but once he pulled himself together and returned to the living room the rest of his brothers had arrived. They were all quietly talking until Nick looked up and spotted him bracing himself against the door jamb.

"You want some of this, bro?" Mike held up a bottle of water, and Ian nodded as he reached a shaky hand out for the bottle.

"You should probably sit so we can tell you what we know," John said, and Ian didn't want to hear anything, but he needed to know. He knew he didn't love her anymore. Those feeling were long gone, and it took that night eighteen months ago, to help him figure that out. Nearly losing Sandy also taught him that what he felt for Colleen was not even close to what he felt for Sandy. Colleen was his past, but she was still part of his history. He'd been in love with her but she'd also been his best friend for most of their childhood. Hearing about her death was like a punch in the gut.

"You should probably bring a bucket. You know how Ian gets." Aaron said. Ian knew it wasn't to make fun, it was because whatever they had to tell him was probably going to make him sick. Before anyone else spoke, James placed a bucket next to Ian.

"What happened?" It was hard to get anything out, but he forced himself to say the words.

"I was on duty today when an APB came in looking for Gerald Morgan." John started.

“Colleen’s brother?” He knew that’s who it was, but he had to try and speak again to make sure his throat would not close over.

“Yes. Gerry’s a person of interest for a double murder in Winnipeg, Manitoba.” John continued.

“Double murder? Gerry?” He found that hard to believe since the guy he knew growing up wouldn’t hurt a fly.

“Almost two weeks ago, they found the bodies of a man and woman in Gerry’s house, and he was nowhere to be found.” John looked away from him and then back up again. “Ian, the woman, was Colleen, and the guy was her husband. His name was Carter Taft.”

“Did you know she’d gotten married?” Mike asked.

“I knew she was engaged.” Ian lay back against the back of the couch and threaded his fingers through his hair. “So, what happened to them?”

“They were both shot in the head. From what Uncle Kurt could find out, they both died instantly.” James picked up because John seemed to be finding it hard to continue. Colleen had been the closest to Ian, but she’d been friends with all of them.

“And they think Gerry killed them?” Ian said.

“He’s a person of interest.” James, always the cop. In Ian’s books, anyone who was being tracked by the police was more than a person of interest.

“Come on let’s call a spade, a spade, bro. The cops think Gerry killed them.” Mike rolled his eyes. Being a lawyer made him more to the point even though he dealt more with family law.

“They need to question him to see what he knows,” John spoke up. It would have been comical to watch the cops and lawyer in his family debate, but right now he was just sick.

“Are you okay, bro?” Aaron sat next to him. As the baby of the family, Aaron was usually the jokester, but he was the most sensitive to people’s emotions.

“I don’t know how I feel. I mean, yeah Colleen was a big part of my life once, but that was a long while ago, but I’d never wish this on her or her husband.”

“The Winnipeg authorities think Gerry may be headed back here because it’s where he’s from,” John said.

“Why? It’s not like he has any family left here. Their parents both passed away, and their other brother killed himself.” Ian remembered Colleen mentioning Luke’s drug overdose.

"It'd be pretty stupid to come back here. The Morgan house isn't even there anymore. The sailing club bought that land a few years back and tore the house down." James said.

Ian listened to his six brothers discuss all the reasons why it would be a stupid move for Gerry to come back home and how they found it hard to believe the man would ever hurt anyone let alone his own sister. Keith wasn't contributing much to the conversation. He was staring out through the window. Keith was never a great conversationalist, but something wasn't sitting well with him.

"Bro, we're heading out. Are you okay?" Aaron asked as he and Nick stood to leave. "If you need us just call."

"I will and thanks." Ian stood and hugged both of them.

"We're leaving too, Ian," John said as James and Mike followed behind. "Are you sure you're okay?"

"I don't know how I feel. I just need some time to process all this." Ian said.

He stood on his front step and watched his brothers disappear from his view. For a moment, he didn't even realize that anyone was behind him, but when he heard the gruff voice, he turned around.

"Don't hurt her again." Keith glared, and at first, Ian wasn't even sure what his brother meant. Then Keith jutted his chin toward Sandy's house.

"Why would I hurt her?" Ian didn't plan on letting any of this interfere with his budding relationship with Sandy.

"I'm just warning you, bro. I know how she feels about you and you fucked things up with her once before because of Colleen." Why was he so concerned about Sandy getting hurt? Sure, she worked for him, but he'd never really warned him about hurting her before.

"I love her, Keith," Ian said.

"So do I." Keith stepped toward him. Ian's mouth dropped open. "For fuck sake, get that look off your face. I'm not in love with her, but I love her the same way I love Jess, Kristy, Isabelle, and Pam."

"Like a kid sister." Ian felt instant relief. Not once had the brothers fought over a woman but he sure as hell wasn't letting anyone take Sandy from him.

"Yes, so don't fuck this up." Keith took a step back and glanced at the open door. "Hey, Sandy." Ian turned, and his body tensed.

"Hi, Keith. I didn't want to interrupt, but I needed to give Ian this." She held out a business card.

"Remember what I said Ian and if you need anything call." Keith nodded toward Sandy and jogged down the driveway to his truck.

"I really didn't want to interrupt, but there was a guy here earlier today." She was still holding the card in her hand. Ian took her hand and pulled her into the house.

"You're not interrupting, but I do need to tell you something." Ian closed the door, and he led her into the living room. "I guess you're wondering why all my brothers were here."

"I was wondering but if it's not something you can't talk about I understand." Sandy looked down at the card she was still holding. Ian pulled it from her hand and tossed it on the coffee table.

Ian grasped her hands in his and stared into her beautiful brown eyes as he explained everything. He'd never talked about Colleen a lot with Sandy because it seemed weird to speak of an old flame with the woman he loved. Plus, she never really brought up any of her previous relationships. When he'd asked, she'd just say they weren't worth discussing.

"I'm really sorry about what happened," Sandy said.

“She didn’t deserve to die like that.” Ian felt the lump in his throat and dropped his head.

“Nobody does Ian, and when someone you care about or once cared about is taken so violently, it’s hard.” She seemed to be talking from experience.

They sat on the couch in silence for a few moments just holding hands. Ian didn’t know how but somehow Sandy seemed to know exactly how he was feeling. When he met her eyes again, tears were running down her cheeks.

“Sandy, why are you crying?” Ian cupped her face and wiped the tears with his thumbs.

“It’s just when I think about someone taking someone’s life so senselessly it makes me sad.” She took a deep breath and forced a smile. “And if you tell Keith you saw me cry, I will punch you.” Ian chuckled.

“You don’t want your boss to know you’ve got a soft heart?” Ian watched her eyes close as he pushed a stray curl back from her cheek.

“I like Keith to think I’m a tough cracker.” Her smile appeared forced.

"I think you're a tough cracker with a beautiful heart and you're incredibly brilliant, and I'm so sorry it took me so long to admit how I feel about you. The one thing that has opened my eyes with all this news today is, life is way too short, and we need to make sure people know how we feel about them. You'd think as a doctor I'd know that long ago." She cupped his face in her hands.

"How about we start right now and never hold back what we feel. I love you, Doc and I'm so sorry for what happened to Colleen and her husband. I hope they find who took them away too soon." He couldn't love her more than he did at that very moment.

"I love you too, Churchie and I hope the person in your life that was hurt gets justice as well. I know you're not ready to talk about it and if you're never ready I understand, but I want you to know I'm always here if you need me." He brushed his lips against hers, and she sighed.

His hand threaded into her hair as his lips molded to hers. She answered his kiss with an eagerness that had his dick turning painfully hard. He'd wanted her for so long and just touching her made him rock hard, but there was something about this kiss that had him throbbing to be closer to her. Her arms slid around his neck, and she pressed against him as her mouth opened and her tongue slid against his. He pulled her onto his lap, and his hands clenched on her hips pulling her tight against the erection straining against his zipper.

“Sandy, I want you so bad.” Ian panted as he pulled his lips from hers. She ground herself against him, and he had to hold her tightly because he almost embarrassed himself. “If you keep doing that, baby it’s going to be over before it starts.” He kissed his way across her jaw and slipped his hand under her tank top. Her skin was like silk, and he ran his thumb below her full breasts.

“Touch me, Ian, please,” Sandy begged.

“Where do you want me to touch you, sweetheart?” Ian whispered and gently bit her ear.

“Please, Ian,” she panted, but he wanted to hear her say it.

“Tell me, baby. Tell me where you want me to touch you.” He ran his tongue down the side of her neck and to the cleft between her breasts. “Tell me what you want, Sandy.”

“I want you to kiss my breasts, touch them.” She gasped when his hands cupped them, and he continued to slide his tongue inside her cleavage.

“Like this?” He could feel her nipples harden under the thin fabric of her bra. He squeezed her breasts gently and groaned when her hips thrust forward rubbing her groin against him.

“Yes! Use your mouth.” She slowly pressed her heat against him. She moaned when he thrust up to meet her. It was driving him crazy. He pulled his hands out of her top, grabbed the neckline and ribbed it apart, and she gasped. “Oh, God. That’s so damn hot.”

“Jesus, you’re fucking beautiful.” He flicked his tongue against her pebbled nipple through her bra. Luckily it had a front clasp. He flicked it and yanked it open. He pulled back and took in the sight of her full firm breasts. “Fucking beautiful.”

“Ian, damn it, take them in your mouth.” Sandy gritted her teeth as she slowly slid her groin against his cock and he could feel her wetness through his jeans and hers. He took her nipple between his lips and sucked it hard into his mouth.

“Ahhh yes.” She moaned.

“Fuck, Sandy I need you naked. Now.” Ian stood up and her legs wrapped around his waist as she nipped at his neck. If she kept this up, he was going to come in his pants like a horny sixteen-year-old. “Baby, you have to stop rubbing against me. You’ve got me so fucking hard. I need to calm down a bit.” Sandy pulled back and gazed into his eyes as he kicked open his bedroom door. She dropped her legs so he could stand her on the floor. She quickly lost her torn top and bra. He couldn’t look away, as she took two steps back and slowly began to open her jeans.

Ian grabbed his shirt, pulled it over his head, and tossed it aside without tearing his gaze away from her. She’d stepped out of her jeans and was still slowly backing toward the bed in nothing but a pair of yellow bikini underwear with the words 'Perfect Sunshine' just above where her wetness had darkened the color of her panties. Then he saw the tattoo.

"Are you just going to stare at me?" She crawled onto the bed on her knees and slid her thumbs into the sides of her panties.

"No. Leave them on for now. I'm getting a good look at that ink I never knew about." His gaze slowly took in the tattoo spanned across her lower abdomen from one hip to the other. It was beautiful and hot as hell.

"We can talk about the tat later. I want to see if you have any I didn't know about." She grinned as he dropped his pants and his boxer briefs. Her gaze slid down his body and licked her lips as she took in his form. When she zeroed in on his erection, her eyes widened, and she bit her bottom lip making him almost lose it.

"If you keep looking at me like that I'm going to embarrass myself." Ian chuckled. He crawled onto the bed and met her in the middle. They knelt facing each other but not touching.

"You're absolutely perfect." She whispered finally touching him with her hands slowly sliding up his arms and across his shoulders. She ran her index fingers down until she reached his nipples. She circled them once and ran her finger slowly down his over his abs. Ian closed his eyes and reveled in the feeling of her gentle touch. “Your body is incredible.” She sighed.

“Your body is pretty perfect too.” Ian opened his eyes and let them slide down her body. He slowly slid his fingers into the sides of her panties and gripped them tightly. “These need to go.” He growled and ripped them from her body.

“Ahhh... that’s so hot.” She gasped when he slid his hand between her legs and drove a finger inside her. “Yes.”

“Baby, you’re so ready for me right now.” Ian covered her mouth with his and eased her back on the bed. “I need to be inside you.” He murmured against her lips.

He reached for the bedside table and pulled out a condom. Sandy took it from his hand, held it between her teeth and slowly pulled it open. He’d never seen anything so erotic in his life. She pushed him to his back, straddled his legs and slowly rolled the condom over his hard length.

“Fuck, Sandy I need to be inside you before I completely explode.” Ian flipped her over onto her back and hovered over her. Her eyes were dark with arousal, and he was sure it mirrored his very own.

“Make love to me, Ian.” She whispered as her arms slipped around his back and pulled him down to her. His erection slid between her folds and found the entrance to her heat. Slowly he pushed inside her. She was so tight and hot that it took everything he had, not to come at that very second. When she started to thrust up to meet his, he grabbed her hip with one hand to stop her from moving.

"Baby, give me a second." He growled and rested his head against hers. "I've been waiting for this for so long I want it to last more than five seconds." Her giggle sent a vibration through her body, and he could feel it from inside her. "Shit, don't do that." He gritted his teeth.

"Ian, I need to move." Sandy panted after a couple of seconds. He'd managed to tamper down the tingling in the tip of his cock and started to thrust into her slowly at first as his mouth devoured hers. She squeezed his ass and pushed him deeper inside. Her soft moaning was like music to his ears, and the combination of that with her whispering dirty words into his ear had him more turned on than he'd ever been in his life. He liked that she seemed to get off on a little dirty talk.

"I'm gonna come, Ian." She screamed when she thrust her hips off the bed and dug her nails deep into the skin of his ass. It was all he needed. One more deep thrust and he lost it. He erupted inside her with such force it took every bit of air from his lungs as he roared out her name.

The vibration of her giggle had him lifting his head from the crook of her neck to see what was so funny. When she met his eyes, she started to laugh harder.

"Baby, that's not something a man wants to hear after making love to his woman." Ian couldn't help but smile when her giggles stopped instantly.

"His woman?" She squeaked, and he kissed the top of her nose.

"That's right, my woman. You're mine Sandy Churchill." Ian whispered and brushed his lips against hers.

"In that case, that makes you my man, Ian O'Connor and don't you forget it." She stretched up and gently bit his lower lip. The action had his still semi hard cock jerk inside her. It was probably going to be a very long, hot night for them.

Chapter 8

Sandy tried to roll over onto her back, but something heavy and very warm had her pinned against the mattress. She opened her eyes slowly and saw the large muscular arm draped around her waist. The body attached to that arm was flush against her back, and she smiled. His hand twitched when she turned her head to gaze into his face. He was still sleeping.

She managed to roll over onto her back and push him over onto his. He murmured something in his sleep, and she turned over on her side to face his sleeping form. She rested her head in her hand and let her eyes take in his form, and he was beautiful. Thick, wavy, auburn hair a little longer than he usually kept it but she always wanted to run her fingers through it. Long, dark lashes curled at the ends surrounded his. Sandy smiled because some women would kill for lashes like his. His nose was long and narrow with a small bump at the top, but it only added to his perfect features. His full lips were slightly opened and were surrounds by a two-day growth of beard a little redder than his hair and sexy as hell.

Her gaze moved down to his muscular chest where she could finally get a better look at the two tattoos on each side. One she knew was a family tattoo because he told her the whole family had the same one. It had apparently been a tradition in their family, and even the women had it. On the other side was a cross with the initials of his grandfather. He said he'd gotten it after his grandfather passed away. She never really liked tattooed men before, but on Ian it was perfection. She continued to ogle his form and scanned lower where his stomach rose and fell with his even breathing. Even in rest, his six pack was visible.

"You look like you're about to eat me." Sandy's head snapped up to see him grinning at her.

"Just enjoying the view." She grinned.

"I'm liking the view pretty well myself." He lifted the blanket, and his eyes raked down the front of her body. He flipped her onto her back and tried to kiss her, but she covered her mouth with her hands.

"Ian, No. I haven't even brushed my teeth this morning." She turned her head when he pulled her hands away.

"I don't give a fuck. I want to kiss you." Before she could protest anymore, he covered her mouth with his, and at that moment she didn't care about brushing her teeth anymore.

His hand caressed her breast, and she pushed her chest harder into his hand. Things were getting hot, and she barely heard the loud knock coming from the front door. Ian pulled back and cursed.

“I’ll fucking kill them,” Ian growled as he grabbed a pair of track pants, and Sandy admired his bare ass while he pulled them on. He yanked a T-shirt over his head as another knock sounded. “I’m coming, hold your fucking horses,” he yelled as he stomped out of the room.

Sandy threw the blankets back and jumped out of bed. She suddenly realized she had no shirt or underwear since Ian had ripped them off. It had been so erotic, but that left her only with the option of going commando. Going without a top was not an option. While she pulled on her jeans and bra, Sandy scanned the room and spotted the shirt Ian had pulled off last night on the floor. She grabbed it and yanked it on but held it to her nose for a moment. It smelled like him.

Ian’s voice drew her attention, and she walked out of the room to see him disappear into the living room. The man behind him jogged her memory from the day before. It was the lawyer that had been looking for Ian. If this was legal trouble, he really should have a lawyer with him. She pulled her phone from her pocket and searched for Mike’s number. Keith had given her all his families’ numbers in case something happened to him during a job. She tapped it and held the phone to her ear.

“Michael O’Connor.” He answered on the second ring.

“Mike, it’s Sandy. I think you need to get here to Ian’s as soon as possible.” Sandy’s kept her voice low.

“What’s going on?” Mike asked.

Sandy explained the visit from Leonard Anderson and that he was with Ian now. There was a muffled voice, and Mike whispered something to the person.

“There’s something weird going on, Mike.” Sandy didn’t like the feeling she was getting just from having him in the house.

“Tell Ian not to say a word. I’ll be there in twenty minutes.” Mike said, and then the call ended.

Sandy walked into the living room, but Ian wasn’t there. Leonard was sat on the couch pulling files out of his briefcase. He glanced up at Sandy and nodded.

“Dr. O’Connor is just making a phone call,” Leonard answered her unspoken question. Sandy nodded and hurried to the kitchen. Ian was leaning against the counter with his phone to his ear.

“He’s not answering, and I know you don't practice anymore but can you just get out here,” Ian whispered. “I don’t know what this guy wants, but he's a lawyer that says he has legal business with me."

"Ian, I called Mike he's on his way here," Sandy said.

"Never mind Nick, Sandy called Mike." Ian listened for a minute. "I know I won't say a word until he's here. Later, bro." Ian tossed the phone on the counter and stared at her.

"How did you know to call Mike?" He raised his eyebrow.

"I told you that guy was here yesterday and gave you his card but we got.... distracted." Sandy crossed her arms over her chest and mirrored his facial expression.

"Oh.... yeah....it was a good distraction." Ian grinned and then it fell. "What the hell does this guy want?" Ian looked over her shoulder toward the living room.

"I don't know, but let him know you're not talking until Mike gets here." Sandy walked over to him and wrapped her arms around his neck. "Mike said he'd be here in twenty minutes." Ian hugged her to him, and he rested his chin on top of her head.

"Thanks for looking out for me, Churchie." He whispered and kissed the top of her head before releasing her and taking her hand. "Come on I'll let him know he'll have to wait until Mike gets here."

Leonard seemed a little put out because he had to wait, but Ian made it clear he wasn't talking to him without legal representation present. Sandy made coffee, and Ian paced the hallway. It seemed like they'd been waiting a lot longer than twenty minutes when Mike finally hurried in through the front door.

"It's about fucking time." Ian snapped as Mike pulled off his jacket.

"I had a late night, and I was still in bed when Sandy called. I had to drive my…. company home before I came here." Mike tucked in his shirt and fixed his collar.

"Another wham bam, little brother?" Ian shook his head, and Sandy had to cover her mouth to keep from laughing.

"Fuck off." Mike pushed Ian's shoulder, but the smile on his face said Ian was right on the mark.

"Mr. Anderson my name is Michael O'Connor. I'm Dr. O'Connor's legal representative." Ian shook Leonard's hand. To see Mike going from telling Ian to fuck off to completely professional was amusing.

"Like I told Dr. O'Connor, having you here really wasn't necessary." Leonard sat back on the couch. "I represent the estate in which Dr. O'Connor was named the sole beneficiary." He held the papers close to his chest as his eyes darted back and forth between

Ian and Mike. "There is also some personal business that Dr. O'Connor needs to know about, but I think we may need some privacy for this." His eyes darted to Sandy.

"Whatever you've got to say can be said in front of my girlfriend." Ian snapped and took Sandy's hand in his.

"It's okay, Ian. I can go home until this is all settled." Sandy didn't want to intrude.

"You're staying." Ian kissed the top of her head, and he sat on the second couch across from Leonard pulling Sandy down next to him.

"I guess that's settled," Mike sat on the arm of the sofa next to Sandy. "Whenever you're ready, Mr. Anderson."

For a moment, he just glanced between Sandy and Ian but then looked down at the files he was holding against his chest. He opened the first one and gave the envelope to Ian.

"Before we get into things you need to read that letter," Leonard handed a large brown envelope to Ian. Ian tore open the envelope and pulled out some papers. From what Sandy could see, it was handwritten and about five or six sheets. Ian shuffled through the papers and glanced up at Leonard.

"This is going to take me a bit to read." Ian stared at the man.

“I’ll wait,” Leonard sat back and folded his hands in his lap.

“Alright.” Ian held the papers in front of him and began to read. After a few minutes, Sandy felt him stiffen beside her.

“Ian, are you okay?” Sandy placed her hand on his knee, and he looked up.

“It’s from Colleen,” Ian whispered and grabbed her hand in his as he continued to read. After what seemed like hours Ian dropped her hand and stood up. “There’s no fucking way.”

“Ian, what’s wrong?” Mike picked up the papers Ian had tossed on the table and began to read. Sandy didn’t like the way Ian was pacing and the paleness of his face.

“Dr. O’Connor these papers say different, and you’re the only family they have,” Leonard held out a photograph. Ian looked at his hand as if he was holding a bomb and started shaking his head.

“Ian?” Sandy didn’t like the way this was affecting Ian. Before she had a chance to ask anything Ian bolted down the hallway and she heard the bathroom door slam.

“Mike, what’s going on?” Sandy looked up as Mike flopped down on the couch next to her.

"Ian is probably getting sick because whenever something shocks or scares him, he throws up." Mike stared at the papers, but he wasn't reading anymore. "Mr. Anderson, you know we'll have to do some tests to make sure this is true."

"Children's services require it." Leonard held out more papers to Mike.

"Mike, what the hell is going on?" She was thoroughly confused.

"Those papers say I have two daughters." Ian's voice made her jump because she hadn't heard him come back into the room. "Two children she didn't tell me about." His face was so white that it looked like he was about to pass out.

"The letter explains everything." Leonard was still holding the photo in his hand.

"And that makes it okay that she hid his children from him?" Mike snapped.

"All that letter says was it was a mistake to keep them from me, and part of it was because she was afraid I'd try to take them from her. Really? She didn't know me at all if she thought that." Ian's voice was trembling.

“Look, gentlemen, I’m only here to give you all the information. I didn’t know Mrs. Taft.” Leonard sounded almost defensive.

“Apparently, I didn’t either.” Ian snapped.

Sandy stood up and took the picture from Leonard’s hand. She glanced down to see two of the most beautiful little girls she’d ever seen but what took her breath away was that one of the little girls looked to be about six to seven months old. The other was older about the same age as Marina and James little boys.

“How old are these little girls?” Sandy asked Leonard, but she was looking at Ian.

“The oldest one is Lily, and she’s six. The younger one is Grace, and she’s eight months old.” Sandy walked toward Ian and put the picture into his hand.

“You need to deal with this. I’m guessing Grace was conceived the night you stood me up.” Sandy walked around him and was about to run out the door, but Ian grabbed her arm.

“Sandy, let me explain,” Ian begged.

“No explanation needed Ian. We weren’t together, and the woman that broke your heart came to town, and things happened. It’s not a surprise. I just wish you’d told me why you stood me up.”

Sandy clenched her jaw because she knew as soon as she was alone the tears were going to start, but she wasn't going to do it in front of Ian.

"I didn't want to hurt you," Ian whispered.

"That worked out really well for you. Didn't it?" Sandy pulled her arm from his grasp and opened the front door.

"Sandy, don't go. I love you." Ian stood in front of her.

"I love you, too, but that isn't always enough, is it?" Sandy stepped around him and almost ran out through the door. The closer she got to her house, the faster she walked. Once inside Sandy fell to her knees and sobbed.

Chapter 9

Ian watched her almost run back to her house, and it took everything he had not to run after her, but everything was so fucking screwed up right now. Ian slammed the front door and started punching it with all he had.

"Fuck, fuck, fuck," Ian growled with each punch to the door.

"Ian, stop." Mike grabbed his arm and pulled him away from the door. "This isn't helping anything. What the hell is wrong with you?" Mike stood in front of him and braced Ian against the wall.

"I've lost her," Ian yelled, but it came out like a sob.

"You haven't lost her. Let her get her head around this. Jesus, bro get your own head around it." Mike shook him.

"How could she not tell me?" Ian rested his head back against the wall and closed his eyes to the burning of the tears that were threatening to fall. "How could she come here fuck me and not tell me I had a daughter eighteen months ago, and then have another one and not tell me?" He slid down the wall and sat on the floor. Mike crouched in front of him and placed a hand on his shoulder.

"I don't know, bro but you need to pull yourself together and get this shit figured out," Mike was right. He pressed the heels of his hands into his eyes and took a deep breath. "You ready to hear the rest?" Ian nodded and jumped up to his feet.

For the next couple of hours, Ian sat and listened to everything Leonard had to say about the two little girls as well as reading the several letters Colleen had left for him. According to Leonard, Colleen's husband knew everything, and there was no chance he could be the youngest girl's father because he was unable to have children himself. Ian let Mike do all the talking while he read the letters. Even though she tried to explain why she kept it from him it didn't help with his anger, but what good did it do to be mad at her now? She was dead. Murdered. He couldn't confront her about it. What was surprising to him was the amount of money that Colleen had left to care for the girls. Colleen's family were blue collar just like his. Her father was a fisherman, and her mother was a seamstress.

"As you can see, financially the girls will be cared for." Leonard brought him out of his thoughts.

“I don’t need her fucking money to take care of these girls if they’re mine. I can afford to take care of them.” Ian didn’t like what Leonard was insinuating.

“I didn’t mean it that way, Dr. O’Connor. All I’m saying is Mr. and Mrs. Taft left the girls with enough money that they will never have to worry about finances. You’ll be the executor of the money and see that the girls use it wisely.”

“They’re what, six and eight months old. I seriously don’t think they’ll blow all that money on candy.” Ian scoffed at the squirming man sitting across from him.

“Ian, take it easy,” Mike said, and he knew he was a complete ass with a man that was only doing his job. It was just a lot to take, and he couldn’t help but worry if this meant the end for him and Sandy.

“Look, I’m sorry, Mr. Anderson. I know none of this is your fault. It’s just a lot to take in.” Ian sat back and threaded his hands through his hair.

“I understand and, to be honest, Dr. O’Connor I’d probably feel the same way, and I don’t mean to seem like I don’t care its just you boys are very intimidating.” Leonard chuckled, and Ian couldn’t help but laugh. Leonard was probably not much more than five feet tall, and his six feet three and Mike's six feet would intimidate anyone.

"So, what happens now?" Ian asked.

"The social worker will be here at three tomorrow with the girls. Even if the tests say the girls are not your daughters, the will states you're the legal guardian, but we will do the DNA test just for verification." Leonard informed him. "It will not cost you anything since that has been all taken care of by Mrs. Taft."

"I'll leave all these papers with you, Mr. O'Connor." Leonard handed everything to Mike. "If you have any questions all my information is on the top there." He pointed to a business card clipped to the top folder.

"Thank you, Mr. Anderson, and again I apologize for being such an ass." Ian held out his hand and shook Leonard's hand.

"I fully understand, Dr. O'Connor but those little girls are the sweetest things I've ever met, and the oldest one is smart as a whip." It was the first time that Ian saw the man smile since he'd arrived. "That's something else in those files. Lily is a gifted child, and all the information on that is there."

"Great, that means she takes after Keith." Mike joked.

"Keith?" Leonard asked.

"Another of our brothers. He has an Eidetic memory which is annoying when you grow up with someone like that." Mike said.

"Well if that's the case then she does take after her uncle. She remembers everything she sees or hears and her IQ is off the charts according to her file." Leonard said.

"And Grace?" Ian asked.

"Well she's a little young, but she's got a beautiful smile." Leonard pointed to the picture turned down on the coffee table. He still hadn't looked at it, but he wasn't sure why.

"Thank you again, Mr. Anderson." Ian shook Leonard's hand again as he walked out through the door.

"Good luck with it all, Dr. O'Connor and I hope you work things out with your girlfriend." With that statement, Ian looked over to see Sandy getting in her car with a suitcase. He quickly texted her because knowing how stubborn she'd probably run him over before she talked to him.

Where are you going? I need to talk to you.

He watched her look down at her phone then look toward him, and for a moment he didn't think she was going to answer him, but his phone beeped just as she backed out of her driveway.

I've got a job in Halifax. I'm out of town for a few days.

It wasn't uncommon for her to have to leave for jobs but he didn't know she was leaving today, maybe it was for the best for now.

I'll miss you, and I love you. Please call me later.

He stared at the driveway as her car stopped at the end of her driveway. Again, his phone beeped, and he held his breath.

I'll try.

His heart felt like it was about to shatter until another beep came in just as she drove off.

I love you, too.

He let out the breath he was holding and closed the front door. When he walked back into the living room, Mike hunched over the table staring at the picture and the files spread across the top.

"I don't think you need a DNA, bro. Those girls are definitely O'Connors." Mike said as he held out the picture. "That older one, Lily, she looks just like Jess when she was little, and the little one got A.J.'s smile." Ian took the picture. His hands shook as he stared down at the two angelic faces smiling back at him.

“Wow,” Ian said mostly to himself because it was hard to believe he helped to create such beautiful children. Both had the O’Connor blue eyes. Lily had waist length auburn curly hair a shade darker than his. Grace had her mother’s dark hair, but Mike was right, she had his youngest brother’s smile.

“A little surreal, huh,” Mike said, but it was such an understatement. There was no word to describe how he felt. “You have until tomorrow until the social worker is here. Did you want to tell the rest of the family today?”

Ian’s heart thundered in his chest as he waited for his entire family to show up at his house. Mike made the calls to his brothers and cousins while he called his parents, uncles, and aunts. Of course, his grandmother lived with his parents, so she was coming with them and of course her friend, Tom.

Nanny Betty would never admit that she and Tom were more than friends, but there was no way to hide the way they acted around each other. They’d been sweethearts in their teens, but a misunderstanding had separated them, but years later they were brought back together by a series of strange coincidences. Now Tom was like part of the family so why shouldn’t he be invited?

“You might want to down this before they all get here.” Mike held out a shot glass, and Ian didn’t have to ask what was in it.

Newfie Screech was his grandfather's drink of choice, and he always said it calmed his nerves. Ian took the glass and downed it.

“Fuck, that stuff burns like hell.” Ian choked out.

“Yeah, but it’s a good burn.” Mike tossed back his own shot and chuckled.

Forty-seven minutes. That was how long it took for the entire family to fill his house. Sure, most of them lived five-minute radius, but it still surprised him how they all come running when called.

“Okay Inky, what’s goin’ on here? I’ve got dough risin’.” Nanny Betty plopped herself down in the armchair next to the door. His grandmother was a force of nature, and of all his family it worried him the most telling her. He didn’t want any of the family to be disappointed in him but her especially.

“Mudder, why are you making bread again today? You baked a dozen loaves yesterday. You need to calm down.” His father stood in the doorway of the living room with his arm resting on his wife’s shoulders. Ian rolled his eyes because his father should know better.

“Sean, Yes, and I’m makin’ more tamara’, and I’ll make it every day if I have ta. Now hush before I bust yer arse.” Nanny Betty pointed at his father and everyone just turned to hide their snickers.

"Sean, why do you consistently put your foot in it." Cora laughed because as Nanny Betty's only daughter, she knew as well as everyone, nobody told his grandmother what to do. "By the way, Ian. Where's Sandy?" With that, his chest felt like it was going to collapse. He'd been trying not to think about her but when he did his chest hurt.

"She had to go out of town on a job," Keith spoke from his spot in the corner of the living room where he leaned against the wall with his massive arms crossed over his chest, and Ian knew by the look Keith was giving him that Sandy had filled him in.

"Ian, it's time you stepped up and admitted how you feel about that girl. You know what I told you," Cora said. Apparently, his aunt had made her prediction for Ian and Sandy. Ian didn't say a word because nobody was permitted to doubt her. Cora the Cupid and her special gift were always right.

"He's got a whole lot more to deal with now," Keith muttered into Ian's ear

"Don't start." Ian snapped.

With everyone settled in the living room, Ian pulled the picture out of his pocket and held it tightly between his fingers. He glanced to Mike for support, and his brother nodded. He felt something tugging on his leg, and he looked down to see his nephew, Mason looking up at him.

"You can do it, Uncle Ian." Mason took Ian's hand. It was odd because even though Mason had no way of knowing what was going on, just by holding his hand, Ian felt like he *could* do this.

"Thanks, buddy." Ian squeezed his hand gently but didn't let go of it. "I don't know how much you all know up to this point, but yesterday I was told Colleen had died, and I don't know all the details, but it wasn't natural." Ian didn't want to go into detail since his niece and nephews were in the room.

"We heard and that's just terrible." His mother said holding her hands against her chest.

"Well, it turns out she was hiding something from me for a while." Ian started. "A year and a half ago Colleen came to town and asked to meet with me because there was something she needed to talk to me about. I went to meet with her and…." How the hell was he going to say this without actually saying it?

"They ended up having a sleepover," Mike interjected with a smile. Ian glanced around, and it seemed everyone understood.

"When I woke up the next morning, she was gone, and I never heard from her again. I also didn't find out what she'd wanted. This morning a lawyer showed up here with her will and a letter for me. It turns out that what she had to tell me was when she left seven years ago she was pregnant, but the sleepover also resulted in the same condition." He knew it sounded stupid, but with Mason holding his hand he was trying to keep the details PG rated.

"Inky, are ya sayin' ya have youngsters?" Nanny Betty asked

"Yes. Two. Daughters." Ian handed the picture to his grandmother, and she covered her mouth with her hand as she studied the picture.

"Oh, my. Such beautiful little angels." She cooed and gave the picture to his mother.

"Where are they, Ian?" His mother's eyes filled with tears.

"Kathleen, let the boy finish." His father didn't sound pleased.

"The social worker will be bringing them here tomorrow, and I know everyone is going to want to meet them, but I'd like to keep it to a minimum until they're settled in," Ian said.

"Of course. Ian, what are their names?" Marina and Stephanie were looking at the picture before handing it off to their husbands.

“The older one is Lily, and she’s six. She also has a lot in common with Keith according to all the information we’ve got.” Ian glanced at Keith, and for a moment his expression was proud but quickly turned back to pissed. “The little one is Grace, and she’s eight months old.”

“Auntie Stephanie, Olivia will have a friend her age.” Danny, his other nephew, crawled up on James’s lap.

“Yes, that’s true, honey.” Stephanie glared at Ian, and the term ‘if looks could kill’ jumped into his head.

“So I think the best thing is when they arrive that only myself and Ian be here,” Mike said.

“Why you?” Nick asked.

“Because I’m his legal representation and I don’t want anything screwing this up for him,” Mike replied, and Ian was glad that someone was going to be there with him.

“Mike, I want mom and dad here too.” Ian heard his mother gasp.

“Oh Ian, really?” Kathleen wrapped her arms around his waist, and he hugged her.

"Yes, Mom because if anyone can make these girls feel at home, it's you." Ian smiled.

Ian was keeping a careful eye on the picture as it was being passed around since it was the only one he had, and he didn't want to lose it.

Mike and his father sat on the couch as his mother headed to the kitchen to see if he had the ingredients for cookies. It was normal for his mother to bake when she was anxious about something, and everyone just let her go. Ian leaned against the wall in the hallway after almost everyone left. Keith was on the back deck staring out at the ocean, and Ian knew he was going to have to talk to him.

Ian stepped out and stood next to Keith. In the distance, he saw a whale jumping, and he focused in on it. He was just waiting for Keith to speak because when he was in these moods, there wasn't any point talking until he was ready.

"She saved my life," Keith murmured.

"Sandy?" Ian didn't know how Keith and Sandy met. As a matter of fact, he didn't know if anyone did.

"Yes," Keith said.

"How?" Ian asked.

"It's not important, but we formed a bond, and I hate that she's hurt because you're an idiot," Keith said gruffly. "She's not as tough as she puts out there, Ian."

"I didn't mean to hurt her, Keith." Ian leaned his arms on the rail and Keith did the same.

"I know, but she's been hurt before by someone and the fact that she even let you this close is a big step for her," Keith said.

"What happened in Yellowknife, bro?" Ian knew that was where they'd met, but when Keith came back, he was different. He'd always been a little more serious than the rest of the brothers, but it was worse when he came back.

"It's not important, and if Sandy hasn't told you then it's not my place to say but let me tell you this. She's a kind, caring person, and for some reason, she's in love with you, and yeah I know you love her, too. I also know Aunt Cora has used her cupid power, and you two are meant to be but, bro, as God as my witness, if you hurt her, I'll make you sorry you did. Brother or not." Keith grabbed Ian's arm and turned him, so they were face to face.

"I need to know something, Keith and I need you to be honest." Ian wasn't sure he wanted to know the answer, but Keith was so emotional about Sandy. "Are you in love with her?" Keith rolled his eyes and pushed Ian back.

“You’re a fucking idiot. No, I told you I’m not in love with her. We just shared a painful experience and like I said she saved my life and almost lost her own in the process. That means something to me, and I’m in debt to her.” Keith said. “Trust me, bro. If I wanted Sandy, you wouldn’t have even gotten near her.” Keith laughed. “Just don’t be a dick.”

“I just hope I haven’t lost her already.” Ian rubbed his hands over his face.

“I’m sure things will work out but you really need to go shower and shave, or you’re going scare the shit out of those kids.” Keith wrapped his arm around Ian’s shoulders and nuggied the top of his head.

“Fuck you, asshole.” Ian twisted and got out of Keith’s grip.

“Congrats on the kids by the way,” Keith said as they both walked into the house. “I know it’s not conventional, but I’m sure you’ll be great.”

“I’m just worried that Lily is going to be smarter than me.” Ian chuckled.

“She probably is, but that’s ok, she still has her Uncle Keith.” Keith teased and waved to Mike and his father as he walked by the living room. He quickly ducked into the kitchen and kissed their mother’s cheek. “If you need anything, call.”

For a few minutes, Ian saw the Keith he grew up with but just before he disappeared through the door that sadness reappeared and Ian wished he knew what had put that look on his brother's face. If Sandy ever forgave him, maybe he'd ask her about their time in Yellowknife, and maybe he could help her with whatever happened.

He didn't sleep that night and when he did finally doze off a loud commotion from his foyer had him jumping out of bed and running to the front door in nothing but his boxers.

"You look... Well.... You're awake." Isabelle peeked over the box she was carrying. Behind his cousin were her two sisters and his two sisters-in-law also moving boxes that looked way too heavy for the five small women.

"What the hell is all this?" Ian grabbed a pair of track pants from the chair beside his bedroom door.

"Well we would tell you, but then we'd have to kill you." Kristy stood up on her toes and kissed his cheek. Then followed Isabelle into his spare room.

"What we can tell you is, when your brothers put their heads together they get things done." Marina walked by him and winked. Stephanie and Jess followed her, and he stared at them as he tried to close his door.

"We bust our butts getting everything you need for your two little girls, and you slam the door on us. Not cool, bro." Aaron pushed the door open. Ian stood back as the rest of his brothers followed the women into his spare room. What he heard next had him, running behind them.

"We can put most of this junk in the attic or the basement," Nick said.

"It's a good thing he's not a hoarder." Jess laughed.

"Okay, just stop," Ian yelled, and everyone turned to look at him. Without a word, he raised his hands and gestured around the room.

"What?" John asked.

"What do you mean, what? You all come in here at the break of dawn and start ransacking my spare room and bring in a bunch of oversized boxes and don't tell me what the hell you're doing." Ian could feel his blood pressure rising. Probably because he was tired and scared shitless. He'd also hadn't heard from Sandy.

"I know you can read, asshole," Keith grumbled as he ripped open one of the larger boxes. Ian glanced at the large writing on the box and then looked at the others. A crib, two dressers, a bed and some sort of toy chest.

"If you could pick your chin up off the ground now and give us a hand. That would be awesome." Stephanie was pulling what looked like blankets out of a large bag.

"The room needs painting, but we won't have time for that before the girls get here." Marina was helping James assemble the bed.

"When did you guys do all this?" Ian was dumbfounded.

"As soon as we left here last night, your brothers dragged us out to St. John's and straight to the Mall. We had exactly two hours to get all this stuff. Not bad huh?" Jess laughed as she held the side of the crib for Keith to bolt together.

"You can't have the kids sleeping on the floor," James chuckled. Ian couldn't believe what he was seeing. His family always came together to get things done, but for some reason, the scene was making it very hard for him to swallow and his eyes were blurring. He turned and bolted for his bedroom. He needed to pull himself together. He sat on the foot of his bed, rested his arms on his knees and covered his face with his hands.

"We're all here to help." Ian recognized the voice, but he couldn't look up at her. Stephanie was Sandy's best friend, and she was pissed. He'd promised not to hurt Sandy, and he'd meant it. This wasn't something he'd expected in a million years, and Sandy was hurt, but he couldn't do anything to change it.

"Thanks," Ian muttered but didn't look at her.

"It wasn't right what she did, Ian." Stephanie's voice cracked. "It wasn't fair that Colleen didn't tell you about your daughters either, but you should've been entirely honest with Sandy and told her why you didn't make it that night." He felt the bed dip next to him and turned his head to look at his brother's wife.

"I know, but I didn't want to hurt her. I love her more than I've ever loved anyone in my life and that night, with Colleen, it made me realize any feelings I had for Colleen were long gone. We were drinking, and I know it's no excuse, but I never wanted Sandy to think Colleen was more important because Sandy means everything to me." Ian scrubbed his hands over his face and stared up at the ceiling. "I just don't know what to do."

For a moment Stephanie didn't say anything but she stared out through the bedroom door, and it was as if she was struggling with something.

"I want you to remember something, Ian. I've got no doubt that Sandy is deeply hurt by what happened, but there's something more that's upsetting her and don't ask me what it is because I can't tell you but when or if she does, be understanding." Stephanie didn't give him a chance to respond she stood, kissed his cheek and left the room.

That afternoon, Ian paced the floor as he waited for his daughters to arrive. His daughters. It was still hard to believe he had two little girls. The thought made his stomach tighten, and he swallowed down the bile rising in his throat. He wasn't letting this happen five minutes before they showed up. He hated that part of him, but his mother always told him it was because he felt things deep in his gut and it was why when things were stressful personally that he'd have to get sick to release all that stress.

The knock on the door made him freeze in the middle of the kitchen. He pressed his hands against his stomach and forced his feet to move toward the door as he took several deep breaths and opened the door.

The first thing to greet him was an older woman with graying hair and a kind face but what drew his attention was the little strawberry blonde in her arms chewing on her fingers. Her blue eyes locked onto him and for a second Ian thought she was going to cry, but she looked at the lady and then reached her small arms out to him.

"She loves people." The woman smiled and nodded as if to give him the okay to take the sweet little girl. "This is Grace, and my name is Milly Anderson and yes before you ask Leonard is related. He's my husband."

"It's nice to meet you, Mrs. Anderson." Ian carefully took Grace from Milly and smiled at the baby. "And it's really great to meet you, Grace." Ian ran his finger down the little girl's cheek, and she grabbed his finger.

"This little beauty is Lily." Milly gently placed her hand on the head of the little girl standing next to her. "Lily, do you know who this man is?" Milly asked the little girl, and Ian started to worry his daughter didn't know anything about the situation.

"Yes. My daddy." Her sweet little voice was soft but very confident as she met his eyes.

"How did you know that this man was your father, Lily?" Milly seemed surprised by the child's knowledge.

"Mommy showed me pictures of him on the computer." Lily folded her hands in front of her. "She told me all about my daddy and his family." The kid was incredible.

"I'm so glad to meet you, Lily." Ian crouched down and reached out his hand.

"I'm sorry mommy didn't tell you about us." She took his hand.

“That’s not your fault, honey,” Ian motioned for them to come inside.

“I know.” She held his hand as she glanced around the hallway.

Ian led them into the living room and as expected his mother was already crying. His father had his arm around her. Mike stood when they entered the room.

“Lily, do you know who these people are?” Ian asked wanting to know just how much Colleen had told her.

“Yes.” She walked over to his mother. “I’m happy to meet you Grandma or do you prefer Nanny?” The shock on his parent’s face must have mirrored his own.

“You can call me whatever you feel comfortable with, but I’m delighted to meet you too, Lily.” Kathleen took both of the little girl's hands and kissed them.

“I’d like to call you Nanny, and I’ll call you Poppy if that’s okay.” She turned to his father and smiled.

“That’s fine with me, Lily,” Sean said, and the surprise in his voice was evident.

"You're Michael, but mommy told me she always called you Mike." Lily turned to his brother who had sat back down.

"That's right everyone calls me Mike." His brother answered.

For a moment, the room was quiet. Everyone seemed to be in shock with Lily's maturity. She was only six. She sat up on the couch between his parents and sighed.

"So, I think that went well." She said so seriously that it sent all the adults into laughter. Ian turned to Milly who was laughing as well.

"You haven't seen anything yet." Milly chuckled. "She can converse with the best of them."

One by one the family started showing up. Not that Ian minded because the truth was he was always more at ease when they were around. He sat on the couch watching his two little girls getting to know their cousins. Olivia and Grace were making noises at each other, and Ian could only think it was some weird baby language that only babies understood. James's little boy Colin was sitting next to them, but he just seemed to be confused. Ian chuckled because it was probably the way every man looked when he sat between two chatting women.

Danny and Mason were playing snakes and ladders with Lily, and she seemed to be having fun. Around the boys, she actually acted like the little girl she was, and it made him smile. He was terrified when he thought about raising two little girls on his own, but one look at them, and he knew he'd do anything for them. There was only one thing that would make it perfect. If the girl next door would forgive him.

"Dr. O'Connor there's a truck outside." Milly entered the kitchen. Ian had completely forgotten she was still there.

"I'm not moving anything." Ian rushed to the front door, and sure enough, a large box truck sat at the end of his driveway.

"Of course, not. The truck has the girl's belongings." Milly smiled. "I meant to tell you that their things would be delivered by six, but it looks like they're early."

"Looks like my brothers and I have more lugging to do, but that truck looks awfully big for two little girls' belongings." Ian turned around.

"We're all here to help, bro." John threw his arm around Ian's shoulder.

"I'm still mad at you, but I'll help too." Stephanie crossed her arms over her chest.

"Thanks so much and Steph I'm going to try to fix things as soon as Sandy is back." Ian wrapped his arms around her and picked her up off the floor. She squealed and wiggled to get away from him.

"John, get your big, dumb brother to put me down." She groaned.

"Maybe you should forgive him, sweetheart." John chuckled.

"Fine, just stop screwing things up with my friend." Ian chuckled when she placed a quick kiss on his cheek. He put her down, and she gave him a little shove.

"Are all of ya jus' gonna stand around or are ya goin' ta get ta da truck and bring in de girl's things?" Nanny Betty stood in the doorway with her fists resting on her hips. "Stop yer lollygaggin' and get out ta de truck."

Ian and his brothers quickly moved because none of them wanted to piss off Nanny Betty and he wanted to make sure the girls had their own things, so they felt at home. Ian couldn't believe that two little girls could have so much stuff.

"Holy shit man, are you sure there's only two little girls?" Nick grumbled as they carried in an enormous wooden box.

"Yeah." Ian chuckled.

"How the hell do two little girls have so much stuff?" Aaron carried in another box that said clothes. Ian lost count of how many of those boxes came into the house.

"Because they're little girls, you big goof." Stephanie pointed to the pile of boxes in the corner.

"This is why I'm single," Aaron grunted.

"Yeah, that's the reason. It wouldn't be because you can't keep a girl for any longer than one night." Mike dropped another box on top of the pile.

"Fuck you." Aaron snapped and then ducked as Nanny Betty slapped his arm.

"Watch yer mouth A.J." Nanny Betty warned.

"Sorry, Nan." He hurried out of the room but not before he gave Mike the finger behind Nanny Betty's back.

Later that evening everyone had filtered out of the house, except for his mother and grandmother. Lily was helping his mother bake cookies in the kitchen. It was comical how they debated which type of cookie was healthier. His chest puffed up with pride when his mother looked down at his little girl and told her she was absolutely right about using honey instead of sugar in the cookies.

“They taste so much better, Lily.” His mother smiled as she ate the cookie.

“I know, Nanny. It’s better for you, too.” Lily sat at the kitchen table with her cookie and a glass of milk. She glanced at him and tilted her head to the side. “Daddy, I think Gracie is tired. She’s rubbing her eyes.”

Ian turned toward the baby he was holding in his arms. Sure enough, she was rubbing her eyes with her little fists. Stephanie had bathed her and put her in pajamas before she left and told him that she’d probably be ready for bed soon.

“I think you’re right, Lily.” Ian smiled.

“She’d gonna want a bottle first.” Lily jumped down off the chair and pulled it over to the counter.

“Lily, what are you doing?” Ian asked.

“I’m making her bottle.” She said as if it was something she was supposed to be doing.

“I can do that, sweetheart,” Marina had made sure he knew how to mix the bottle before she left.

“It's okay, Daddy. I do it all the time.” Lily flicked on the electric kettle. Anger began to build in his chest. What the hell had

Colleen been doing? It wasn't right for a six-year-old to be doing this. It was the parent's job, and he was going to let Lily know she could be a little girl, not a mother.

"Lily, it's not your job to do that. You're supposed to be a little girl." Ian soon felt like the biggest ass in the world when she jumped down off the chair and ran out of the kitchen.

"What did I say?" Ian handed Grace to his mother.

"That's what you need to find out." She nodded toward where Lily bolted out of the kitchen.

"Maybe she likes ta help wit, Grace." Nanny Betty said.

Ian searched the house and beginning to panic when he finally found Lily huddled in the middle of his bed. He took a deep breath and let it out slowly. His heart almost broke when she looked up at him with tears running down her cheeks.

"Lily, I'm sorry." Ian sat at the foot of the bed. "I didn't mean to make you cry." He reached over and wiped the tears from her cheeks.

"It's okay." She sniffed.

"No, it's not. Why did you get so upset?" Ian asked.

“Mommy used to let me make Gracie’s bottle and then she’d read a book while we fed Gracie together.” Lily sobbed. It broke his heart and made him want to kick himself in the ass.

“We can do that too, sweetheart. I just didn’t know you did that.” Ian took her hand and pulled her into his lap. “This is all new to me.”

“I miss mommy.” She hiccupped and lay her head against his chest.

He swallowed the lump in his throat and closed his eyes. He had no idea what it was like to lose a parent, but the thought was heart-wrenching for him as an adult, but he couldn’t imagine what it would be like as a child.

“I’m sure you do, honey, but you know what?” He hugged her tightly to him.

“What?” She whispered.

“Your mom is in heaven watching over you.” Ian kissed the top of her head.

“Do you really believe that?” Lily looked up at him.

“Yes, I do,” Ian did believe it.

“I never got to say goodbye.” Lily sniffed and put her head on his shoulder again. It was then he realized Colleen didn’t have any family to claim her remains, besides the brother, everyone thought killed her. Maybe having a service for Lily would give his daughter some closure as well as himself. He’d get John or James to look into having Colleen’s remains brought home.

“Maybe we can have a service so you can say goodbye,” Ian whispered.

“Like the funeral Carter’s friend had?” Well at least she knew what a funeral was and it made him wonder if Carter had any family either.

“Yes, just like that. I’ll get Uncle John or Uncle James to check into it for you, okay?” Ian felt her body relax a little and she nodded.

For a few moments, he sat holding his little girl and thinking maybe he really could do this. She’d been putting on such a brave front for everyone, but Lily really was just a little girl who lost her mother, and no matter how smart she was, it was still hard to understand. It was hard for adults to understand.

“Can we go feed Gracie now?” She wiped her eyes, and Ian nodded. She jumped down from his lap and ran out of his room.

"I think this little one might be ready for a story, too." His mother stood in the doorway with Grace resting her little head on his mother's shoulder.

"I think so too." Ian lifted the baby from his mother arms.

"You're going to be a great father, Ian." Kathleen kissed his cheek and walked away from him.

"So, Gracie. Do you think Nanny is right?" Ian studied the round face of the baby girl. She grabbed his nose and babbled. "I'm going to take that as a yes. Let's go out and have story time with your big sister." Then maybe when they went to sleep he'd call Sandy because as hectic as it had been all day, he missed her like crazy. He just hoped she answered.

Chapter 10

Sandy stared out the window and watched a small bird eat from the bird feeder in the back garden. She really loved visiting this house, even though it brought a lot of bad memories back but it was something she needed to do so she wouldn't have to keep looking over her shoulder and give Keith the peace he deserved as well.

Then there was his brother. The one she couldn't get out of her mind because she'd completely overreacted with everything. Considering what happened in the past, it wasn't a surprise. It still hurt to think about how Ian blew her off for the woman who broke his heart. Especially, to know for sure that they didn't just talk.

"Why are you acting so self-righteous considering what you're hiding from him," Sandy whispered to herself. "If he knew everything, he'd probably run for the hills."

The door to her room opened, and she turned to see the familiar face come through the door holding a tray. Ruby was the older sister of one of her dearest friends, and she'd become a good friend to her as well. Tessa's life had been short and tragic and was one of the reasons Sandy wasn't giving up on finding the bastard that took Tessa's life and left her little girl without a mother.

Evie was another reason Sandy kept in touch with Ruby because she'd fell in love with Tessa's little girl. Sandy took it upon herself to help Ruby with the little girl.

"Alexandra, you haven't eaten all day. I brought you a sandwich and some tea." Ruby said, and Sandy cringed. She hadn't used her given name since she'd left Yellowknife. She hated it, but Ruby refused to call her anything else.

"Thanks, Ruby." Sandy met her at the door and took the tray. "You really didn't have to do that."

"Do you think I don't know a broken heart when I see it? I saw that look on you before." Ruby sat on the foot of the bed.

"Ian is nothing like him." Sandy snapped a little louder than she intended.

"I see." Ruby stared at her. "So, what did this Ian do?"

"Nothing really. It wasn't Ian's fault, and I overreacted." Sandy plopped down on the bed.

"I seem to remember you thinking that about someone else." Ruby reminded her.

Sandy's body trembled as her thoughts drifted back to the day she almost lost everything.

Nine years earlier.

Keith O'Connor had to be a crazy man because there was no way the man sitting in her living room was the same man Keith described to her. Scott Coates was her husband, and she knew him better than anyone. Didn't she? The man Keith described was a cold, cruel man, but the one sitting in her living room wasn't him. This one agreed to marry her even though she was pregnant with another man's baby.

"Hey, babe didn't hear you come in." He stood up and stretched.

"Sorry, I was just watching you." Sandy lied.

"You look exhausted. Maybe you need to rest." He walked toward her, and before he got within arms reach she blurted out the question swirling around in her brain since she'd left Keith's office.

"How do you know Tessa?" Sandy asked.

His face turned red with anger, and his hands fisted at his sides. In the short time, Sandy had known him not once had she seen the expression of hatred on his face. She gasped when he grabbed her shoulders and shook her.

"Don't ever mention that fucking name in front of me again." He was squeezing her shoulder so hard it was hurting. "Do you understand me?" She nodded and pulled away from his grasp.

"I was just wondering." She whispered as she backed up toward the kitchen and cupped her hands over her swollen stomach.

"Well stop, because that bitch almost ruined my life with her lies and one of these days she'll get what's coming to her." He growled as he pulled his phone out of his pocket. He read something on the screen and snatched his coat from the hook.

"Where are you going?" Sandy asked.

"None of your fucking business." With that, he slammed the door behind him.

Sandy walked into the nursery and looked around. He'd helped her put the whole thing together. He helped her get excited about the baby. She grabbed the white teddy bear on the dresser and hugged it to her. Keith was right. Just the mention of Tessa's name turned Scott's face into a menacing snarl. Obviously, Tessa wasn't mistaken. Scott had been the one to rape her when she was just fifteen years old. What made Sandy's stomach clench was he'd gotten off with it because Tessa was too terrified to testify against him. According to Keith, there were also stories that Tessa wasn't the only one, and he was still a person of interest in some missing person cases.

It terrified her that she really didn't know him at all but what was she supposed to do. She was twenty-three years old, pregnant and the only family she had was her father in Newfoundland, but she'd never even met him and as far as she knew he wanted nothing to do with her.

She picked up the phone to call the one person who'd become like a brother to her since she'd moved to the north. He'd help her figure out what to do.

Sandy shook her head back to the present and sighed when she realized Ruby had not left the room. If it weren't for Ruby, she would have had nowhere to go on that terrible week, and Evie would be in foster care.

"Evie will be home from school soon," Ruby said. "She's looking forward to spending some time with you, Alexandra."

"I feel guilty for not coming to visit more often." Sandy picked up the sandwich and took a small bite.

"You have no reason to feel guilty. Evie knows you love her. She's a smart little girl, and she keeps those teachers on their toes." Ruby grinned.

"I'm so glad you agreed to take custody of her. I didn't want to see her lost in the system considering I was the one that turned her into an orphan at two weeks old." Sandy stood up and moved to the window.

"Don't be so hard on yourself. That man is the reason Evie was orphaned, and the reason why your baby is gone and I pray some day we'll get justice." Ruby snarled, and Sandy stared at her because she was usually so quiet and refined, but the man took Ruby's sister, so she had every right to hate him.

It was still hard to believe that it had been eight years, and there wasn't a day she didn't think about her little girl. The one Scott took away with one bullet along with her ability to have children. Well, the doctor never said she'd never be able to have any, but the chances were less than ten percent. The bullet damaged her uterus as well as caused her to lose one of her ovaries. She'd been so devastated that she'd spent a year living with Ruby to help her with Evie. It took her a little while to hold Evie at first, but when she did, it was like it helped her heal.

She spent the entire evening playing with Evie and making cupcakes. She felt a connection to Evie, probably because Evie lost her mom the same day Sandy lost her child. There wasn't a day that went by that she didn't think about what her daughter would look like and what kind of personality she would have. She missed Tessa too. She'd been her only friend when she needed one.

“Alexandra, we should have a movie night tomorrow night since it's Friday.” Sandy could hear the hopefulness in Evie’s voice.

“That sounds like a good idea. What movies would you like to watch?” Sandy asked as she tucked Evie in bed.

“I like Frozen, but nobody ever wants to watch it. Aunt Ruby says she’s tired of princesses.” Evie rolled her eyes.

“I’d like to watch it with you.” Sandy smiled.

“Yay!” Evie jumped up and wrapped her arms around Sandy. “I love you, Alexandra.”

“I love you too, Baby Doll.” Sandy kissed the top of her head and hugged her tightly.

With Evie sleeping soundly, Sandy sat in her room and read through the numerous texts she’d received from everyone back home. Stephanie had sent her a picture of Ian’s little girls and raved at how cute they were. Stephanie really didn’t mean to make her feel bad but it so hard to think she’d never be able to give him a child.

Stephanie apparently gave Ian shit. Sandy appreciated it, but he didn’t deserve it at least not with what he was dealing with. Her friend urged her to tell Ian everything. Besides Keith, Stephanie was the only ones outside her sister and Ruby that knew everything.

Keith's texts were more about getting information. He was hoping their lead panned out, but of course, as usual, everything they received on Scott never turned up anything. He seemed to be able to vanish every time they got close. What was worse, nobody ever remembered seeing him.

Eight years ago…

"Keith, you have to get me out of here," Sandy shouted when he finally answered.

"Did he hurt you?" Keith growled into the phone.

"No, but I asked him about Tessa and the look in his eyes... Keith, he was so pissed." He looked like he could actually hurt someone.

"Put together what you need, and I'll be there to get you in thirty minutes," Keith said. "Sandy, if he comes back don't let him know I'm coming, okay?"

"Okay." Sandy hung up the phone with a shaky hand and quickly put a bag together. She placed it next to the door and stared at the clock. It seemed like it wasn't moving at all. Thirty minutes never seemed so long. When her back door finally opened, she jumped.

"Where the hell are you going?" Sandy turned slowly at the sound of his voice.

"I'm just going out to visit a friend." Sandy knew her voice was anything but calm.

"Babe, do you think I'm a complete idiot? You're not going anywhere in your condition." That's when she noticed the gun in his hand and the blood on his clothes.

"Scott, what did you do?" She backed toward the front door to put as much distance between them as possible.

"Don't worry about it. All you need to know is that bitch won't be spreading stories about me anymore." Sandy gasped at his admittance, but before she could respond, her front door flew open.

"Sandy, grab your stuff and go out to the car," Keith growled.

"She's not goin' anywhere with you." Scott snapped.

Sandy noticed his hand was behind his back and she remembered the gun. She opened her mouth to warn Keith, but he stopped her.

"Sandy, go out to the car," Keith said.

It was as if everything happened in slow motion. Scott lifted the weapon and pointed it straight at Keith. Without a second thought, she shoved Keith. A loud crack caused her ears to vibrate. Keith slammed against the wall, and Sandy felt as if someone punched her in the stomach. She was jolted back against the counter knocking the wind out of her lungs. She slid to the floor as she gasped for air and everything around her started to blur. She blinked her eyes to clear her vision and saw Keith point his weapon at Scott. The last thing she remembered was glancing down at her stomach to see her shirt soaked in blood.

She woke up in the hospital with Keith holding her hand. For a moment, she wasn't sure what had happened. Keith somber expression had it all flooding back.

"You saved my life." He whispered as he kissed the top of her head.

"Why am I here?" She could barely speak.

"Sandy, you were shot," Keith whispered. The memory of her blood-soaked shirt flashed in her mind.

"My baby?" Her other hand went to her stomach, and she knew.

"I'm sorry, Sandy," Keith whispered. "The baby... She didn't make it."

"He killed my .... How could I have married someone like him?" She sobbed.

"That's something I meant to tell you when I got you out of there. Your wedding wasn't real. You're not legally married to Scott. The guy who performed the ceremony wasn't certified to perform wedding ceremonies." She couldn't believe what she was hearing.

"I don't want to hear any more." She just wanted to curl up in a ball and cry for her baby. The little girl never got a chance to live, and she would never get to hold her daughter.

"Keith, it's Tessa." A bald man entered the room, and the look on his face told her it wasn't good.

"What?" Keith stood up.

"He got to her, man."

"No!" Keith whispered. "I was supposed to protect her and Evie."

"The baby was with Ruby." The man was one of her co-workers she knew as Bull.

"Take care of her." Keith roared as he bolted out of the room. Sandy turned to her side and let the tears she'd been holding

back flow. Bull sat next to her and held her hand while she mourned her baby and one of her best friends.

Sandy jolted awake to the beeping of her phone. She grabbed it off the nightstand and stared at the screen. It was Ian.

I miss you, please call me. Please

Tears flowed down her cheeks like a river. Sandy needed to talk to him because the truth was, she missed the man so much it was hard to breathe. No matter what happened, nothing was going to change how much she loved him. She just didn't know how he would handle her secret, but how could she tell him without telling Keith's too?

I'll call you tonight. I miss you too.

Okay.

Sandy's first priority was to call Keith. She needed to find out how much Keith wanted people to know. If he was okay with any of it. Then she'd tell Ian, but she was doing that face to face. She owed him that much. Especially with the way she reacted to something he had no control over. The only thing that she was afraid to tell him was, her inability to have children. Would it be too much for Ian to handle? Then there was dealing with her own acceptance of his two little girls. Colleen gave him the one thing that Sandy couldn't. Could she accept that?

Chapter 11

It had been a long day, and it didn't take long for the girls to fall asleep, but as exhausted as he felt, standing in the doorway to his daughters' bedroom watching them sleep was strangely calming. The first night had been a little bumpy but thanks to his mom, grandmother and Lily, it ended with Grace falling asleep before they'd even finished the book and Lily telling him he did a great job.

Ian smiled as Lily sighed and rolled onto her side. The little girl was such a contradiction. She was six years old, but she seemed to have such an old soul. Gracie babbled something in her sleep, and Ian chuckled when she giggled. At least she was young enough that it would be easier for her to adjust, but Lily worried him.

"Ya did a great job, Inky." His grandmother whispered as she stood next to him. Ian wrapped his arm around her shoulder and kissed the top of her head.

"Thanks, Nan. I hope I can be all they need." Ian whispered, and Nanny Betty closed the bedroom door before she turned to him and grabbed his hands.

“Ian William O’Connor yer exactly wat dem babies needs and don’t ya forget it, but ya need ta get yer act together and work tings out wit, Sandy. I like her, and Cora says she’s yours.” She squeezed his hands gently, and Ian tried really hard not to roll his eyes at his Aunt Cora’s name. He knew better than to scoff at Cora the Cupid, and what he and his brothers referred to it as her Cupid power.

“I’ll try my best, Nan. I love her, but with all this, it’s a lot for someone to accept.” That was his biggest fear and finally admitting it had his stomach turning. What if Sandy couldn’t live with the fact he had two little girls that weren’t hers? He loved her so much, but his priority now was his daughters.

“She’ll deal wit it better den ya tink. Ya jus’ needs ta be as understandin’ as ya want her ta be.” Nanny Betty said. “Now, I gotta go. Tom’s pickin’ me up and bringin’ me home because da man tinks I shouldn’t be walkin’ at night by meself.” She rolled her eyes. Ian chuckled because if the woman really wanted to walk home, nothing or no one would tell her any different. His grandmother really didn’t mind Tom fussing over her.

“I’m not going to say I disagree.” Ian held her coat.

“I’ll drop by tamara’ and help out fer a bit if ya wants.” Nanny Betty kissed his cheek as she pulled open the door. Tom stood on the front step ready to knock.

"Thanks, Nan. I'll let you know." Ian hugged her. "Hey Tom, thanks for driving Nan home." Ian shook hands with the older man.

"It's my pleasure even though Elizabeth complains when I fuss over her." Tom held out his elbow, and Nanny Betty linked her hand into his arm.

"I don't complain and stop callin' me Elizabeth." She snapped.

"Of course, Betty my dear, a slip of the tongue." Tom placed his hand over hers, and Ian smiled when she grunted on their way to the car. If his father, uncle, he or one of his brothers said anything like that to her, she'd smack them, but Tom seemed to get away with a lot.

Ian was pouring a cup of coffee when his phone vibrated in his pocket. He pulled it out expecting to see his mother's number or even one of his brothers. Sandy's beautiful smile showed on the screen, and his heart started to thud in his chest. He swiped the screen and cleared his throat.

"Hello."

"Hi." Sandy's voice was quiet and almost unsure.

"I'm glad you called." Ian rested his hip against the counter.

“I wanted to hear your voice.”

“What’s wrong, sweetheart?” It wasn’t like her to sound so defeated.

“I miss you.” She sighed.

“I miss you too. I was worried I wouldn’t hear from you.” Ian admitted.

“I just needed to do some thinking,” Sandy said. “I need to talk to you when I get home.”

“That doesn’t sound right.” His heart started to pound in his chest.

“There’s just something you need to know before we can even think of a future together.” Now he was anxious.

“Can’t you tell me now?”

“It’s not something I want to do over the phone, but I wanted to let you know I’ll be home tomorrow and…. I love you.” she whispered the last three words, but it echoed in his brain.

“I love you too, Sandy,” Ian whispered.

“How are things with your daughters?”

“Hectic and terrifying. I don’t know if I’m going to be a good father.” Ian said.

“You’re going to do great, Doc. Look, I need to run, but I’ll see you tomorrow night.” Sandy said.

“Okay.” He didn’t want her to go.

“But Ian….” She stopped.

“Yeah.”

“I do love you.” Before he had a chance to respond, she ended the call, but he sent her a text.

You hung up before I could tell you. I love you too, and I can’t wait to see you tomorrow.

She didn’t answer, but she’d read the message. Ian couldn’t wait to see her and have her meet his daughters. A sudden pang of guilt hit him in the chest like a punch. He’d hurt her by not being honest with her back then, but he wasn’t losing her again no matter what.

He jerked upright in the bed when a small warm hand touched his cheek. At first, he was confused, but he heard her little voice, and he turned. Lily was kneeling on the bed still in her pajamas. He didn’t remember falling asleep, but he glanced down and realized he was still wearing his jeans and T-shirt with his phone resting in the middle of his chest.

“You sleep really loud.” Lily tilted her head and stared down at him.

“I snore when I’m tired.” Ian laughed and glanced at his phone. It was a little after eight. “Is Gracie awake?” Ian sat up in the bed.

“Yep, she got all her blankets tossed on the floor. She likes to do that when she wakes up.” Lily didn’t follow him, and he stopped at the door.

“Is something wrong, Lily?” Ian asked when he noticed.

“Who’s Sandy?” She asked, and Ian bit back a curse.

“She’s my next door neighbor.” What else was he supposed to tell a six-year-old?

“You said you loved her. Is she your girlfriend?” She did that head tilt thing.

“When did you hear me say that?” Ian had been careful the day before because he didn’t know how Lily would react. He needed her to know she and her sister were his first priority.

"When you were asleep." She smiled. "Can I meet her?" The kid was incredible.

"She's away for work, but she'll be home tonight. You can meet her if you want." Ian held out his hand. "I think right now we better get Gracie before she tips over the crib." Ian could hear the crib banging off the wall, and he figured Grace was getting impatient waiting.

Ian was glad Colleen had involved Lily so much with the baby because while he didn't have trouble getting Grace changed and dressed, but he was a little out of his element with picking out things the child could eat. Lily must have seen the fear on his face and pointed to the box of baby cereal on the counter.

"You're an excellent helper, Lily," Ian told her while he was trying to get Grace to keep most of the food in her mouth.

"I like to help." She informed him as she dug into a bowl of Cheerios. She'd insisted they were the healthy option.

"Good, because I'm learning and I'm gonna need all the help I can get." Ian groaned as Grace spit yet another spoonful of cereal at him, but this time she didn't miss his face. Lily started to giggle as he wiped it off.

"You think that's funny." Ian smiled at her, and she nodded. "Maybe I should get you to feed her."

“She doesn’t spit at me.” Lily giggled.

“Well let’s see about that.” Ian pushed the high chair next to Lily and handed her the bowl. He stood back and crossed his arms over his chest.

“Look, Gracie, it’s a plane, vroom.” Lily held the spoon in the air and slowly brought it to Grace’s mouth, and Ian smirked. Any second the baby was going to make a mess, but Grace opened her mouth and took the whole spoonful of mush into her mouth without spilling a drop. All he could do was stare. Grace flopped her arms up and down with each spoonful Lily gave her.

“And why didn’t you tell me she liked the airplane game?” Ian narrowed his eyes at Lily.

“Because it’s funny when she spits it at you.” Lily giggled as Grace took the last spoonful of food and looked up at Ian with a grin.

“So, you think it’s funny to do you?” Ian reached down and tickled the baby’s stomach making her squeal with laughter.

“That’s probably the only girls you can get to squeal for you.” Ian didn’t need to turn around to know the mocking voice.

“Good to see you too, A.J.” Ian cleaned Grace’s hands and face.

"Hi Uncle A.J." Lily smiled as she brought the dishes to the dishwasher. "I'm gonna go get dressed, Daddy." She said as she dashed out of the kitchen.

"She seems to be settling in fast." Aaron poured himself a cup of coffee and sat in the chair next to Grace. "How's this little dolly doing?"

"So far, so good but I think Lily is helping with that. I'm a little worried at how well Lily is doing. Last night she had a little breakdown, but today she seems fine." Ian admitted.

"At least she's got lots of support with the family." Aaron was letting Grace play with his fingers.

"I hope you washed your hands before you let my daughter touch them." Ian sat across from his youngest brother.

"I had a shower at home before I came here, ass…. jerk." Aaron stopped himself when Grace giggled as he tickled her.

"I see. So you slept in your own bed last night." Ian chuckled, and Aaron put his hand over Grace's ears.

"Fuck you," Aaron said in a hushed voice.

"Danny said Nanny Kathleen puts pepper on your tongue when you say bad words." Ian and Aaron looked toward the door where Lily stood with a brush in her hand. “Uncle A.J. you’re lucky Nanny’s not here.” She held out the brush to Ian.

“You know James’ boys have big mouths.” Aaron sipped his coffee.

“Can you brush my hair?” Lily asked, and Ian felt a sudden wave of panic.

“I can try,” Ian said taking the brush. Lily’s hair was a mass of curls, and as he gently tried to pull the brush through her hair, the brush got stuck. “Well, this isn’t going well. I’m going to call my mom to come over and do this.”

“Come over here, Lily.” Aaron sighed and glared at Ian.

“This should be interesting.” Ian scoffed.

Five minutes later, Aaron had Lily’s hair tangle free and pulled into a ponytail at the back of her head. Ian stared in shock and then grinned.

“Don’t even think about laughing,” Aaron warned.

“Where did you learn to do that?” Ian pulled Grace out of her chair.

“While all my big brothers were busy ditching our annoying female cousins and leaving Nick and me at their mercy, they taught us a few things that come in handy with the ladies." Aaron wiggled his eyebrows. "Besides with the older girls, ponytails come in handy."

"Watch it, bro." Ian nodded toward Lily who was staring up at Aaron waiting for him to continue.

"What? It comes in handy when we're eating, and their hair is in the way." Aaron gave him an innocent smile that was nothing close to innocent.

"Thank you, Uncle A.J." Lily left the kitchen.

"What are you doing here anyway?" Ian asked as he put Grace in her playpen with her bottle.

"I wanted to see how it was going." Aaron plopped down on the couch.

"Come on A.J. you don't just drop by to see how it's going," Ian said putting air quotes around the how it's going.

"Fine, mom asked for one of us to drop by every day to make sure you're not getting overwhelmed because you'd know it if she was here every day. So today I pulled the short straw." Aaron said.

"I figured she'd be dropping by every day, but I guess she has the cavalry looking out for me." Ian rolled his eyes.

Aaron stayed until supper, and he didn't know who was having more fun playing crazy eights, Aaron or Lily. Lily was winning most of the hands, but Ian was sure Aaron was letting her because when she'd win, he'd make a big deal about losing and if she was cheating. It made her giggle when he'd slam his cards on the table and exaggerate his whining. Grace seemed to enjoy it too because he'd turn to her and ask her if she was helping Lily cheat.

Aaron entertaining the girls gave him a chance to shower and tidy up around the house. It also gave him the opportunity to run to Isabelle's restaurant and pick up supper. If he was being honest, he was enjoying the day with his brother. Aaron was always the jokester, and although he was a bit of a playboy, he still had a heart of gold.

"I'm telling your daddy you're cheating." Aaron picked Lily up off the chair and tossed her in the air making her squeal.

"You're just a sore loser." Lily wiggled away from him and ran out of the living room.

"You're a bigger youngster than she is." Ian shook his head as he handed Aaron a cup of coffee.

"She's a great kid, bro," Aaron said.

"It's only been a couple of days, but she seems to be comfortable with the family and me. I just worry that she's keeping everything inside."

"Kids bounce back pretty quick but shouldn't she see a shrink to make sure she's dealing with that shit? I mean losing her mom and her step-dad has got to be rough on her." Aaron had a point, and Ian knew it. Lily was dealing with the death of her mother a little too well.

"I think I'll give one of my old classmates a call. He's a pediatric psychologist." Ian said.

"Maybe she's like you and just keeps everything locked up tight," Aaron was probably right. It's why he always got sick in stressful times.

Over the years, Ian hadn't been great at expressing how he felt and when he was hurt he usually kept it deep down. He knew from experience it wasn't good to keep things locked up.

Aaron left as he was getting the girls ready for bed. It was a little awkward bathing them, but part of his life now. Ian got Grace's bottle, and when he walked into the living room, Lily was already sitting on the couch with a book. He looked at the cover, and his heart sank. The book was called '*We're making breakfast for*

Mother,' and he knew that Lily could read so she had to know the name of the book.

"Is that the book you want to read, honey?" He tried to sound casual as he settled Grace in the crook of his arm. Grace quickly popped the bottle in her mouth and snuggled into his chest. He smiled as he glanced down at the baby.

"I like this story." Lily climbed onto Ian's lap and opened the book. "Mommy read it all the time."

Maybe it was her way of feeling close to Colleen. He wasn't going to rock the boat by asking her if it would be a better idea to read another book.

As he read, Lily turned each page, and Grace drifted off to sleep. He was constantly glancing at Lily to gauge her reaction, but all he could see was her lips moving as she silently read along with him. By the end of the book Lily's eyes were droopy, but emotionally she seemed to be fine.

"I think it's time for sleepy little girls to go to bed." Ian stood with both girls in his arms. Grace was sound asleep, and Lily rested her head against his shoulder as he made his way to their room. Ian sat Lily on her bed and carefully settled Grace into her crib. The baby babbled something and sighed when he covered her.

When he turned around, Lily curled up in her bed staring at him. He pulled the covers over her and sat on the side of the bed. She still didn't speak, but her eyes never left his face.

"You're a good daddy," Lily said sleepily and tucked her hands under her cheek.

"Thank you, and you're a terrific big sister to Gracie." Ian smiled remembering all the times his mother would tell him how great a big brother he was to his younger brothers. It always made him feel good as a little boy even though John and James were older than him, it still made him feel like he was king of the world that his mother would give him that compliment.

"Can you sing like Uncle A.J.?" She asked. Aaron had been singing with her earlier and had made the mistake of mentioning the band his brothers had. He'd also told her that Ian could sing and play the guitar. It wasn't that he couldn't, it was just that it was something he did alone.

"Well Uncle A.J. is probably a better singer but don't tell him I said that." Ian tapped her nose with his finger, and she giggled.

"Can you sing me a song?" There was no way he could deny her when she used those big blue eyes on him.

"Sure, honey." Ian tucked her hair behind her ear and sang the first song that came to his head. Irish Lullaby was a song his mother would sing to them before bed time as kids, and since it was a lullaby, it just seemed fitting to sing to his little girl.

He'd been about half way through the song when she yawned and closed her eyes, and for a few minutes, he just watched her sleep. He didn't know what she was going through and it was killing him. He still had his mother and the thought of something happening to her made his chest hurt.

He closed the door quietly as he left the room. Sandy was going to be back that night, but he hadn't heard from her. Maybe she'd changed her mind about coming to talk to him or maybe her flight didn't get in. He missed her and prayed with all the changes in his life, they could still move forward in their relationship. He couldn't change what happened that night as much as he wanted to but it killed him to know it hurt Sandy.

He grabbed a beer from the fridge and settled in on the couch to wait for Sandy. It was the first time he'd sat down to relax since he got out of bed that morning. How the hell did his parents raise seven boys? He was dead on his feet with two little girls, and they weren't nearly as rambunctious. Was he really going to be able to raise two girls by himself? What did he actually know about raising kids especially girls? ure, he grew up around four female cousins, but all he remembered about that was terrorizing them. He needed to talk to someone who knew about raising girls, and the only one he could think of was his Uncle Kurt.

Chapter 12

Sandy was never so glad to see her driveway in her life. The last twenty-four hours were a roller coaster, and it wasn't over yet. She still had to talk to Ian and the thought of telling him she could probably never give him any more children was terrifying. Reliving that night was not easy for her, and she hadn't talked much about it to anyone.

She walked into her house and dropped her bag in the foyer with a thud. Every part of her body was exhausted, but she had no time to rest. She pulled her cell phone out of her pocket and checked it. There were no missed calls or messages, and it made her heart drop a little. Part of her was hoping to see something from Ian.

She called Keith to let him know she was back and to make sure he was still okay with her telling Ian about Yellowknife. She needed to know he was okay with her coming clean with Ian. Their relationship was never going to work if she kept this secret from him.

Her heart pounded as she waited for Keith to answer the phone. She was so worried he would tell her to keep his name out of it that she was on the verge of having a panic attack. When he finally answered, she yelled into the phone.

"Hello," Keith answered with his usual deep, gruff voice.

"Hey, it's me," Sandy said louder than was necessary.

"Is there a reason you're yelling at me?" Keith chuckled.

"Sorry. Listen….ummm…. I want to make sure you're still okay with me telling Ian about Yellowknife." Sandy stumbled over her words and felt like a complete idiot. He was like a brother to her even before she knew she had a brother.

"I already told you I was okay with it." He said.

"I'm afraid this is going to change how he feels." She blurted out.

"I think you should tell him. Especially now, but I honestly don't believe it will change anything," Keith said.

"I hope not." She leaned against the wall.

"I know Ian loves you and he'll understand. If he doesn't, I'll kick his ass." Keith said.

"Yeah, that'll help." Sandy rolled her eyes. "I'm going over to talk to him before I lose my nerve." Sandy pushed herself off the wall and opened the door.

"Do you want me to be there when you tell him?" Keith asked.

"Thanks, but I think I need to do this alone." Sandy sighed.

The whole way to Ian's house she prayed because it would kill her if he couldn't accept it. Considering he came from a large family and they'd talked about what kind of families they wanted one day, Sandy knew Ian wanted a big family.

The screen door was closed, but the door inside was slightly ajar. Sandy opened it and listened before calling out to Ian. It was a little after ten, and she figured the girls were probably asleep. There was no response, so Sandy walked further into the house. The light from the television was flickering, Ian was slouched down on the sofa, and she smiled when she heard his soft snore.

She pressed her head against the door jamb and watched him for a moment. He must have been really exhausted to fall asleep so early. She was disappointed, but it appeared their conversation had to wait.

Sandy turned to leave and saw a little girl standing in the hallway in a pink nightgown with the word Frozen written across the front. Sandy knew the Disney movie well since Evie made her watch it numerous times. Sandy crouched down as the little girl walked toward her.

"Hi," Sandy gazed into the same blue eyes as Ian had. There was no doubt the lovely little girl was Ian's child.

"Hi." The little girl said. "You're Sandy."

"Yes, I am." Sandy was a little taken back that the little girl knew her name.

"I'm Lily." She flicked her wavy hair back from her face.

"It's nice to meet you, Lily. How did you know who I was?" Sandy asked.

"I saw your picture on his phone while he was sleeping and he said he loved you while he was asleep." Lily glanced into the living room and then back at her. "He says it a lot in his sleep."

The little girl seemed so much older than six years old. There was also a lot of sadness in her eyes and with good reason. She'd lost her mother, and if anyone knew how that felt, it was Sandy.

"I see." Sandy didn't know what else to say as she glanced back at Ian softly mumbling on the couch.

"He sleeps really loud." Lily's serious expression made Sandy chuckle.

"He's probably tired." Sandy smiled.

"Yeah." Lily sighed and her eyes filled with tears. Sandy knelt on the floor and took the little girl's hands.

"Lily, what's wrong?" It was a stupid question because the child was probably missing her mother terribly.

"I had a bad dream," Lily said in a soft broken whisper.

Without hesitation, Sandy pulled the little girl into her arms and hugged her tightly. She should probably wake Ian and let him know Lily was upset but something inside her wanted to be the one to help.

"Bad dreams aren't nice, but you know what?" Sandy whispered into the little girl's ear.

"What?" She sobbed

"I'm excellent at scaring away bad dreams. My mommy used to sing me a song that kept all my bad dreams away." Sandy smiled as she thought back to the song her mother sang to her when she was little. It was a silly made up song, but it always made her feel better and at times when she was feeling overwhelmed she'd sing it to herself.

"Where's your mommy?" Lily tilted her head to the side, and her blue eyes searched Sandy's face.

"She's in heaven." Hopefully Lily knew what that meant. Not everyone taught their children about religion these days.

"My mommy's there too." Lily dropped her head.

"I know." What else could she say?

"Can you sing the song to me?" Lily looked at her with such hope that there was no way she could refuse.

"I can, and I'll even teach you the words so you can sing it too." Sandy stood and lifted the little girl into her arms and headed back to the room she'd seen Lily exit.

"We got to sing quietly 'cause Gracie is sleeping," Lily whispered.

"Okay," Sandy whispered and helped Lily into her bed. She glanced around the room. Ian certainly pulled things together quickly, but chances were his family had helped.

"I'm ready." Lily snuggled down into her bed and pulled a ratty-looking bunny into her arms.

“First you need to know that the song has the same music as twinkle, twinkle little star but the words are different,” Sandy explained.

“I know that song. Gracie loves it.” Lily whispered.

“Okay, so listen to the words and then we’ll sing it together, all right?” Sandy said.

“Okay.” Lily smiled.

“I’ll use your name in the song instead of mine.” Sandy knelt next to the bed, and Lily nodded. “Okay, here we go, ‘There’s a place in our minds, where our hopes and fears unwind. Sometimes they are scary things, sometimes they will give you wings. But there’s one thing you must hear, dreams can never hurt you, dear. Lily you must always know, that your daddy loves you so.’”

“I like that song.” Lily yawned.

“You want to try singing it with me?” Sandy asked, and Lily nodded.

Sandy started off slow singing the song again, but Lily never missed a word and not only did she know them but the little girl had such an angelic voice. Sandy stopped singing and just listened.

“That was superb, Lily.” The voice startled Sandy.

“Sandy taught me a song.” Lily’s eyes fluttered. “Her mommy helped her stop the bad dreams.”

“It sounds like a great song.” Ian smiled down at the little girl, and Sandy fell a little bit more for him. If that was even possible.

“Her mommy’s in heaven too.” Lily yawned and closed her eyes.

“I know, sweetie. You go back to sleep, and we’ll be out in the living room.” Ian tucked the blankets around Lily and peeked in the crib at the baby. Sandy hadn’t had a chance to get a glimpse of the baby, but from what she could see there was no doubt she resembled her father.

“I’m sorry, you were asleep, and she was really scared, and I remembered mom singing me that song, and it made me feel...” Ian stopped her babbling by pressing his lips against hers. She stiffened for a moment but the warmth of his mouth and his arms pulling her into him she melted into the kiss.

“I missed you,” Ian whispered.

“I missed you, too.” She pressed her lips against the side of his neck, and he moaned.

"Don't ever leave me like that again." Ian pulled back and cupped her face in his hands. "I know this was all a shock, and you were hurt."

"It wasn't that Ian. It's… well, there's something you don't know and... Only a couple of people know." She tried to look away, but he held her face forcing her to meet his eyes.

"What is it, Sandy? You know you can tell me anything." She wanted to believe him, but she was so afraid it would change how he saw her.

"I just don't want it to make a difference and…. with all the changes in your life this could be too much and…." Sandy stopped and pressed her lips together. It had to be like pulling off a Band-Aid. Just tell him and then answer his questions, but the minute she gazed into his eyes, the words stuck in her throat.

"Sandy, are you sick?" The pained expression that came over his face made her cringe. Since his brother James had lost his first wife to cancer, the whole family probably worried about it.

"No. I'm not sick... I'm... I lost a baby eight years ago, and I can't have children anymore because of what happened." Sandy blurted out so fast she wasn't sure he even understood what she said.

"You can't?" It was almost as if he couldn't believe what he was asking.

“No.” She shoved her hands into the front pockets of her jeans and stared at the floor.

“You said only a couple of people know about this. So, Stephanie knows?” Ian asked.

“Yes.” She glanced up to meet his eyes, but he’d walked out of the room. Her eyes blurred with tears because it was just as she feared.

“Who else knows?” His voice startled her. She turned, and he was holding two bottles of beer. One of which he held out to her.

“My sister Kim, Stephanie and….” She took the bottle, and her hand shook. She was worried about telling him Keith knew.

“And who?” Ian raised the bottle to his lips but stopped just before it touched them.

“Keith,” Sandy whispered.

“My brother.” Ian’s jaw clenched, and it was evident he didn’t like Keith knowing.

“I don’t talk about this, and the only reason Keith knows is that he was there.” Sandy watched his expression turn from anger to concern.

“What happened?” Ian asked

"It's a long story, but I want to tell you if you want to know. I need you to know, but it's tough for me to talk about it." Keeping her emotions under control when she spoke of her baby was almost impossible.

"Was Keith, the father?" Ian asked but before she had a chance to answer a familiar gruff voice answered for her.

"Don't be a fucking ass. No, I wasn't the baby's father." Keith snapped.

"What are you doing here?" Ian stomped past her and plopped down on the couch.

"I knew Sandy was going to tell you and I wanted to fill in the parts she didn't know. Ian nobody else needs to know about this." Keith stood in the center of the room and crossed his arms over his massive chest. She always referred to it as his 'I'm intimidating you' stance.

"Stop with the cloak and dagger shit, Keith. Just tell me what the hell this is all about." Ian rolled his eyes, apparently not the least bit intimidated by his younger brother.

Her stomach churned even thinking about how it all started. She wasn't proud of that time of her life. After her mother had passed, she went a little wild. Drinking and sleeping with men she hardly knew. The very reason she got pregnant in the first place was because of a wild night of drinking way too much and screwing around with a man she just met.

"Go ahead, Sandy." Keith nodded and sat down next to Ian. "You keep your trap shut until she's done." He poked Ian in the chest with his finger.

Nine years earlier...

Sandy scanned the small tavern for a target because getting hammered and taking a random guy home seemed to be the only thing that helped her forget the pain of losing her mother. Even while she was at work, she couldn't ignore it, but she couldn't mix her promiscuous lifestyle with her job. Being one of only two women on the Yellowknife police department, she'd heard the men talk about the other female officer and how she was easy. She didn't want them disrespecting her the same way.

She saw him the minute his gaze locked onto her. He was a little older than she preferred but he had a nice face and a friendly smile. Sandy wasn't egotistical, but she knew men were attracted to her curves. Of course, the tight jeans and top she was wearing accentuated it. She winked and stalked toward him like a lioness stalking her prey.

"Hello, gorgeous." His voice was deep, and he smelled like Ivory soap.

"Hello, yourself, handsome." She ran her finger up his arm and licked her lower lip. It always worked, and when his gaze slowly moved down her body, she knew she had him.

"What's your name, honey?" He asked.

"Alexa." It wasn't really a lie because it was part of her name.

"No last name, huh? I'm Dennis, and I'm very happy to meet you." His green eyes sparkled when he smiled, and before all this, she could see herself getting to know him, but now she just wanted a release.

A few shots of whiskey and God knows what else, they brought the party back to the small motel behind the club. He wasn't much taller than she was and not muscular, but he had a decent body, and he was a pretty good kisser. Things got hot pretty fast, and it was over almost as quickly. She slid out of bed and was about to get dressed, but he grabbed her hand and pulled her back to the bed.

"That was way too fast, honey." Dennis grinned. "Come back here, and I'll show you what I can really do." Sandy smiled. She had to admit she was interested, but her rule was once and done.

"Sorry handsome, I have to run, but maybe I can catch you next week." Sandy grabbed her clothes and winked as she hurried into the bathroom. It had been over a month since she went searching for sex to forget her grief and like every other time, it didn't work. Nothing was going to help her get over her mother's death. It was time for her to deal with it the right way.

Six weeks later….

Sandy swore she'd never walk into the club again in case she'd run into Dennis again. Now here she was waiting for him to show up because their one night had turned into a lifetime commitment. How was it when she'd decided to face her grief and stop sleeping around, the last man she screwed gets her pregnant?

She'd been sitting in the club for over an hour, and it was the fourth night in a row. The worst thing was she couldn't ask anyone because she didn't even know his last name.

She stood up about to leave when someone tapped her on the shoulder. She turned and met the eyes of a man she didn't know. He was dirty looking with unkempt, greasy hair and a beard that was tinted yellow with nicotine, but it was his smile that made the hair on the back of her neck stand up.

"I've seen you here the last couple of days." The man said stepping a little too close.

"I was looking for someone, but it looks like he doesn't come here anymore." Sandy pulled on her jacket and zipped it quickly when he leered at her breasts.

"You were here with Dennis a few weeks back." He grinned, and the smell of his breath made her stomach turn but if this guy could help she'd have to talk to him.

"Do you know him?" Maybe he could get in touch with Dennis, then she could let him know about the baby. She wasn't looking for anything, but he could be as involved as he wanted. He could step up, or he could be absent like her own father. Either way, she didn't care because she'd decided to keep the baby.

"I did." When the man leaned closer, Sandy stepped to the side.

"What do you mean did?" She was really getting a bad feeling.

"He got killed in a Skidoo accident about two weeks ago," The man reached seemed to take the hint and stepped back.

"He's….he's dead?" Sandy stammered. The man nodded. She backed away, turned and ran out of the club. She heard the man yell something after her, but she didn't know or care what he said.

She remembered the accident because the department had sent officers out searching for the man that went missing. She never did find out who he was, but now she knew. Her baby's father was dead, or at least she assumed it was the same, Dennis. The man at the club said he'd seen her with him. What was she going to do?

The next couple of weeks passed in a blur. How could she do this by herself? Sandy had no family to help unless you counted her father but she'd never even met him, and she was sure he wouldn't help. The only friends she had were Tessa and Ruby, but Tessa was pregnant herself.

She also had to let the department know, but the minute they found out, it was desk duty for her. They'd been trying to get her behind a desk since she'd started because of her computer skills. She'd always declined the offers, but now she didn't have a choice

At five months, the superintendent put her behind the desk and saddled her with research just as she predicted. Not that she didn't like working with computers, but the job she was doing wasn't exactly all she could do. Then again there weren't a lot of cyber criminals in Yellowknife.

She'd received several calls from Tessa throughout the day asking weird questions about a friend of hers that was going to be dropping by to talk to her. At first, Sandy thought Tessa was setting her up on a blind date, but then she said something weird about him knowing what she needed. That statement made her extra nervous.

She was getting ready to head home when the Superintendent called her into his office. She had a feeling he was probably going to talk her into going on leave until the baby was born but when she walked in she ran into a wall of solid muscle. She slowly raised her head up and up until she met his amused eyes. He had the bluest eyes she'd ever seen.

"Alexandra, I'd like you to meet Keith O'Connor." Superintendent Moss motioned to the brick wall.

"Nice to meet you, Mr. O'Connor." Sandy held out her hand.

"My father is Mr. O'Connor. Call me Keith, and it's a pleasure to meet you too." He was a Newfoundlander. There was no covering the accent.

"I'll let you two talk and Keith it's good to see you again." The superintendent walked out of the office leaving her alone with the large man.

"Let me get right to the point. I need a computer analysis, and I'm told you're the best." He crossed his arms over his massive chest and stared down at her. If he thought, he was going to intimidate her with that stance he was mistaken.

"I'm sure there's better somewhere in the world I guess." She liked giving herself the little ego boost.

"Good. I'm here to offer you a job with my security company, and I need you to start right away." Keith held out a folder full of papers.

"There's no beating around the bush with you, is there?" Sandy took the folder.

"Nope. When I want something, I go after it. Usually, I get it, and I want you, Alexandra. First, I've done a background check on you, and I know your education as well I know you're from Newfoundland." Keith braced himself back against the door and crossed his legs at the ankles.

"Why do you want me?" She was curious as to why he would hire a total stranger.

"As I said, I heard you're the best and that's all I hire. That has everything you need to know." Sandy glanced down at the yellow folder in her hands.

"You do know I'm pregnant?" Sandy opened the folder and began to scan the papers without looking back up to gauge his reaction.

"Yes I do, and I also know the father of your baby is dead." Sandy's head snapped up, and her mouth dropped open.

"How?" She gasped.

"Tessa. I know everything about you." Keith raised an eyebrow.

That look told her he knew what she'd been doing since she arrived in Yellowknife. She was pissed. Not because Tessa told him about her but because it was as if he was looking down on her. Who gave him the right to judge her?

"I don't see how my lifestyle would cause problems with how I do my job." Sandy snapped.

"It doesn't. I don't care if you screw the entire male population of Yellowknife. I'll give you twenty-four hours to read over that contract, and I'll be back tomorrow for your answer." Before she had a chance to say anything he was gone leaving her with her mouth hung open.

When she got home, Tessa and Ruby were taking up supper. The West sisters had become her best friends since she arrived up north, but at that moment she wanted to smack Tessa for telling Keith about her.

"Hey there." Ruby sat down at the table.

"Hi." Sandy opened the fridge and grabbed a bottle of water.

"So tell me." Tessa grinned.

"Tell you what?" Sandy leaned against the counter and rubbed her hand over her swollen belly.

“Come on Alexandra. Keith told me he talked to you.” Tessa rested her hands on her own swollen belly.

“How do you know this guy anyway?” He wasn't remotely like any of Tessa's other friends. Most of her male friends were either losers or bigger losers.

“He’s friends with my brother,” Tessa said.

“It figures he would be friends with Lane.” Her brother was much like Keith. Tall, handsome and full of muscle.

“Actually, he doesn’t call my brother Lane. All the guys that work with Keith have stupid nicknames. They call Lane, Shadow.” Ruby rolled her eyes.

“Look, Keith is a good guy, and Newfoundland Security Services or as Lane calls it N.S.S, is a great company,” Tessa said.

“How do you know so much about it?” From everything, she read the contract N.S.S, was a private company. They were hired strictly through government agencies.

“Lane asked Keith to help him investigate some missing women around Yellowknife as well as the assaults happening around here over the last five years. Lane’s convinced it’s the same guy.” Tessa’s face paled a little, and her eyes became glassy.

"The same guy that attacked you?" Sandy asked. Tessa had told her about the man that raped her when she was fifteen. He'd left her for dead. Tessa was now twenty-years-old, but there were times she seemed so much older because of what happened to her.

"Yes." Tessa's voice was barely a whisper.

"Are they having any luck with it?" Sandy sat next to her friend and took her hands. Ruby had dropped her head down and sniffed.

"I don't know. I don't ask." Tessa smiled, but it wasn't her normal happy smile. It was the one she used when she was putting on her happy front. Sandy knew it was time for a subject change, but she would ask about it when she told Keith she was accepting the job.

So, began her job with Newfoundland Security Services and the big burly men that worked for the equally big burly Keith O'Connor.

To people who didn't know them, the men could be intimidating, but to her, they were like big brothers. Keith, Bull, Shadow, Hulk, Trunk, Smash and Crash were larger than life and treated her like a princess. Their names were a little crazy, but of course, they weren't their real names. For the most part, they referred to each other by their nicknames. Even Keith went by Rusty with the guys, but she was warned to call him Keith. He hated the nickname he'd received because of his hair.

In her sixth month, Tessa and Ruby had to go to Edmonton to take care of their grandmother. It left Sandy alone. The following week she met Scott Coates at a coffee shop. The small café was full, and he asked if he could sit with her. At first, she was going to decline, but she figured once he'd seen her swollen belly he'd back off. To her surprise, he was sympathetic to her situation, and before she knew it, she agreed to have supper with him the same evening.

Fast forward one month, and she was moving in with him. She'd developed feelings for him, and he waited on her hand and foot. He even drove her back and forth to the office because she couldn't fit behind the wheel and he said he didn't want her walking. It was sweet, but when he suggested they get married, she was a little taken back, but he said he loved her and wanted to be there for her and the baby. It was the one thing she'd never had as a child, and her baby needed a father. She agreed, and a week later they were married by a minister at Scott's friend's house.

She called Tessa to let her know about the marriage, and her friend was upset at first because she wanted to be there. Sandy told her they'd have a celebration when Tessa got back to Yellowknife. Tessa told her she was hoping to be back soon and she had news of her own.

While all this was going on, she'd noticed a change in Keith. He didn't seem as surly as he usually did and she'd even caught him whistling a few times on his way into his office. He'd been going back and forth between Edmonton and Yellowknife, but Sandy didn't know why. When she'd asked him about his mood, change all she got was a shoulder shrug.

She was completely in the dark until the day Tessa called to tell say she and Keith had eloped. She was shocked. She didn't even know Tessa and Keith were dating. It hurt that her friend hadn't told her, but when she thought about it even when she did talk to Tessa, she was so wrapped up in her own life that she didn't ask Tessa about hers. Keith wasn't the baby's father because Tessa had gotten pregnant from her last boyfriend. Sandy hadn't met him, but from what she knew he was married and ran like a jack rabbit when Tessa told him.

Tessa returned to Yellowknife three weeks before Sandy was due to have her baby. Tessa had given birth just days before her arrival. Of course, everyone fell in love with sweet little Evie and Sandy was no different. The little girl favored her mother with dark hair and olive colored skin. Tessa and Ruby were of Aboriginal descent, and it was evident in the baby.

Sandy was miserable and couldn't wait for the baby to come. She was uncomfortable, not sleeping, and all the men around her had turned into complete idiots. Scott had been out of town for a few days, and Sandy was staying with Keith and Tessa until he got back. Ruby was still with their grandmother, and Tessa said her sister was enjoying being in Edmonton. It was nice to spend time with her friend, but she was still in the dark about how Keith and Tessa ended up together. They certainly didn't act like a newlywed couple, but she just chalked that up to dealing with a new baby. When she asked Tessa about it, she would smile and tell her that they'd found safety in each other. It didn't make sense, but they seemed happy enough.

The next day Sandy walked into the office or waddled as seemed to be the way she moved at that point. She was surprised to see the office decorated with balloons and streamers. A mountain of wrapped gifts sat on her desk, and a bunch of large men grinning like idiots had her eyes filling with tears. Stupid hormones. She had a feeling Tessa had put most of it together when she stepped out from behind the men.

Her phone rang just after four o'clock. It was Scott. He'd come back to town early and was just pulling up in front of the office. She told him to come in because she wanted to show him what her co-workers and friends had done for her.

When Scott walked into the office, Sandy heard a gasp, and when she turned, Tessa had run into the bathroom. Before she got a chance to check on her friend, Keith had entered the bathroom and closed the door. A few minutes later he returned. His face was tense, and his jaw clenched, but all he said was Tessa wasn't feeling well.

With the gifts loaded, Sandy was about to get in her car, but Keith asked if she could stay for an important meeting. Scott offered to wait, but Keith told him that he would drive Sandy home. Scott kissed her cheek and drove off as Keith wrapped his arm around her and guided her into the building.

That was when everything went to hell. Tessa was in Keith's office with tears in her eyes and clinging to Evie. Bull was pacing the floor, and the rest of the team seemed to have vanished.

"Sandy, I think you need to sit for this," Keith guided her to the chair across from Tessa.

"What's going on? Is Ruby okay? Lane?" Sandy didn't want to sit she just wanted to know what was wrong.

"Sandy, I'm sorry. I never knew his name." Tessa sobbed.

"Whose name?" Keith crouched in front Sandy and took both her hands in his.

"The man that raped Tessa and could be responsible for a lot of missing women here in Yellowknife," Keith said with the softest tone she'd ever heard him use.

"They caught him?" Sandy had prayed they'd find the bastard that hurt her friend.

"Sandy, Tessa recognized him," Keith said.

"Recognized who? Will you just tell me?" Sandy had a knot in the pit of her stomach. She knew what he was about to say, but she didn't want to believe it.

"It was Scott." Keith gently squeezed her hands. Sandy shook her head.

"No. Tessa you must be mistaken." Sandy glanced at her friend, but she knew the story of Tessa's attack and how the man made her look at him while he raped her. Tessa had told her many times she'd never forget the man's face.

"Sandy, I want you to come home with us," Keith said, but she was already half way out of the office.

"No, he won't hurt me. I'm going home." The whole walk home seemed like a blur, and she didn't feel the chill in the wind because she was numb.

Present day...

The night Keith came to pick her up was burned in her brain, and it would never go away. Scott screaming at her when she mentioned Tessa's name then waiting for Keith to come and get her out of the house before Scott got back home. The worst was when

Scott came back covered in blood holding a gun and then the loud crack of the gunfire.

"What the fuck, Keith?" Ian stood in front of his brother with his hands on his hips. "Why the hell didn't you tell us you were married and had a kid?"

"Because it wasn't what you think," Keith admitted.

"Well, what was it then?" Ian hadn't even looked at her since she'd told him everything.

"It doesn't have anything to do with you or Sandy." Keith stood up and begin to pace. She'd noticed when he was agitated he did it a lot. It seemed that all the brothers did it.

"Nobody knows you were married?" Ian pushed.

"No, and nobody needs to know. Now drop it and listen to the woman you love." Keith stalked out of the kitchen leaving her alone with Ian.

"Why the fuck is he being so secretive about all this?" Ian threw his hands up in the air and finally turned to face her. "Why were you so secretive?"

"Keith's story is his to tell, but the reason I've been so secretive is easy." Sandy sat on the edge of the couch and covered her face with her hands. She heard him move toward her and covered her hands with his as he knelt on the floor in front of her.

"So, tell me." He gazed into her eyes and all the emotion she'd been holding in all these years, all the hurt that she'd probably never be a mother came flowing down her cheeks in a river of tears. "Sandy, tell me."

"Because I didn't think you'd want me if you knew," Sandy admitted.

"Sandy, that wouldn't have mattered to me. I love you." Ian cupped her face in his hands.

"But you've got two little girls now, and they need you." The pang of jealousy in the pit of her stomach made her want to throw up. She'd never be able to give him what Colleen did.

"And they've got me, but that doesn't mean we can't be together." Ian dropped his hands to his sides and sat back on his heels. "Or does it?"

Could she be with him and accept the little girls that weren't hers? For a moment, she studied his face, and she could see the worry. Sandy was about to tell him it didn't matter because she wanted to be with him and she loved him with all her heart, but before she got a chance to answer, he was on his feet and pacing the floor.

“I guess the silence answers my question.” Ian snapped and stalked out of the living room. The next thing she heard was the click of his bedroom door.

“What just happened?” Sandy whispered and glanced up to see Keith’s massive frame stomping toward Ian’s bedroom. She jumped up and ran to stop him from going in the room but before she got to him he pushed the bedroom door open so hard that it slammed against the wall behind it.

“What the fuck?” Ian stood up, but before Sandy knew what happened, Keith had Ian pinned against the wall.

“I fucking warned you to listen to her.” Keith pulled his fist back, and Sandy knew what was about to happen. She pushed between the two huge men.

“What the hell is wrong with you, Keith?” Sandy yelled as she braced her hand hard against his chest and her other hand against his fist. “There are two little girls in the room down the hall, and you’re going to scare the shit out of them the way you’re acting. This is between Ian and me. Stop acting like an overprotective dick.” She pushed with all her strength, and he stepped back but only because he decided to step back. There was no way he would’ve moved if he didn’t want to.

“He’s being an ass,” Keith growled.

“So are you.” Sandy snapped. “Now go out there. Make sure you didn’t wake the girls and let Ian and I talk.” She stood with her hands on her hips. Keith turned around and stomped out of the room. The next thing she heard was Ian chuckling. “You think that was funny?”

“Not funny. Amazing.” Ian was still leaning against the wall. “You're probably one of the few women not intimidated by Keith.”

“Keith’s like the little brother I never wanted, and no I’m not intimidated by him or any of the giant apes that work with me. I’m intimidated by you, though.” She admitted.

“Me? Why?” He pushed himself off the wall and walked toward her, but she held up her hand to stop him.

“You’ve got the power to break my heart into pieces.” It was her biggest fear.

“You’ve got that power too.” Ian took her hands and pressed them against his chest.

“How are you so calm about everything that you’ve found out in the last few days?” She’d never been so out of control of her emotions in her life. “You just seem to be taking everything in stride, and you go on. I don’t understand how you can do that.” She could accept Ian’s daughters, but it was going to take some time. She loved him with all her heart, and she’d love any part that came from him.

"You think I'm not scared shitless?" Ian continued and rested his hands on her hips. "Sandy, I'm terrified. Of being a good dad to those little babies, of losing you. I don't care if you can have babies or not, but I can see it's devastating to you and I don't know how to make that sadness go away."

"Ian, the sadness is because I'm scared you can't accept that I'm damaged." It was the only way to explain how she felt about herself. Damaged was the only way to explain it.

"You're not damaged, and with all the scientific breakthroughs these days nothing's impossible, and if it is, there are other avenues to explore. Right now, I want you, and to me, you're perfect." She didn't know when the tears started and she hated crying in front of anyone, but she just couldn't hold them back. What he said was so beautiful, and it made her feel like the happiest woman in the world.

"There's something else you need to know," Sandy said. "Ruby has custody of Tessa's daughter, Evie. I've asked them to come live in Hopedale with me because Scott's still out there. It's my fault that Evie lost her mother." Ian stepped back, and his eyes went completely full.

"What? He's not in jail?" Ian gasped.

"During all the commotion, he was shot in his hand by one of the cops. He slipped out of the hospital when they were taking care of him. He's sent a lot of threatening emails to me over the years saying I was the reason he was on the run. It's the reason Keith has Trunk and Crash doing security for Ruby and Evie."

"Trunk and Crash?" The look of utter confusion on Ian's face made her smile.

"They work for Keith, and before you ask, no that's not their real names." Sandy took a deep breath and slowly let it out. "He swore he'd take away the most important people in my life." Ian cupped her cheeks.

"I'm sorry that you've had to go through this but aren't they safe where they are? Isn't that putting them in more danger to bring them where you are?" She knew Ian was just asking, but for some reason, it struck a cord, and she pushed him away.

"Do you think I'd bring her here if I thought I couldn't keep them safe?" Sandy stomped away from him.

"I didn't mean anything by that." Ian reached out to her, but she pulled back. "Are you doing this because of my girls?" With those words, all she could see was red.

"This has nothing to do with your girls. I've wanted Evie close to me, and now that Ruby has agreed to move here too, I can give her what she needs." How dare he insinuate she was bringing Evie to live with her because she was jealous of his daughters? Did he even know her at all?

"Sandy, don't get pissed at me. I was just asking...."

"You think this is all of a sudden? I've been struggling with this for years. You've got no idea how it feels to know that a child lost their mother because of you and you lost your own child because you were stupid. No, you have no idea. Of all people, I thought you'd understand, but I guess I didn't know you as well as I thought I did." Sandy spun around and ran out of the house ignoring Ian's demand for her to come back.

She didn't need him. Fuck him. The only thing she cared about now was bringing Evie and Ruby to Newfoundland and being able to see the little girl every day. She still had her brother and sister. She was sure Brad and Kim would love Evie as much as she did. Ian O'Connor wasn't going to be as supportive. Her heart felt like it was shattering in her chest.

She made it to the front door of her house, and when she got inside, she slammed the door and fell on her knees. She was devastated. Tears streamed down her cheeks, and her body shook with sobs. She cried over the man she'd been in love with for years and the relationship that never had a chance.

Chapter 13

What the fuck just happened?

He stood on the deck of his house staring at Sandy's front door that just slammed so hard he heard the glass in the door rattle. Why had she gotten so upset with him? She was the one who kept a huge secret and now was bringing a child into her house that was possibly in danger. All he did was ask if it was safe.

"What did you say?" Keith walked next to him, and Ian turned to face him.

"I have no fucking idea." Ian shook his head. "All I asked was if she was sure it was safe to bring the kid here. She flipped at me and took off."

"You, stupid asshole." Keith threw his hands up in the air.

"What?" Now he was baffled.

"Maybe she wanted you to say you'd help her keep Evie safe." Keith tipped his head and raised his eyebrow.

"Well, how the fuck was I supposed to know that. I'm a doctor, not a cop or bodyguard." Ian pushed by Keith and stomped into the house.

"She just wants your support." Keith followed him.

"Of course, I'll support her." Ian snapped.

"Well, maybe that's what you should've said." Keith sighed. "Look, she's scared that dickhead is going to go after Evie. I don't know why the hell he's out to hurt Sandy because I was the one who finally got him arrested."

"And nobody has any idea where this guy is?"

"I've got some friends in the RCMP, and they've been looking for him since he escaped, and he slips through their fingers every fucking time. The bastard is like a snake, but he's also a fucking predator who's raped at least six more women since he escaped and that's only the ones we know about, and he's not gonna stop until someone stops him." Keith growled through gritted teeth. Ian was sure his brother wanted to be the one to stop the bastard.

"Why didn't you ever tell us about Tessa?" Ian finally asked.

Keith walked into the living room and slowly lowered himself onto the couch, but his expression didn't change. He rested his elbows on his knees and clasped his hands together.

“Because I was so obsessed with taking down the guy who raped her that it ended up getting her killed and almost got Sandy killed.”

“Did you love her?” Ian sat in the armchair directly across from Keith.

“I cared about her but thinking about it now I don’t think I loved her like a husband should love a wife.” Keith sighed. “She was pregnant and even though Evie isn’t mine. I love the kid.”

“You were trying to be her hero.” Ian didn’t mean it as an insult. It was what Keith did all his life. He always stood up for the underdog and protected people who couldn’t defend themselves. It didn’t matter how it affected him.

“I didn’t want people to look down on her because she was pregnant and alone.” Keith sat back on the couch and rested his head against the back. “Please don’t start with the hero complex shit again.”

“It’s not shit, you’ve been doing it all your life, and I’ve got a feeling you always will.” Ian stood up and stretched. “I need to head to bed. Those little girls are cute, but they like to get up really early. You can stay if you like and crash on the couch.”

“You’re just afraid Sandy is going to come back and kill you in your sleep.” Keith chuckled. “I think I will crash here, though.”

"I don't think I'll be getting much sleep, but I've got to try." Ian plowed his hands through his hair. "It's so weird not to be working and feel more exhausted than if I worked an eighteen-hour shift."

"When are you going back to work?" Keith asked.

"I've taken four months' paternity leave, but I'm pretty sure I won't be going back to the ER once it's over. It won't work with the girls."

"Going to take up the old man's offer?" Keith chuckled.

"I think it'll be the best option." His father had wanted him to go into practice with him ever since he completed his residency.

"Do what's best for you. You know the family will give you all the help you need." Keith was right, but Ian didn't want to think about that now. He was too worried about Sandy and if they'd ever work things out.

"There's extra blankets and pillows in the window seat." Ian nodded toward the large bay window.

"Thanks, bro, and don't worry. Just talk to Sandy in the morning. She'll have time to calm down because you know she's like a firecracker." Keith said.

Ian knew Sandy was passionate, but the way she reacted to his question made his stomach feel like it was in knots and his chest hurt. He couldn't lose her now not when they'd finally found their way to each other.

"Fuck it seems like one hit after another." Ian flopped down on his bed and stared at the ceiling. He pulled his phone from his pocket and found nothing from Sandy, but he wasn't surprised. He had to let her know he'd be there for her whatever she decided. He started and deleted the text a half a dozen times before he finally sent one.

The last thing I wanted to do was upset you. I just wanted to make sure that bringing the little girl here wouldn't put both of you in more danger. You know I love you, and I can't take anything happening to you, and I know if something happened to Evie it would be devastating because I've got a feeling she's taken the place of the baby you lost. I'm sorry, please don't shut me out. I love you.

He stared at the screen for a few minutes waiting to see if she read the message, but it seemed that she wasn't even going to check it. He tossed his cell next to him on the bed and rolled onto his side. His life had taken such a one-eighty in the last couple of days. He finally admitted his feeling to Sandy, then found out he had two little girls that he hadn't known about and then he was told Sandy had a roller coaster of her own she was riding. He closed his eyes and for the first time in a long time he prayed.

Ian sat upright on the bed with a start. At first, he didn't know what the buzzing sound was, and then he glanced at his phone. He'd forgotten to turn off his alarm for work and getting woke at five in the morning when it was after three when he finally fell asleep made him want to smash his cell against the wall. He sat on the side of the bed and cursed. Hopefully Lily and Grace were still sleeping so he could at least take a shower to feel somewhat human.

After confirming the girls were still sleeping, he quickly showered and trimmed his beard. Once he threw on a pair of track pants and shirt, he headed to the kitchen.

Lily's soft voice had him stopping and peeking into the living room. She was talking to Keith and Ian stifled a laugh because his brother looked downright uncomfortable.

"Did you have a sleepover with daddy?" She asked Keith. He looked like he hadn't slept much either.

"I guess you could say that, kiddo." Keith yawned and stretched his arms over his head.

"My name's not kiddo. It's Lily. Did you forget?" Lily stood with her little hands on her hips staring down Keith.

"No, I didn't forget. Kiddo is just a nickname." Keith looked up and met Ian's amused expression, but Keith wasn't amused.

"But I'm not Uncle Nick," Lily said, and Ian almost choked on his laughter.

"I didn't mean Nick as in Uncle Nick, I just meant… never mind." Keith was smart because he would be fighting a losing battle with Lily.

"Are you gonna make breakfast?" She asked.

"I think your dad is gonna do that." Keith pulled on his shirt.

"You got a lot of tattoos, and you're really bumpy." Lily pointed to the tattoos on Keith's arms, and his brother glared at him.

"Hey, kiddo look, your dad is up." Keith nodded toward Ian.

"I'm Lily, not kiddo." She said as if he'd insulted her.

"You know you really talk a lot." Keith sighed.

"I like to talk." Lily sat next to Keith, and his brother looked like he was about to run.

"Lily, why don't you go get dressed while I make breakfast." Ian stepped into the living room and to give his brother a reprieve from the curious little girl.

She skipped out of the room and disappeared into her bedroom. Ian heard her talking to Grace and knew it wouldn't be long before the baby made it known she wanted to be changed and fed.

"That kid is intense." Keith stood up and followed Ian to the kitchen.

"Well, she must take after you." Ian chuckled.

"Fuck you, asshole." Keith shoved him lightly.

"You better watch what you say, or she'll tell mom." Ian began to prepare breakfast for the two little girls.

"There are so many kids around now, you can't say shit." Keith lifted the cup to his lips and stopped. Ian turned around to see Lily standing in the doorway with her hands on her hips.

"Daddy, your brothers sure say a lot of bad words. Nanny Kathleen must have used a lot of pepper when they were little." Lily was shaking her head as she turned to leave the kitchen again.

"She's like a fu…. freaking ninja," Keith mumbled, and Ian burst into laughter.

Breakfast was enjoyable with Lily always telling Keith, her name wasn't kiddo. Keith seemed a little uncomfortable with how Grace was staring at him. It wasn't like his brother wasn't used to kids because he played with his nephews all the time. Maybe it was because they were little girls. When Ian thought about it, Keith always looked uncomfortable around John's little girl too.

Ian was still trying to get his head around Keith's secret marriage. It didn't make sense why he hadn't told anyone, but as the brothers did, Ian would keep it to himself until Keith was ready to tell everyone.

Ian did his best to keep his mind off of Sandy, but it wasn't easy. She hadn't returned his text, and her car wasn't in her driveway. He kept screwing things up with her, and he didn't know if he could fix it this time. Stephanie and Marina had come by to take the girls for a sleepover, and although they'd only been with him for a few days, he missed them. He also realized that he hadn't gone for a run since they arrived. He did his best thinking when he was running, so maybe taking a long run could help him figure out how to make things right with Sandy.

He found himself on the beach an hour later tossing rocks into the waves. The beach always gave him a sense of peace, and he went there when he needed to think. He hadn't come up with any epiphany, but it made him realize that April winds were hard on the lungs. Spring wasn't a season that often appeared in Newfoundland, and from the chill in the wind, there was a good chance that it would probably snow before the week was out. When he turned to head up from the beach, he was sure he saw someone standing at the edge of the wharf watching him but by the time he made it to the road the only thing that was there was a smoldering cigarette butt.

He made his way across Beach Street and walked onto Glory Road. If he didn't drop in to see his mother, she'd disown him. Besides, he was starting to feel the chill of the wind in his bones. He jogged up the driveway of his childhood home as he'd done so many times in his life.

"Mom, you home?" Ian called as he opened the front door. Just because the door wasn't locked didn't mean someone was home. His parents still refused to believe that Hopedale was the type of place you locked your doors.

"Yar mudder jus' went ta da shop." Nanny Betty's voice floated from the kitchen along with the smell of fresh homemade bread.

"How's the best grandmother in the world?" Ian asked as he entered the kitchen and gave his grandmother a kiss on the cheek.

"Hmm.... Now would me bein' da best grandmudder have anyting ta do wit da bread I jus' pulled outta da oven?" Nanny Betty raised her eyebrow as she brushed butter over the top of the hot loaves in front of her.

"Nan, you know you're the best in the world." Ian smiled as he poured a cup of coffee.

“Inky, I wasn’t born yesterday.” Nanny Betty shook her head. “but since yer here ya can take a loaf home wit ya.” She pointed to the bread that was already in bags on the counter.

“Thanks, Nan.” Ian sat at the counter and watched her finished buttering the last loaf.

“So wat brings ya here t'day?” Nanny Betty sat next to him.

“Steph and Marina took the girls for a sleepover, and I went for a run. I wanted to drop in before I head home.” Ian smiled when she cut a slice off of one of the hot loaves of bread and put it in front of him with a bottle of molasses.

“And yer tryin’ ta figure out how ta get yerself outta da dog house wit Sandy.” Nanny Betty took a sip of her tea as she met his eyes. Her eyes were a similar blue to his own, but she always insisted their blue eyes came from Grandda Jack.

“How did you know?” Ian sighed.

“Stephanie was here when Sandy called her.” She explained.

“You know everything?” Ian didn’t need to ask.

“I know wat I needs ta know.” She said.

“What’s your advice?” Ian asked because of all the people in his family Nanny Betty was always the one that knew how to fix things.

“Inky, when a woman's told havin’ babies is not in da future, it’s devastatin’. After Cora had Pammy, she almost died, and as ya know she wasn’t able ta have any more youngsters. It took her a long while ta even function. It’s not somethin’ a woman gets over. They jus’ learn ta live wit it. I think dis little girl gives Sandy wat she can’t have and considerin’ wat ya did ta her, I’d suggest ya be understandin’ and support her.” It was a hard pill to swallow that his grandmother was disappointed in his transgression, but she was right that he just needed to help Sandy and let her protect Evie.

He walked up to his driveway and played the conversation with his grandmother over in his head. Sandy’s car still wasn’t back, so she was either gone to get Evie or was staying with her sister to avoid him.

He leaned against the wall trying to find a solution to the problem but something moved out of the corner of his eye, and he raised his head.

“Ian, please don’t call the cops.” The scruffy man held up his hands in front of him. A split second later Ian had the man on the floor with his hands behind his back.

"Who the fuck are you and what the hell are you doing in my house?" Ian growled as he twisted the man's arm behind his back.

"Fuck, Ian it's me." The man moaned. "Gerry." It took a moment for the name to sink in.

"Gerry who?"

"Morgan." He groaned. "Colleen's brother." Ian's blood ran cold as he remembered the police suspected Gerald of killing Colleen and her husband.

"You, son of a bitch. You killed your sister." Ian turned him over and pulled him up off the floor. Gerald was never a big man, but he was nothing but skin and bones, so it took no effort for Ian to slam him into the wall.

"Ian, I didn't kill her," Gerald grunted.

"That's not what the police think and if you didn't, why did you run?" Ian was trying hard not to beat the hell out of his old friend.

"It's a long story, but you've got to believe me, man. I wouldn't have done that to Colleen. Jesus Christ, she's all the family I had left next to the girls." Gerald sobbed, but the mention of Lily and Grace made Ian see nothing but red, and he punched the wall behind Gerald.

"Leave my daughters out of this conversation, because until you can prove to me, you had nothing to do with taking their mother away from them, you'll be no family of theirs," Ian growled through his teeth.

"I get it. Let me explain. Please." Gerald begged, and Ian grabbed him by the jacket collar and dragged him into the living room.

"Start talking." Ian practically pushed Gerald onto the sofa.

"I didn't kill my sister or Carter, but pretty sure I know who did." Gerald clasped his shaky hands together.

"Who?" Ian asked.

"I don't know what his real name is. He always went by Lefty because his left hand is lame. I don't think anyone knows his real name." Gerald was trembling, and Ian started to feel guilty. It looked like he hadn't eaten, or showered in a long time.

"You look like shit." Ian sighed. "How long has it been since you ate or showered for that matter," Gerald's lowered his eyes.

"About a week since I've had a decent meal and I've been hiding out in the old camp in the woods. You know the one we built when we were kids. It's in rough shape, but it's out of the elements, and it gave me a place to hide out until I could figure out what to do." Gerald wouldn't look at him.

"Come with me." Ian left the living room and headed to the guest bathroom with Gerald following him. "Go get cleaned up. I'll give you something to throw on. I'll get you a bite to eat, and you can tell me the rest."

"Thanks, Ian but where are the girls?" Gerald asked.

"They're fine and won't be back tonight." Ian wasn't telling him anything more about Lily and Grace until he could be sure Gerald was innocent.

"They're safe where they are, right?" Gerald looked genuinely concerned.

"Very." Ian pulled out a couple of towels from the closet and tossed them to Gerald. "Get cleaned up, and I'll leave some clean clothes on the counter."

Ian turned and left the bathroom. He had a war raging inside his head. He really should call the police because as far as he knew, Gerald was a fugitive, but this was Gerry. The same kid that used to follow him and Colleen around. He went to school with Keith. Could he be capable of killing his sister?

Ian found an old pair of track pants and T-shirt in his dresser. He tossed it on the counter in the bathroom and headed to the kitchen to make a couple of sandwiches. He had to give Gerald the benefit of the doubt. The man he knew would never hurt a fly, let alone kill his sister. Maybe he should call his Uncle Kurt, John or James. He squashed that idea because they were police and would have to take Gerald in custody. He could call Keith but knowing his brother, he'd probably make Ian call the authorities. No, he was waiting until Gerald told him everything and then he would decide what to do.

Chapter 14

"What did you expect, Sandy?" Her sister sighed as she closed the dishwasher. "I mean you tell him you want to take in a child of a woman that was murdered and the man that killed her has been threatening you."

"I don't know, Kim." Sandy flopped back on the small love seat in her sister's small apartment. She really didn't know how Kim could live in such a tiny place.

"Look, I know my initial introduction to the O'Connors, was shall we say less than honorable but I've changed, and it's partly because of them. When I was dating John, I was a bitch." Kim said. Sandy chuckled because it was the truth.

"You laugh, but you know it's the truth. The fact any of the O'Connors even talk to me shows what kind of family they are. Hell, Stephanie and Marina hired me to do their hair and makeup for their weddings, and Nanny Betty comes to me every month to get her hair done." Kim laughed because Ian's grandmother was not a big fan of Kim in the beginning.

"I know all that." Sandy sighed.

"Ian is a great guy, and yes the situation is entirely screwed up, but you don't want to lose him, do you?" Kim asked.

"No, I've been in love with him for years, but I feel responsible for Evie." Sandy sighed.

"But Ruby is taking care of her, so Evie is not your responsibility." Kim was right of course.

"It's hard to explain. Ruby understands, which is why she agreed to move here with Evie." Sandy had the conversation with her friend, and Ruby never hesitated.

"And I'm sure Ian would understand if you'd given him a chance." Kim sat next to her and nudged her with her shoulder.

"I hate it when you're right." Sandy poked her back.

"I must get my brains from my big sister." Kim grinned, and Sandy rolled her eyes. The fact that there was only a total of four months between the two of them didn't really mean Sandy was that much older.

"Have you seen Brad or our wonderful father lately?" She needed a subject change from talking about Ian or Evie. Things were already in motion. Trunk was flying in with Ruby and Evie in the morning while Crash drove the moving truck with their belongings.

"Brad seems to have turned into a bit of a womanizer, but that doesn't surprise me because he's been spending a lot of time with A.J. lately." Kim laughed.

"Jesus, A.J. and Brad? Someone needs to warn the single women of the province." Sandy chuckled.

"And probably some of the married ones." Kim laughed. "Dad has been pretty quiet lately. He calls me at least once a week to ask about you, and when I tell him to call you, he changes the subject." Kim had always been closer to their father than she or Brad because he took Kim in after her mother died. Kim was still a teenager at the time, so he felt responsible, or so he said.

"I guess it's too hard to punch in my number." Sandy rolled her eyes. "I'm going to head to bed. Ruby and Evie's flight is supposed to be in at nine in the morning."

Sandy walked into Kim's small guest room and flopped down on the bed. She pulled her phone out of her purse and turned it on. She'd been ignoring calls and texts from everyone because she just needed to get her head together. There were a bunch from Stephanie and Marina as well as a couple from Keith telling her to call him before he found her and kicked her ass. That made her scoff because he knew that would never work with her. The last message made her heart race.

Sandy, we need to talk.

The message from Ian was short, but it could have been a novel for what she read into it. Was the conversation going to break her heart into pieces or was it going to make her happier than she'd ever been in her life? She wouldn't know unless she called.

She opened up her phone and scrolled to Ian's number but before she had a chance to tap it her cell rang and Keith's name flashed on her screen. If she ignored him, he would just keep calling back. It could be a job, or maybe something could have gone wrong with Ruby and Evie's flight.

"Hello." She answered.

"Well hello to you too." She didn't miss Keith's sarcastic tone.

"What's up?" She tried to sound casual.

"Let's see the price of gas, unemployment and yes my fucking blood pressure because someone doesn't know how to return texts or calls." Keith snarled.

"Oh, stop being a drama queen. I needed some peace and quiet." Sandy said.

"Peace and quiet? At Kim's? Ha, that's funny." The asshole knew where she was but he was right, Kim was anything but quiet. Her personality had changed a little since she'd been stabbed and left for dead by Brad's crazy ex but she could still be loud and obnoxious at times.

"So, if you knew where I was, why is your blood pressure up?" Sandy asked.

"Because I hate being fucking ignored and I was wondering if you were going to suck it up and go talk things out with my brother instead of acting like a spoiled princess who didn't get her way," Keith said.

"Fuck off, Keith." She snapped.

"He loves you, kiddo. Call him." Keith used the name he used when she was going through the depression of losing her baby.

"I will." She was going to call him.

"Tonight." It wasn't a question from Keith, it was an order.

"Yes, boss." Sandy used her usual sarcastic tone that she knew pissed Keith off.

“I mean it, Sandy,” Keith warned.

“If you must know, I was about to call him, but you called, and I had to answer because you hate when you're ignored.” Sandy smiled when she heard him growl.

“Fine and make sure you bring my girl to see me when you get back to Hopedale. I miss the little fart.” Keith was a big part of Evie’s life since the day she was born, and he’d kept in constant touch with her. She even called him Uncle Keith which was weird considering technically he was her step-father. He was also paying for her schooling because, like Sandy, he felt responsible.

“I will.” She tapped the screen to end the call, and her finger hovered over Ian’s number for a moment. “Just bite the bullet and call him.” She whispered and tapped his number.

The phone rang several times which was not usual for Ian. He generally kept his phone close to his hip, but since he was on leave, he probably didn’t need to have it close all the time. After the fourth ring, she was about to end the call but a voice she didn’t recognize answered, and it was a woman.

“Hello.” The female voice was pleasant, but it didn’t give her a nice feeling.

"Umm…. I'm sorry... I must have the wrong number." Sandy stumbled over her words. She programmed his number into her phone, so it wasn't the wrong number.

"Are you looking for Ian?" The woman asked.

"Ahhh... Yes." She wanted so badly to ask who the hell was answering his phone.

"This is Sandy, right?"

"Yes, who's this?" She hoped her question sounded casual.

"Isabelle. Ian left his phone here at Aunt Kathleen's house. I was just on my way to drop it off before I went to town." Of course, it was Isabelle. How could she think anything else but one of his family? "Did you want me to give him a message? Like he's a huge ass, and you want to kick it all over Hopedale?" Isabelle chuckled.

"I see news spreads fast." She should have known they would all know by now.

"How long have you known my family?" Isabelle laughed.

"Good point. Just tell Ian, I'll call him tomorrow." She laughed.

“I will and if you need anything Sandy you know you can call any of us,” Isabelle’s offer caused tears to form in Sandy’s eyes because she knew it was from the heart

“Thanks. I’ll talk to you soon.” Sandy ended the call and flopped on the bed. She was exhausted, but sleep was not her friend over the last few days. The only day she’d slept well was the night she spent in Ian’s arms.

Two hours of tossing and turning was enough. Sandy threw her legs over the side of the bed and sat up. So, here she was not able to sleep, and it was after midnight. The worst thing was she couldn’t even do any work because she wasn’t home. Part of it was because she hadn’t heard from Ian. She did tell Isabelle that she would call him tomorrow, but she usually got a text from him every night.

She walked out into the dark kitchen. Kim lived on the fourth floor of the apartment building just on the edge of St. John’s. Her view sucked. The only thing she could see was the highway that ran by the back of the apartment building. Kim liked it because since she’d opened her salon and spa with an old friend of hers in Hopedale, it was an easy commute. Why she just didn’t get a place in Hopedale was beyond Sandy, but Kim didn’t always make sense.

Sandy stared at the cars flying up and down the highway. There weren’t many because it was late, but someone was always driving in or out of the city. She was in such a trance she almost missed the vibration of her phone in her pocket. Without even looking at the screen she answered.

"Hello." Sandy hoped it was Ian and couldn't help her disappointment when she heard the voice on the phone.

"Hey, Sandy. It's Smash." Smash a/k/a Gage Hodder was also a computer analyst with Newfoundland Security Services as well. He'd had the task of trying to track anything he could find on Scott. It was too personal to Sandy which is why Keith gave him the job. Her boss was worried that she would go after Scott on her own if she tracked him down.

"Hi, Gage." She said.

"I was wondering if you could check out a photo." he asked.

"Thinking about changing your profile picture on Facebook?" Sandy laughed.

"Now that wouldn't be fair to all the other guys on that site." He chuckled.

"Your modesty is so refreshing, Gage." Sandy rolled her eyes.

"I know, but no. Rusty is probably gonna give me shit for this because he told me not to involve you in this, but you knew this dick better than any of us." Sandy's heart thudded in her chest. He was calling about Scott.

"You've got a picture of him?" Sandy tried to keep her voice steady.

"It's from a surveillance video in Moncton dated about a week ago. I'm almost positive it's him." She could hear the clicking of the keys as Gage spoke.

"Send me the picture." Sandy blurted out. If he was in Moncton, it could mean he was on his way to Halifax. Maybe he knew where Evie was and he was on his way to get her. "Send it now."

"Holy shit, you've been around Rusty too much. You sound just as bossy." Gage said. "Just sent it to your email."

"Hang on." Sandy opened her email and groaned. She had over two hundred unread emails. Her hand trembled as she opened the email from Gage.

"Did you get it?" She heard Gage ask.

"Yes, hold your horses. It's coming up now." The black and white picture opened on her screen, and she stared at it. It wasn't the clearest picture, but there was no denying it. The picture was fuzzy, but there wasn't any doubt in her mind. It was Scott. Now it wasn't just her hands trembling.

"Sandy?" Gage's voice echoed through the earpiece of her phone.

"It's him." She put the phone to her ear and closed her eyes.

"You're sure?" Gage asked.

"Yes." Sandy took a slow deep breath. "Call Keith." She ended the call before Gage could say anything else. Ruby and Evie were at a hotel next to the Halifax airport. Trunk was staying with them at the hotel. He needed to know to be extra careful and keep a close eye on Evie.

She was in a complete state of panic when the fourth call to Truck went straight to voicemail and was in the process of looking up the number to the hotel when Trunk's name flashed across her screen.

"What the hell took you so long to answer the damn phone?" Sandy snapped as soon as she answered.

"Probably because the fucking thing has been ringing like something possessed for the past half hour." Trunk's deep voice rumbled through the phone. "Between Smash, Rusty, Crash and you I've been ready to heave it out the window."

"They told you about Scott being in Moncton?" Sandy asked.

"Yes, and Ruby and the princess are safe." For some reason, Trunk always referred to Evie as the princess. Sometimes Sandy wondered if he even knew the little girl's name.

"What time are you going to the airport tomorrow?" She knew the time the flight arrived, but she didn't have all the details of their departure time.

"Rusty changed our flights, we're actually leaving in an hour for the airport. We'll be getting in St. John's about three in the morning." Sandy cursed under her breath when she glanced at her watch.

"Well, it would've been nice if he'd let me know that," Sandy grumbled.

"Maybe if you hadn't been harassing Trunk with phone calls, you'd have read the text I sent you." Sandy gasped and dropped her phone.

"What the fuck, Keith?" Sandy snatched her cell off the floor but not without giving Keith the death stare. "Thanks, Trunk. See you in a few hours."

"You know, your sister's building needs better security." Keith opened the fridge and pulled out a bottle of water.

“Just make yourself at home there, asshole.” Sandy snapped. “How did you get in here?” They’d locked the door, and it was a secured building.

“I told you the security here sucks,” Keith finished gulping down half of the bottle of water.

“I’ll be sure to alert my sister that you broke into her apartment to prove her security is the shits.” Sandy leaned against the counter and crossed her arms over her breasts.

“I’m serious, we should amp up her security. I mean she’s your sister.” Keith finished off the bottle of water and put the cap back on it. He held it up, and she pointed to the recycling bucket next to the fridge.

“I’ve been trying to talk her into moving to Hopedale,” Sandy admitted, but Keith was right. Lots of times she’d come to visit Kim and people would open the security door and let her in without even checking to see if she knew anyone in the building.

“Considering that’s where her salon is it would make more sense.” Keith propped his shoulder against the fridge shoved his hands in his pocket.

“Yeah.” Sandy turned and stared out the window.

"You know he isn't getting near Evie with Trunk there, right?" Keith stood next to her.

"I know." She did know, but until Ruby and Evie were in front of her, she wasn't going to be able to relax. Knowing Scott was close made her blood boil. She wasn't afraid of him, but it terrified her that he could hurt Evie or Ruby just to get to her.

"Ummm…. Why is there a mountain in my kitchen leaning against my fridge?" Kim yawned.

"Hi, Kim!" Keith chuckled when she tried to push him out of her way to get into the fridge.

"I didn't hear the buzzer." She pulled a bottle of water out and closed the fridge.

"Probably because your neighbors don't care who they let in the building." Sandy laughed.

"What?" She looked back and forth between Keith and Sandy.

"Let's just say I'm sending one of my guys to put in better locks and a security system in your apartment," Keith told her.

“And how exactly am I paying for that?” Kim raised her eyebrow and gave him that defiant stance that seemed to run in their family.

“Just a haircut.” Keith smiled.

Kim had become the O’Connor family hairdresser, but Keith always had her come to his house because he wasn’t stepping foot inside a beauty salon.

“Sounds good but you have to come into the shop.” Kim grinned.

“Don’t hold your breath waiting for that, doll.” Keith chuckled.

“Okay, I know you aren’t here at this hour to test the building security. What’s up?” Kim asked.

Sandy filled Kim in on the flight change but not why. Her sister didn’t need to be worried about Scott since she was still getting over her trauma of being stabbed. She still hid most of her scars with long sleeve shirts and high necklines, but she would never admit they bothered her.

Sandy stood at the bottom of the escalator that brought the passengers to the gate. She was bouncing on the balls of her feet watching every person that came through the door.

“Where are they? Are you sure Trunk got them on the flight?” Sandy asked Keith.

“They’re on the flight, kiddo. Have some patience for Christ’s sake.” Keith said, and she turned and elbowed Keith in the ribs. Of course, it didn’t bother him.

“I hate you.” She sighed when he laughed at her attempt to hurt him. As she glared up at him, he nodded his head toward the escalator. She looked up as Evie was trying to maneuver her way around people in front of her. Every time she got by someone she’d stop and wave to Sandy.

“Alexandra, Uncle Keith,” Evie yelled as she jumped the last two steps and ran full speed toward Sandy.

“Hey there, princess.” Keith’s face lit up when he lifted Evie into his arms and hugged her. “I missed ya.” Keith kissed her cheek.

“Maybe you should’ve come to visit more often,” Ruby walked up next to Sandy and wrapped her arm around Sandy’s shoulder.

“Sorry, Rubes.” Keith grinned sheepishly. “At least I’ll get to see you more and get lots of that great banana bread.” Ruby laughed.

“Can I have Evie now, please?” Sandy asked because he was still holding her.

“Alexandra, I’m so glad we’re gonna live with you.” Evie practically jumped into Sandy’s arms.

“Me, too, but here everyone calls me Sandy.” Sandy reminded Evie.

“Sorry, I forgot.” She hugged Sandy and whispered. “I don’t think Aunt Ruby will care.”

“Probably not.” Sandy giggled.

They headed back to Kim’s from the airport, so Ruby could rest, and Evie could hopefully take a nap. Kim fell in love with Evie the minute she entered the apartment. She also had made some sandwiches for them. Trunk and Keith stayed as well since they weren't comfortable with the building's security.

“Did Keith put an ad out to find the biggest and best-looking men in the country when he hired these guys?” Kim whispered as she followed Sandy out of the kitchen with a second platter of sandwiches.

“Probably.” Sandy laughed.

Kim was the one to finally convince Evie to take a nap with her in her huge bed, and Sandy led Ruby to the guest room where the woman almost fell into the bed. Sandy was sure she was asleep before she left the room.

Trunk and Keith were taking up practically the entire couch while they quietly debated who was going to end up in the playoffs for the Stanley Cup. She flopped down on the love seat and curled up on her side. She wasn't actually paying any attention to them until Keith mentioned Ian's name. She wasn't really sure what he said, but the mention of his name had her heart hurting. She regretted the way she ran out on him without explaining how she felt. She closed her eyes and drifted off to sleep wondering what he was doing at that moment.

Chapter 15

He was pacing the kitchen when his front door opened, and he ran to see who it was. All he needed was someone to come in and find Gerald in his house before he got a chance to see what the man had to say. He almost bowled Isabelle over as he rushed through the doorway.

"Isabelle, what are you doing here?" He sounded rude, but the water shut off in the shower and he didn't know if Gerald would just come out of the bathroom before checking.

"Nice to see you too, cuz." He didn't miss Isabelle's sarcasm, and he felt like shit.

"Sorry, I just wasn't expecting anyone," Ian said.

"It's okay. I'm only here 'cause you left your phone at your parent's house, and I told Aunt Kathleen I'd drop it off to you. I'm on my way to town to spend the night with Kristy."

"Shit, I didn't even realize it was gone. Is everything okay with Kristy? It's kind of late to be going to town." Ian took his phone from Isabelle and checked the time.

"Yeah, she's just having some guy issues," Isabelle said as she walked back to the front door.

"Who is he? I'm sure one of us will kick his ass." Isabelle, Kristy, Jess, and Pam were like the little sisters they didn't want, but Ian and his brothers would kill anyone if they hurt them.

"She's fine. The guy is the one who's playing hard to get." Isabelle rolled her eyes. "He thinks he's too old for her."

"I see. Well, let me know if Kristy needs anything." Ian wanted to know more about the guy, but Gerald could pop out of the bathroom at any moment.

"I will." Isabelle hugged him as she walked through the door. "Oh, I almost forgot, Sandy, called. She said she'd call you tomorrow." Ian cursed under his breath.

"She's certainly grown up." Ian turned when he heard Gerald behind him. He looked a lot better with the scruffy beard gone and the week's worth of dirt washed off. Gerry finally resembled the boy that grew up in Hopedale.

"Yeah, they all have." Ian locked the front door and motioned for Gerald to follow him into the kitchen. He wanted to call Sandy so badly, but he couldn't take any chances that Gerald would take off or decide not to talk.

Gerald almost inhaled the two sandwiches Ian put in front of him. Then downed two bottles of water and a cup of coffee as Ian put the third sandwich in front of him. Ian felt awful that someone he grew up with was in a situation where he was practically starving.

"I probably shouldn't be eating this so fast, but it's just been a while since I ate." Gerald seemed embarrassed.

"Don't worry about it." Ian sipped his coffee as Gerald sat back in the chair and let out a long sigh. The first thing Ian noticed was Gerald didn't have any marks on his arms, and it surprised him because he was supposed to be a drug addict. Even though he was ravenous and was probably thinner than a man his height should be, he wasn't showing any of the signs of an addict who was strung out. No sweating. No shaking and although he looked tense, it wasn't the type that you see in drug abusers.

"Before you ask, no I'm not a druggie." Gerald seemed to be reading his mind.

"What makes you think I was going to ask that?" Ian asked.

"I've heard the stories going around about me, Ian." Gerald rested his elbows on the table.

"Stories don't start out of nowhere, Gerry." Ian sat across from him and sat back in his chair. The man dropped his head and then sighed.

"I know, but it wasn't me that was doing drugs. It was Luke." The crack in Gerald's voice said he was having a hard time with his brother's suicide.

"I'm sorry about Luke," Ian said.

"When it came out that he was supposed to have killed himself, I knew something wasn't right. He'd been clean for six months, and he was straightening himself out. He'd promised Colleen he'd be there for her when…." Gerald stopped and looked at Ian. "I'm sorry she didn't tell you about the girls."

"Not your fault." Ian didn't want to talk about Colleen. "So, you don't think Luke killed himself?"

"No, that's why I started hanging out with Lefty. I knew the ass had something to do with it but to get the information I had to get in with that crowd. I know I'm not a cop or anything but Luke was my brother, and I couldn't let people believe he'd killed himself." Gerald pulled his hand down over his face and shook his head.

"So, this Lefty, what did you find out?" Ian asked.

"Not enough to get him arrested and when he showed up at Colleen's the week before she and Carter…." He stopped and swallowed. "He told me he knew what I was up to and if I didn't back off, Luke wouldn't be the only one six feet under."

"He threatened Colleen?" Ian tried to remain calm, but it was getting harder the more Gerald was telling him.

"I thought he was threatening me. He never said anything about Colleen, but I didn't care about myself. I saved all the stuff I'd found out about Lefty and his operation. I gave it to Colleen and told her if anything happened to me, she had to bring it to the police. When she asked me what was going on, I told her everything. Carter warned me to stay away from Lefty because he'd heard the man was crazy. I told him I had to get justice for Luke and left." He held up his empty cup, and Ian refilled it.

"Go on." Ian put the cup in front of him and sat down again.

"The next thing I know my sister and her husband are dead and the police are looking for me." It was with that Gerald finally cracked, and he sobbed. "Ian, I swear I didn't know he'd go after Colleen. I was so glad the girls were with the sitter. She was the one that told me the police were blaming me. She said when Colleen dropped off the kids that day, Colleen looked worried and told her that if anything happened to her to get in touch with the Andersons. Leonard was her lawyer, but you probably know that. Anyway, the sitter helped me get out of Manitoba but please don't tell anyone that. I don't want her to get in trouble."

"You need to tell the police all this." Ian was ready to call his Uncle.

"I don't know what Colleen did with the information I gave her. There was a lot of shit on that USB stick, and there was more I never even got a chance to look at."

"How do I know you aren't trying to get this USB because it proves you're the one that killed Luke and Colleen?" Ian had to ask. He'd seen enough crime shows to know desperate people would do anything to keep their asses out of jail.

"You don't. The only thing I've got is my word and the fact that you've known me almost my whole life. Do you honestly think I could kill anyone?" Gerald looked Ian straight in the eyes. "I. Didn't. Do. This."

"I believe you, Gerry but you need to talk to Uncle Kurt or John or James. Hell even Nick or A.J. could help." Ian told him.

"Jesus, I knew John and James were cops but Nick and A.J. too?" Gerald shook his head.

"That's why I'm taking a huge chance having you here. My girlfriend's a cop too." At least he hoped she was still his.

"I'm sorry for putting you in this situation. Maybe you're right. Who do you think is the best one to call?" Gerald clasped his hands in front of him and closed his eyes.

"The best one would be Uncle Kurt." Ian held his phone in his hand and waited for Gerald to give him the okay to make the call. He was going to call regardless, but Gerald needed to think he was in charge.

Ian tapped Kurt's cell phone number and waited for him to answer. It was after midnight, so he was probably asleep. Kurt would know something was wrong because of the late call, but since he was the superintendent of the Hopedale division of the NPD, Ian figured he was the best choice. Besides his girls were at John's house and the last thing he wanted was them in the middle of the situation.

Kurt arrived ten minutes after Ian hung up the phone. His hair mussed, but what made Ian wish he'd not called him, was the glare his uncle gave him when he saw Gerald sitting at the kitchen table.

"Please tell me you aren't harboring a fugitive?" Kurt growled.

"No that's why I called you." Ian handed Kurt a cup of coffee hoping the caffeine fix would ease the grumpiness.

"Gerry, you're in a lot of trouble, young man." Kurt sipped the coffee.

"I know Kurt, but I didn't do this." Gerald's eyes filled with tears.

"Lots of people in jail say they're innocent. Most of them aren't." Kurt propped himself against the counter and crossed his ankles.

"Tell him what you said to me, Gerry." Ian sat down at the table.

Kurt's expression didn't change the whole time that Gerald spoke. The only time he moved was to refill his cup, and then he returned to leaning on the counter. Gerald kept glancing at Ian for support and then back. Ian heard Kurt could be a hard ass cop, but it was the first time he'd actually seen it.

"You expect us to believe that this, Lefty is the one that killed Luke and made it look like a suicide, killed your sister and her husband to keep you quiet?" Kurt's voice was monotone, and even Ian couldn't tell if he believed it or not.

"Kurt, I've got a lot of evidence against him, but I don't know what Colleen did with the USB I gave her." Anyone could hear the desperation in Gerald's voice.

"You know I've got to take you in?" Kurt said.

"I know." Gerald stood up and held his hand out to Ian. "Thanks for giving me the benefit of the doubt." Ian shook his hand and glanced at Kurt.

"I'm drained and going into the station to deal with this at this hour is not going to make my mood any better." Kurt placed his cup in the sink. "If you can give me your word you'll be here when I come back first thing in the morning, we'll do all this after you get a good night's sleep." Kurt stood directly in front of Gerald.

"I'll be here as long as it's okay with Ian for me to stay for the night." Gerald glanced at Ian, and he nodded.

"Gerry, I'm only doing this because your parents were good friends of mine and I've watched you grow up. Don't make me regret this." Kurt held out his hand, and Gerald shook it.

"May God strike me down dead, I'll be here when you come back." Gerald's face relaxed as Kurt nodded and motioned for Ian to follow him. Ian told Gerald to get something else to eat if he wanted and followed Kurt to the front door.

"I got the feeling he's genuine," Ian said.

"He is." Kurt opened the front door. "I hate to put this responsibility on you, but please make sure he doesn't run."

"I'll keep an eye on him."

"What you need to know is the police aren't looking for him because they think he killed Colleen and her husband." Kurt lowered his voice.

"What do you mean?" As far as Ian knew the police were looking for Gerald.

"They think he's in danger and it was a way to keep him safe if the one who did kill them thought they were blaming Gerry." Kurt sighed.

"I'm assuming you don't want me to tell Gerry?" Ian figured since Kurt didn't say anything in front of Gerry.

"We'll fill him in tomorrow," Kurt said as he slid into his car.

Ian closed and locked the door. His phone vibrated in his pocket, and he pulled it out. It was a text from Keith.

Sandy's at her sister's place. Had to change the flights for Evie and her aunt. Had a sighting of Scott in Moncton. I'll keep you up to date... Ass.

Thanks for letting me know…. Dick.

At least he knew Sandy was safe. He hoped having the little girl with her made her happy.

"From your girlfriend?" Ian looked up as Gerald came out of the kitchen.

"No, it's Keith," Ian said.

"I missed all you guys." Gerald's eyes glistened, and Ian had no doubt his old friend had been dealing with more in his life than he'd ever expected.

"Maybe when we get all this cleared up we can have a beer and talk about old times," Ian said.

"I'd like that." Gerald smiled.

Ian knew he wasn't going to sleep, so he gave Gerald his bed, and he lay on the couch. At least he'd be able to keep an eye on his guest this way. He actually believed the man, and he could tell Kurt did as well. Whoever this Lefty guy was, he was a heartless bastard. Maybe it was because Ian had dedicated his life to saving people's lives, but he couldn't ever see himself taking someone's life.

He didn't remember closing his eyes, but he woke up crumpled up on one side of the couch. He managed to work the kinks out of his neck and back when he stood up and reached his arms above his head. He glanced toward his bedroom. The open door made his heart race. He hurried to the room to see the bed made and no Gerald.

“Fuck, fuck, fuck.” Ian plowed his hands through his hair and grabbed his keys off the hook. He knew he probably looked like a bag of shit, but needed to get to Kurt’s place to let him know Gerald was gone. He yanked open the front door. Gerald was sat on the front step sipping from a cup and staring off into space. He didn’t seem to hear Ian open the door and jumped when Ian spoke.

“Gerry, you should’ve woke me,” Ian felt terrible for thinking the worst.

“I guess the keys in your hand mean you thought I took off?” The hurt was evident in his eyes.

“Sorry.” Ian sighed. “Why don’t you come in and we’ll get a bite to eat before we go see Kurt.” Gerald dropped his head and let out a ragged breath.

“I’m gonna be locked up. Ain’t I?” The tension was apparent in the way he held his shoulders, and Ian was tempted to tell him the truth.

"I don't know, bud. Maybe the police found any USB's when they checked Colleen's place." Gerald didn't move, and Ian rested his hand on the man's shoulder.

"I miss her so fucking much." Gerald's voice trembled. "I never got to say goodbye to her. At least we were able to have a funeral for Luke. I don't even know what they did with her remains." Gerald sobbed.

"My family's having her, and her husband's bodies brought to Newfoundland. We're going to have a service for them." Ian promised his daughter she could say goodbye to her mother. It seemed Gerald needed the closure as well because when he stood up, he grabbed Ian's hand and shook it vigorously.

The whole drive to the station, Gerald stared through the side window. His hands were resting on his legs, and one leg was shaking. Gerald was scared. Was there more to what Gerald knew?

Ian paced the lobby of the police station for what seemed like days. He'd asked Stephanie to keep the girls with her until he called and she asked if everything was okay, but he didn't know the answer to that question.

He'd seen at least three other officers enter the room where Kurt brought Gerald. One of them didn't look familiar. He was either from the St. John's division or the Manitoba police.

For what seemed like the hundredth time the door opened, and someone walked out. The man glanced at Ian and then put his phone to his ear. It was one Ian didn't know. What made his heart pound was when the man shoved his phone back into a pocket and headed toward Ian.

"Dr. O'Connor, I'm Staff, Sergeant Isaac Hunt. I'm investigating the deaths of Colleen and Carter Taft." He held out his hand, and for a moment, Ian almost seemed to forget what the gesture meant. Just hearing him say he was looking into the deaths of Colleen and her husband suddenly made it real.

"Call me Ian, please." Ian shook his hand, but he wanted to give the man his opinion before he started shooting questions at Ian.

"I don't know how much Gerry has told you. We're aware he was working to find out what happened to his brother and we warned him it was dangerous. Lefty and his boss are very dangerous, but he didn't listen." Isaac motioned to the row of chairs against the wall. Ian sat, and Isaac sat next to him.

"So, you knew he was looking for evidence on this guy Lefty?" Ian asked.

"Yes, and I thought he'd been convinced to let the authorities handle it, but with his sister's murder, we knew he didn't stop, and all this is only because Gerry got to close to the truth about Luke." Isaac looked like he was taking all this a little too personally.

"So, killing Colleen and her husband was a warning to shut up Gerry?" It made sense to Ian.

"Yes, but the other victim wasn't Colleen's husband," Isaac explained.

"I'm confused. The man murdered wasn't Carter Taft" Ian asked.

"Oh, it was Carter Taft." Isaac turned his head to look at Ian.

"Carter Taft was married to Colleen." Ian knew that for sure.

"Colleen thought the man she married was Carter Taft. The truth is the man she married was Lefty's boss, and we don't have any information on him. He'd stolen Mr. Taft's identity. The real Mr. Taft was a drug addict. We think Lefty and his boss kept Taft supplied with meth and when Gerry started to figure things out they killed his sister. They had to kill the real Taft because they must have known we'd check fingerprints. He's a smart bastard too because he took every photo of himself. Every picture frame was empty. We only know him by the description Gerry just gave us." Isaac said.

"They killed the real Carter and put him in the house with Colleen?" It was like something out of a spy movie.

"You got it. The man's face was in such bad shape that the only way to identify him was by his fingerprints." Isaac said.

"What happens with Gerry now?" Ian was worried about his old friend.

"We wanted to put him in protective custody, but he said he's not leaving Newfoundland again," Isaac explained. "Right now, we're trying to find a place here in Hopedale where he can stay. Your Uncle mentioned your brother has a security company. Gerry agreed to stay with him. I'm waiting for approval." Isaac said.

"I don't know if Keith would accept money for watching out for Gerry. We all grew up together." Ian said.

"I know, and your uncle said the same thing, but I'm gonna do my best to get it approved," Isaac said as he stood up. "You know I've met some of your family since I've been here the past week. They made me feel at home."

"That's the Newfie way, b'y." Ian didn't use the word b'y very often, but it was a one Newfoundlanders used. Like most Canadians used eh.

“So I’ve been told.” Isaac chuckled. “Your uncle warned me if I don’t show up to your parents’ for Sunday dinner, your grandmother will come looking for me.”

“Jesus Christ, you don’t want that. You’d better be there.” Ian stood up.

“She was here yesterday, and I have to say, she’s certainly entertaining.” Isaac held out his hand.

“That she is. By the way, thanks for helping Gerry.” Ian shook Isaac’s hand. “I just hope you get the bastards that did this.”

Not long after Isaac disappeared into the room again, Keith showed up with one of his guys. They were immediately told to go into the room by one of the other officers and Ian knew at that point, he could leave and get his girls. Knowing what was going on made him want to keep them close so they would be safe.

Chapter 16

Trunk was driving the car, and stayed close behind the moving truck Crash was driving. Evie was bouncing in her booster seat as they turned into Hopedale and Sandy was bouncing for a different reason. She still hadn't talked to Ian and getting closer to her house was making her heart thunder in her chest. Ruby was quiet which was fine because Sandy was too nervous to talk.

"Your place is so cute." Evie squealed as she pointed toward the ocean. It wasn't like the child hadn't seen the ocean before, but they lived in the city. The beauty of Hopedale was all new to the little girl.

"You'll love it here, princess." Trunk pulled into the driveway.

"I'm so excited, Trunk." She giggled as Ruby unbuckled the seatbelts.

Sandy looked toward Ian's house. It was early, but she was sure the girls were probably up, and she tried to stop her shaking hands. Evie was in the front yard spinning around while Sandy unlocked the door. When she turned to tell Evie to come inside, she couldn't help but laugh.

"Evie, it's April, not July. The ground still has frost. Put on your shoes." Ruby shook her head when Evie skipped through the grass toward her.

"We never had grass like this by our apartment." Evie sat on the ground and slipped on her shoes.

"That's because we lived in the city," Ruby said.

"Well, the city sucks." The little girl stood up and ran up the steps toward Sandy.

"I can't say I disagree with that statement." Sandy chuckled.

Sandy's living room looked like a storage locker. Ruby left most of her furniture except for the bedroom sets and personal belongings. Apparently, there was a lot of personal things belonging to Evie. Ruby complained about Keith spoiling Evie with the constant gifts he sent to the little girl. Sandy knew it was because Keith was trying to compensate for his guilt. Like Sandy, Keith blamed himself for Tessa's death.

"So we've got the beds set up in the rooms upstairs." Crash jogged down the stairs. "What I'm trying to figure out is why a single woman needs a house with seven bedrooms."

"Maybe she plans on having lots of kids," Evie said, and Sandy had to swallow the lump in her throat. Evie didn't know.

"Or maybe she just likes lots of room," Ruby knew about Sandy's inability to have children.

"Will Crash and I take the bedrooms down here?" Trunk asked, and Sandy's head snapped up.

"You're staying here?" She didn't remember agreeing to have them stay with her.

"Rusty's orders." Crash walked by with a box of Evie's toys.

"I can toss a rock and hit Keith's front door. I don't think it's necessary for you guys to stay in the house." Sandy pulled out her phone and tapped Keith's number.

"No arguments. They're staying until we find the fucker." It didn't surprise her Keith knew why she would be calling him.

"I do work for you too. I'm trained." Sandy snapped.

"Yep. You do, and you are." Keith said.

"Why do the guys need to be here, too?" Sandy was fighting a losing battle, but she wasn't backing down easy.

"Because I said so," Keith said.

"Really? That's your answer?" Sandy rolled her eyes when Trunk glanced down at his phone and chuckled. He held it up for her to read.

Don't leave that house without my okay.

"That's my answer. By the way, have you talked to Ian?" The asshole had to bring that up.

"None of your business." Sandy snapped and ended the call. Her phone buzzed a couple of seconds later.

Which means, no. CALL MY BROTHER!!!!

"I miss the days when you could hang up on someone, and that was the end of the conversation." She read the text and sighed.

Trunk and Ruby laughed as she tossed her phone on the table in her living room. She was going to call Ian when she was alone. She didn't want everyone to see her apologize for overreacting. Then again if they were going to be together, he would have to get used to that little flaw of hers.

She sat back on the couch, closed her eyes and let out a deep sigh. She'd had a very long day, and the constant reminders for her to call Ian coming from Keith were getting on her last nerve.

"You know he keeps looking over here." Sandy opened one eye. Crash was peeking out through the window that looked out at Ian's house.

"Et tu, Crash?" Sandy groaned.

"Hey, I'm the last person to give advice on relationships but from what I've heard Keith's brother is a good man and he loves you." Crash took a sip of the coffee and turned toward her. "Call the man or better yet, go over there and work things out."

"Is Keith harassing you too?" Sandy smiled at him.

"Yes, but that's not why I'm saying this. Being alone is the shits, trust me. If you can find a happily ever after, do it." With that statement, he walked over to where she sat and crouched down. "Call him." He stood up and left the room.

Evie was sleeping, and Ruby had gone to bed as well. Crash and Trunk were watching a hockey game which gave her the opportunity to do what she'd wanted to do since she got home. Go next door and see the only man that made her feel like everything would be okay. That was if he forgave her for being a jerk.

Chapter 17

Lily was finally asleep again, but Ian didn't know for how long. She'd woken up twice crying since she went to bed and would ask where Sandy was because she wanted her to sing the song about bad dreams. Lily remembered the song, and he sang it with her, but it seemed his daughter had fallen in love with Sandy after just one night knowing her. Like father, like daughter.

His heart hurt. He'd seen Sandy pull up with her friend and the little girl earlier that day. He'd hoped she'd call or come over to introduce the little girl, but Sandy hadn't left the house. Then there were the two large apes going in and out of her house. Of course, Keith made a point to let him know the guys were there for security, but he didn't feel any better. Especially when every time Ian looked over at the house one of them caught him.

He'd called Keith to find out how things were going with Gerald, but only half listened to the conversation. He was worried about his old friend, but he felt lost not knowing if or when Sandy would talk to him again.

He'd grabbed yet another cup of coffee and entered the living room. He heard Lily sobbing again and hurried into the bedroom. He found her sat up in the bed clinging to her bunny.

"Lily, did you have another bad dream?" Ian lifted her into his arms and left the bedroom just in case Grace woke. That was the last thing he needed.

"I need Sandy to sing the song." Lily sobbed and rested her head on his shoulder.

"I don't know when Sandy will be home, sweetheart." He lied.

"Is she mad at you?" Lily lifted her head and stared into his face.

"I'm not really sure but how about we lay on the couch and find a movie to watch." Ian hoped the distraction would work, but his daughter wasn't buying it.

"I heard Aunt Stephanie say you were being a man again," Lily tucked her head under his arm on the couch.

"Did she now?" As much as he loved his sister-in-law, her being mad was the least of his worries.

"I'm not sure, but it sounds like you're in trouble." Lily wiped her eyes with her fists, and he pulled the blanket up over her. He prayed she'd fall asleep again.

"Everything's fine, Lily. How about we watch this movie?" He pointed to the screen where he'd brought up one of the many Disney movies that he watched over the last few days. He was relieved when Lily nodded her head and snuggled into his side.

"Will Sandy ever come over again?" Lily yawned. Ian was about to answer when he heard a soft voice from the doorway.

"Of course." Ian looked up, and his heart melted.

"Sandy." Lily jumped off the couch and ran, right into Sandy's arms. "I had bad dreams, and Daddy helped me sing the song, but the dreams didn't go away."

"Did you want me to sing it to you?" Sandy asked. Lily nodded and glanced at Ian.

"Goodnight Daddy." Lily smiled, but Sandy didn't move toward the girl's room. She met his gaze, and he smiled.

"Is it alright with you if I put her to bed?" Sandy asked.

"It's more than alright," Ian smiled.

He stood next to the patio door staring out at the fog rolling in over the water. Another evening of rain, drizzle, and fog. It was kind of fitting considering how he'd been feeling. Sandy seemed to be in the room with Lily for what seemed like an hour. Seeing her in his doorway was the best thing he'd ever seen in a long time. Ian worried she would end things and had all kinds of scenarios running through his head. He was ready to go in and drag her out of the bedroom, but he saw her reflection behind him through the window.

"She's out like a light," Sandy said.

Ian turned around and braced his hands on the windowsill. She stood there nervously playing with the edge of her T-shirt and doing everything to avoid his eyes.

"For some reason, the song only works when you sing it," Ian pushed himself away from the window and walked toward her.

"I think she just misses having a woman around." Sandy shoved her hands into her pockets and glanced at the television.

"She's been with the women in my family all week. It's you." Ian stood in front of her but didn't touch her.

"Maybe it's because she knows my mom died too." Sandy lowered her head and wouldn't meet his eyes.

"It's you." Ian lifted her chin with his finger, so she had to look at him. "It's only you." This time he wasn't talking about Lily.

"Ian…," Sandy whispered just before his lips brushed against hers.

"I love you, Sandy and I'll stand by you whatever you want to do." Ian cupped her face in his hands, and her hands covered his.

"I need to keep her safe, Ian." Sandy's eyes filled with tears. "I feel responsible."

"I know. I see why you and Keith are so close now. You both feel the need to protect everyone you love." Ian smiled and used his thumb to wipe away a tear that was slowly sliding down her cheek.

"I love you," Sandy whispered.

"I want to be the one to protect you." Ian looked deep into Sandy's eyes. "I want you to feel safe in my arms and know I'll do anything to keep you and those you love safe."

"I don't want to put you and your girls in danger." She touched his cheek.

"I know I'm not Keith or his tribe of apes, but I can keep you and Evie safe too." Ian pulled her into his arms. "Just don't shut me out."

“Do you know how to use a gun?” She asked, and Ian furrowed his brows.

“Uncle Kurt made sure all of us knew how to use guns,” Ian explained. Although he hadn’t been to the range in a long while, he could handle a gun if he needed.

“Good.” Sandy pressed her hands against his chest and stared at them. “This guy is crazy, and we’ve had a sighting of him in Moncton.”

“He’s coming for Evie, isn’t he?” Ian thought he knew the answer to the question.

“No. Scott’s coming for me. Evie was just the way he was going to get to me.” Sandy looked up and met his eyes.

“He’s not going to get near you,” Ian growled, and she lay her finger against his lips.

“I need you to promise that you’ll protect yourself and your girls,” Sandy said. “Let me and the guys take care of Scott.”

“Sandy, I can’t promise you I won’t protect you if I have to.” Ian hugged her against him.

"I know you're a big tough O'Connor, but he doesn't care who he hurts and when he knows the best way to hurt me is to go after Evie, you and your girls, he won't hesitate."

"I'm not afraid of this guy, Sandy."

"I'm sorry for running away again." She whispered.

"Please don't run from me again." Ian pressed his lips against her forehead.

"Can you just hold me right now?" Sandy pressed her cheek against his shoulder.

"I'll hold you forever if you want." The music of the Disney movie played in the background while he wrapped her in his arms. Her tense muscles slowly relax, but she didn't speak, and neither did he. He was just happy to have her in his arms. Any talking they had to do could wait until she was ready.

Chapter 18

Two weeks of having her co-workers constantly around and she was about to go insane. Her house had apparently become the main base for Newfoundland Security Services, and Keith was sending out jobs from her house. She'd taken to spending most of her time working in her room.

The guys seemed to be bothering Ruby too because she'd taken to spending a lot of time at Kim's salon. Kim had offered a job helping with answering phones and keeping the place clean which kept her busy. Evie was enrolled in school and loving her new teachers, but Keith made sure Crunch could be at the school always to keep an eye on her. It was a good plan since all the O'Connor children went to the same school. Keith kept them under protection detail as well. Like her, Keith knew Scott would go after anyone, and he didn't care if it was a child or not.

Lily loved having a friend close to her age around who liked Disney princess movies too. Apparently, her male cousins weren't big fans of the movies.

Ian decided to go into practice with his father. He'd concluded that it would be easier with the kids. He'd been going back and forth between her house and his dad's clinic to set up his office. Although, he'd said he wasn't going back to work for another month.

Sandy spent her time during the day trying to find anything she could on Scott, but like usual he seemed to have vanished. It pissed her off that Scott could disappear so easily, but there was something in the pit of her stomach telling her he was close.

The O'Connor family had a memorial service for Colleen and the murdered man. They knew he wasn't the man Colleen married, but they were doing their best to find out who that guy was. All signs pointed to him being the murderer. The man they called Lefty was involved somehow, but from the information, Gerry had given them Lefty was crazy. Something told her she knew the guy, but she didn't see how that was possible. The guy was from Manitoba, and she'd never been to the province.

"Smash, have you found anything else." Sandy looked up as Keith walked into her room on his phone. He seemed to think he could do that without knocking and she'd gotten tired of telling him he didn't own her room. "I know, but Sandy is dealing with Coates. I want you looking for this Lefty and his boss. My nieces need justice, and so does Gerry." Keith listened for a minute. "Talk to him again.

Maybe he remembers something." Keith tapped his phone and shoved it into his pocket.

"No luck on his side, either?" Sandy sat back in his chair.

"No. Why do the scum of the earth always hide so easily?" Keith bent over the desk and scanned the screen.

"Nothing." Sandy sighed.

"Don't worry, kiddo. We'll find the bastard. I was talking to Shadow, and he's supposed to be heading out this way, but he's not sure when." Keith said.

"He's never going to give up until he gets justice for his sister." Lane struggled with Tessa's murder. Any brother would when someone took their sister's life. He'd made it his mission to find Scott. The only thing that worried her was the lengths he was going to go to get justice.

"That's why I want him here. That way I can keep him from doing something stupid." Keith headed out of the room and left her staring after him. She remembered him being ready to be pretty crazy after Tessa's death, but she wasn't going there with him now. He'd managed to keep himself from going over the deep end.

"Are you busy?" Sandy glanced back to the door. There was the man that made her heart pound every time he smiled or even frowned.

"For you, I'll stop being busy." Sandy stood up and met him halfway across the room. She wrapped her arms around him and pressed her lips against his. His arms snaked around her waist and pulled her against his hard body. His mouth was soft and warm, and she melted into the kiss. He always did this to her when he kissed her.

"As much as I would like to continue, I've got something to ask." He sighed against her mouth.

"Well if you must." Sandy placed one quick kiss against his lips and pulled back from him.

"The girls asked me last night if they could have a sleepover at my house," Ian said. "I think they're getting overwhelmed with all the people here. I just wanted to know if that would be okay with Ruby and if you could possibly not leave me alone with all those little girls." Ian stuck out his bottom lip in an exaggerated pout.

"To be honest, I'm feeling overwhelmed with everyone here, too. I'm sure Ruby would be okay with it, and I'd never leave you to deal with a little girl's slumber party. Dear God that would be torture." Sandy giggled as he pulled her against him.

"Thanks. Plus, when the little girls go to sleep then I can have my own slumber party with you." She felt his hard length against her stomach and groaned when he squeezed her ass.

"Well, I hope their slumber party isn't like the ones I had as a little girl. We'd be up all night." Sandy kissed his chin, and his beard tickled her nose.

"Lots of warm milk." Ian kissed his way down the side of her face to her ear. "No sugar for them." When he sucked her earlobe into his hot mouth, she gasped.

"I'm sure they'll appreciate that." Sandy giggled when he gave her a quick smack on her ass.

"Ruby said I could sleepover." Evie's excited voice floated in from the hallway as she ran into the room.

"Yep, lots of warm milk," Ian mumbled into Sandy's ear.

"That's great." Sandy's smiled and lifted Evie into her arms.

"I know. I haven't had a sleepover ever and Ian, I don't like warm milk." Evie informed him. Ian's expression made her laugh.

When Sandy put Evie back on the floor, the little girl ran out of the room singing some song from the Frozen movie. Sandy turned into Ian's arms and gazed up at him.

"I'm really starting to hate that movie." Ian sighed. Sandy stood up on her toes and pressed her lips against his.

"The joy of having little girls." Sandy ran her tongue across his lower lip and his eyes closed.

"They won't actually stay awake all night, will they?" Ian slid his hand under her shirt and cupped her breast while she kissed her way down the side of his neck.

"I'm sure they'll fall asleep at some point." Sandy slid her hand down the front of his shirt until she reached the hard length of his erection through his jeans. She squeezed gently making him moan and drop his forehead onto her shoulder.

"Baby, that feels so good," Ian whispered.

Sandy stepped back from him, closed her bedroom door, and locked it. She pulled her T-shirt over her head and tossed it on the bed. Ian's gaze slowly traveled down her body, and the heat of his stare made goose bumps form on her skin.

"I fucking love that tattoo," Ian pulled off his own T-shirt. She could say the same to him, but everything about the man's body was beautiful. From this muscled chest down his well defined six pack and to that v that would make any woman lose her mind. The man was perfection.

"Why don't you come here and get a better look?" Sandy teased as she unbuttoned her jeans and slowly slid out of them. In only her matching bra and panties that had 'big girl' written across the ass, she backed toward the bathroom. She'd locked the bedroom door, but Keith would still come in without knocking. He'd never go into her bathroom.

"I'm trying, but you keep backing away." Ian dropped his own jeans, and the sight of him made her mouth water. His white boxer briefs were super snug and showed off every glorious inch of his erection.

"Come in the bathroom, and you can get a better look." Sandy turned and walked out of the bedroom. She made sure that her hips gave that extra swing just to entice him a little more.

"Big girl, huh?" Ian closed the bathroom door and pulled her back against him as he slid his hand slowly into the front of her panties, and she pressed her ass against his hardness. "You're so damn hot."

She pressed her ass against him, and his finger slid between her wet folds making her moan. He kissed the side of her neck while he slowly slid his finger inside her. Her head fell back against his chest as he continued to plunge his digit into her heat. Her legs started to tense and trembled as the first wave of her orgasm flowed through her body.

“Ian, yes.” She moaned as her body trembled with pleasure.

Ian pulled his hand out of her panties and spun her around. He covered her mouth with his, and his tongue slid into her mouth as he fumbled with her bra and panties. She slid off his boxers, and his cock slapped against her bare stomach. Ian lifted her into his arms, and she wrapped her legs around his waist. With a quick spin, he had her back against the wall and plunged inside of her.

“Fuck, yes.” Ian groaned with every thrust he slammed into her. He moved in and out with such force that Sandy could hardly breathe or move. This was going to be fast but so damn hot. His fingers dug into her ass while he held her and she loved every minute of it. Another orgasm was building, and her legs tightened around his body.

“Ian, yes.” She panted as he thrust once more bringing her over the edge.

“So. Fucking. Hot.” Ian pumped with each word, and then his body shook with his release.

For a few minutes, Sandy didn’t move. She couldn’t even if she tried. Ian’s full body weight had her pinned against the door, and thankfully she didn’t have to hold herself up because she was literally weak in the knees.

"Do you think anyone heard us? Ian whispered as he pulled out of her.

"Probably not." Sandy smiled, but her smile faded when Ian looked down and then up again.

"Fuck, I'm so sorry." Ian plowed his hands through his hair.

"What?" She was baffled why he looked like he was about to jump out of his skin.

"I didn't use a condom." Ian started pacing the small bathroom.

"Ian, it's okay. I haven't been with anyone in a very long time." Sandy hoped he would say he hadn't since the last time with Colleen. That thought still hit her in the gut like a punch.

"You already know how long it's been for me, but I'm not worried about that stuff. I know we're both clean. I mean…" He stopped pacing and pulled her into his arms. "Shit, Churchie I forgot. You can't... I mean…."

She realized he'd forgot about her inability to have children. That familiar lump formed in her throat. The one that she always got with the reminder she could never have another baby.

"It's okay." Sandy cupped his face. "I think we're okay with going bare." She forced a smile, and he covered her hands with his.

"I love you, Sandy." He stared into her eyes, and she gazed into his blue depths. She loved the way they sparkled when he smiled, but at that moment she could see his concern.

"I love you too." She kissed his lips with soft feathery touches. "I always will."

"Finish up in there, I've got work for Sandy and Lily is looking for you, Ian." Keith's voice boomed from the other side of the bathroom door.

"Didn't you lock the bedroom door?" Ian pulled on his underwear.

"Yes, but even locked doors don't keep him out." Sandy sighed as she pulled her robe off the hook and wrapped it around herself.

"Would you mind leaving the room so we can get dressed, you fucking asshole?" Ian opened the door a crack and growled at his brother.

"Don't take too long. I've got something for Sandy to check out." Keith said, and then the bedroom door closed.

"I'll be having a chat with my little brother about barging into your room without knocking first." Ian left the bathroom and pulled his jeans on.

"Good luck with that. I've been telling Keith that for years." Sandy giggled when Ian stopped half way through putting on his T-shirt.

"I'll kick his ass if he doesn't start respecting your privacy," Ian growled and continued to dress. Sandy smiled and wrapped her arms around his waist.

"It's okay, Doc. He always makes sure I'm working before he just drops in." She gazed up into his face. "I love you for wanting to kick his ass, though."

"I love you too." Ian kissed her lips tenderly.

"Can we please get back to work." Keith opened the door, and Sandy had to hold Ian back.

"You really need to knock before you walk in," Ian growled.

Keith didn't seem to hear a word Ian said. He hurried over to the bank of computers and pulled his phone out of his pocket. Sandy moved next to him to see what was so urgent it would have Keith touching her computers. He knew she didn't like anyone at her equipment.

“I’ll let you guys get to work.” Ian kissed her cheek and left the room.

“Smash, send those photos now.” Sandy glanced at Keith. The clenched jaw and tapping fingers showing his impatience. Keith didn't give her a chance to touch her computer. He snatched the mouse from the side of her desk and opened the email. Half a dozen pictures popped up on his screen, and Sandy covered her mouth.

The first were of two women very similar in appearance to her. The next two pictures had her wanting to vomit. The women’s brutally beaten bodies lay naked and bloody on what appeared to be a concrete floor.

“I want all the information on these murders.” Keith listened for a minute. “I don’t give two fucks. Call Uncle Kurt and get him to talk to the detective in charge. We know who did this and he’s getting too fucking close to home.” Keith tapped his phone and tossed it on her desk.

“Scott did this?” Sandy knew the answer. Keith nodded and slammed his two fists on her desk.

“Both women were from Halifax, and were killed at least three weeks ago.”

“You think he’s in Newfoundland?” Sandy was afraid to mention how similar the women looked to her.

"Yes. Sandy, I know you see it. Do you know what this means?" Keith turned to face her, but she couldn't look away from her screen.

"They look like me," Sandy whispered.

"He's coming after you." Keith turned her to face him.

"I knew he would." Sandy stepped back. "I'm not afraid of him, Keith."

"I know, but he knows the best way to scare you. He's coming after the people you care about." Keith didn't have to tell her that. She already knew.

Chapter 19

Lily and Evie were curled up on the couch watching the third princess movie for the evening. Grace had gone to bed at her normal time which was a relief, and it looked like Lily and Evie weren't going to be awake much longer. He was surprised that Sandy hadn't come by since she had told him she would be by to help.

I can't handle any more princesses.

He sent the text hoping she'd text him back and let him know she was on the way. He waited but nothing. Something was wrong, and he could feel it in the pit of his stomach. That feeling he always got when something was going to send him running to the bathroom.

He glanced over at the two little girls. Both were asleep, and he didn't have the heart to move them. They were curled up on opposite ends of the couch covered with a blanket. He turned off the television and quietly left the living room.

In the kitchen, he poured a cup of hot chocolate and sat at the table. His life had changed so much over the last few weeks, and it was a shock to find out he was a father, but he was enjoying every minute of it. His relationship with Sandy was going well, but he felt terrible they hadn't had an official date. He needed to do that as soon as things settled down.

His phone buzzed, and he pulled it out of his pocket. At first, he thought it might be Sandy, but Keith's name was on the screen.

"Hey bro, what's up?" Ian answered.

"It's not Keith. It's me." Sandy's voice sounded strange.

"Hey, did you get lost on your way to my house?" He joked.

"I'm on my way over now."

"Why are you using Keith's phone?" Not that it mattered.

"Smash has to put some new software on mine." She sighed. "I'll explain when I come over."

While he waited for her to arrive, he checked on the girls. Then, he checked on Grace and couldn't help but smile when the baby giggled in her sleep. It was weird how he couldn't relax for the night unless he checked on them. It had become the norm so fast that he didn't even realize it.

When he walked out of the room Sandy was standing in the foyer with Keith behind her. Ian didn't like the stress lines across his brother's forehead and the tense set of his jaw. His gaze moved to Sandy, and his stomach flipped. Her face was pale, and her eyes had lost that twinkle.

"What's wrong?" Ian felt that bubble in his stomach that always threatened to lurch when he was expecting bad news. He followed his brother and Sandy into the kitchen where she placed her laptop on top of the table and opened it.

"I know you're a doctor and probably have seen a lot worse than these pictures, but you need to prepare yourself. They're kind of gruesome." Keith said as Sandy clicked on the keys opening several files.

"Okay." Was all Ian could say because he was expecting the worst at this point. Sandy turned her laptop toward him, and the images of two bloodied bodies filled the screen. Keith was right he'd seen some pretty severe injuries in his life, and some were just as bad as what he was seeing in front of him.

"They were murdered over three weeks ago," it was the first time Sandy had spoken since she'd walked into the house.

"Am I supposed to know these women?" Ian hoped not.

"No, but here's what they looked like before that." Sandy clicked on a few more keys and pictures of two attractive women popped up on the screen. The thing that made him tense was their resemblance to Sandy. It made his stomach lurch.

“Do you need a glass of water, bro?” Keith was familiar with Ian’s reactions.

“Yeah.” Ian sat down and plowed his hands through his hair. Keith placed a glass in front of him, and Ian sipped it slowly.

“You ready to listen to all this?” Keith asked. Ian nodded, but he wasn’t sure if he wanted to know.

“We’re pretty sure Scott Coates is responsible for this, and it’s a message to Sandy that he’s coming for her.” Keith started to pace.

“Keith, for the love of God. Can’t you be a little less dramatic.” Sandy sighed. Ian didn’t think his brother was being dramatic at all.

“Sandy, I’m telling him the facts. He needs to know, and we’ve got to put a plan together to make sure you and anyone you care about is safe. That includes him and the girls.” That statement had Ian covering his mouth and holding up his hand as he hurried out of the kitchen. He got in the bathroom, but he managed to keep everything down by splashing water on his face and taking several deep breaths.

"You okay, Doc?" Sandy asked when he entered the kitchen a few minutes later. He nodded because he wasn't sure it was safe to speak at that point.

"This is the plan, bro. One, you and the girls either stay with me or at Sandy's place. Our security is much better than yours, and there'll always be at least two of my guys close. Two, I want you carrying at all times." Keith braced his fisted hands on the table in front of him. "I know you can shoot, but it's no good if you don't have it close."

"I don't need a gun, Keith. I can protect myself and the girls." Ian didn't want to carry a gun all the time.

"You can't block a bullet with your hands or a kick," Keith growled.

"I'm not carrying a gun." Ian stood up and faced his brother.

"Bring up the picture of that bastard," Keith told Sandy, but he kept his eyes trained on Ian.

Ian heard Sandy click on the computer keys again and turn the laptop toward him again.

"Look at that picture. Memorize that face. That's the asshole who's out to kill Sandy. He wants to do what he did to those girls, to the woman you love but he's a sly bastard. So, if you don't realize it's him then he could get to her before you get a chance to drop kick his ass." Keith pointed to the smiling man on the screen, and at first glance, the man looked harmless. Like someone, he could probably be friends with, but Ian knew the truth, and the smile suddenly looked sinister and taunting.

"Do you know where he is?" Ian met Sandy's gaze. She shook her head, and he walked around his brother and crouched down in front of her. "Do you want me to carry a gun?" Ian didn't give a fuck what Keith said. She'd asked him not long ago if he knew how to shoot.

"I'd feel better if you did." She cupped his cheek, and he covered his hand with hers and kissed her palm.

"Then I will. For you and the girls."

"Hi, Uncle Keith." Lily's sleepy voice had them all turning toward the kitchen door.

"Hi, Lily." Keith closed the laptop even though the only picture on there was Scott.

"Did you want something, sweetheart." Ian quickly went to her and lifted her in his arms.

"I'm thirsty." She wrapped her arms around his neck and smiled at Sandy.

Ian carried her while he pulled a juice box out of the fridge. Lily took it and sipped it like she hadn't had anything to drink in days. She reached out to Sandy and Ian placed her on Sandy's lap.

"Are you sleeping over tonight, too?" Lily asked when she finally put down her empty juice box.

"I think so." Sandy glanced back and forth between Keith and Ian.

"Of course, she is." Ian glared at Keith daring him to disagree, but his brother just crossed his arms over his chest.

"You sleeping over too, Uncle Keith?" Lily asked, and Ian chuckled at Keith's expression. He seemed to have a nervousness around the girls.

"I've got some things to do at home. I won't be staying tonight." Keith answered.

"Why were you looking at a picture of Carter?" Lily pointed at the laptop. "He's in heaven with mommy."

"That wasn't Carter, honey that was someone we are trying to find," Sandy explained, and Lily must be confused.

"That was Carter, but he had longer hair in that picture." Ian tensed, and Keith stood up straight. Sandy's eyes looked like they were about to pop out of her head.

"Are you sure that's Carter, Lily?" Keith asked, and the little girl nodded. Keith opened the laptop and pointed to the picture still on the screen. "This man was the man married to your mom?"

"Yes, didn't you hear me a second ago?" Lily shook her head and looked at Sandy. "I think he might have something wrong with his ears."

"My ears work fine. Lily, you need to be sure." Keith bent down to Lily's level, and Ian was worried his overgrown brother was going to frighten her.

"You can be really cranky sometimes, you need to eat more fiber." Lily leaned toward her uncle and Ian had to try to hold back his laughter. "But if you don't believe me, I can show you." With that statement, she jumped down from Sandy's lap and ran out of the kitchen. Ian was about to follow her, but she returned a few minutes later holding a wooden box that looked like an old chest. Stickers and colorful beads covered the top and sides.

Lily put the box on the floor and used a small key to open it. Ian watched her as she searched through the little chest. His daughter seemed to be having trouble finding something. She sat down and pulled it between her legs as she took everything out one by one and placed it carefully next to her side. Ian glanced at Sandy. She was watching Lily like the little girl was about to pull out the best treasure in the world. Keith didn't look as impressed, but that was his brother.

"I know it's in here. Mommy gave me the picture and told me to keep it with the rest of my treasures." Lily seemed to be speaking mostly to herself.

"Do you want me to help you, Lily?" Ian asked.

"Oh no, Daddy. These are my secret treasures." Lily's eyes went wide as she explained how her mom told her only the two of them could look in the chest and Grace when she was older.

For what seemed like forever Lily pulled one thing after the other out of the box. It was starting to look as if the thing had no bottom. Ian sat back against the wall and pulled his hands down over his face. Sandy leaned over with her arms resting on her knees and her hands clasped together. Keith sat on the chair and rested his chin on his fist looking as impatient as ever.

"Here it is." Lily squealed and held up a folded photo waving it in the air. Keith jumped up and almost yanked it out of the little girl's hand.

"That was rude." Lily furrowed her brows and glared at Keith.

"Sorry, kiddo. This is really important." Keith seemed genuinely apologetic.

"I'm Lily and just ask next time." Lily shook her head as she carefully put everything back in the chest.

Keith opened the picture and studied it. Ian glanced over his brother's shoulder to get a glimpse of the photo. It showed a smiling Colleen holding Lily's hand and her other hand on a very pregnant belly. Four men stood next to her one was Gerald. The other two Ian didn't know, but the man with his arm wrapped around Colleen gave him chills. Lily was right.

"Lily, come here and tell me who all these people are in the picture." Keith crouched down on the floor. Ian was puzzled because Keith seemed to know some of them.

"You have really bad manners." Lily closed her box and stood up.

"I'm sorry." Keith sighed. "Could you please come here and tell me who all these people are?"

Lily stood next to Keith and looked down at the picture. She pointed to everyone and called each of them by name.

"That's Mommy, that's me, that's Uncle Gerry, That's Carter, That's Carter's friend, I don't know his name. He smelled really yucky. That's the man that did the wedding." Lily looked up at Keith.

"Thanks, Lily." Keith had apparently learned Lily was waiting for him to use his manners. "Can I keep this picture for a few days?" Lily looked up at Ian, and the panic in her eyes made his heart hurt.

"I don't have any more pictures of mommy." Lily's eyes were filling with tears, and before Ian had a chance to comfort her, Sandy was on her knees and taking Lily's hands in hers.

"I promise you I'll make sure Uncle Keith brings that picture back to you," Sandy said.

"You promise?" The sadness in Lily's voice made Ian's chest hurt.

"I promise." Sandy crossed her heart with her finger.

"Okay, Uncle Keith." Lily looked up at Keith and gave a weak smile.

"I think it's time to go back to sleep." Ian didn't want the little girl hearing anything that Keith and Sandy were about to say.

Lily nodded, and Ian picked her up and brought her back to the living room where Evie was still sleeping soundly.

"Daddy, is everything okay?" Lily whispered when Ian tucked her in.

"Everything will be okay, honey. Don't you worry." Ian kissed her on the top of the head, and her eyes fluttered closed.

Ian stood and stared down at her for a moment. Was everything going to be okay? Did Colleen know what kind of man she married? What had she been involved in and had that got her killed? If anyone could find out, it was his brother.

Chapter 20

Sandy knew what it was like to only have a few pictures of people who had passed away. She had lots of pictures of her mother, but she only had one picture of her friend, Tessa and she kept that in a safe place. She'd scanned it to make sure if something did happen to the photo that she would always have it.

When she made that promise to Lily, she meant it. Keith stood there staring at the picture as he held his phone to his ear. Sandy still hadn't looked at it, but she wasn't sure she wanted to. She was almost afraid of who she would see.

"Bring Gerry over to Ian's house and take an overnight bag 'cause you'll be staying here tonight." Keith listened for a minute. "I need him here."

"Just hold on a sec there, bro. I don't want Lily seeing him yet." Ian walked into the kitchen. Keith held up his finger as he continued to listen.

“Okay, come in through the back of the house because we don’t want anyone to know he’s here,” Keith said.

“Have you looked at the picture yet?” Ian glanced down at Sandy, took her hand and pulled her up from the chair. Automatically she wrapped her arms around him, and he hugged her tightly to his body. It was as if being in his arms made every muscle and nerve in her body calm. She closed her eyes as she rested her cheek against his chest. The steady thud of his heart was even more calming, and she almost forgot about everything. Almost.

“No.” He must have sensed she didn’t want to talk because he hugged her and kissed the top of her head.

“Okay, Sandy. I need you to look at this and see if you know any of these guys before Gerry gets here.” She heard Keith say right after the beep of his phone meaning he ended the call.

She opened her eyes but didn’t move. Keith tilted his head to the side. Keith had to know how hard this was for her. Scott or Carter or whatever his name was a monster, and she wasn’t the only one to have fallen for his tricks.

“Come on, kiddo.” Keith held out the picture, and before she reached for it, Ian took it from Keith’s hand and held it up in front of her.

The first thing Sandy saw was the woman. Obviously, Colleen. She was beautiful and certainly looked happy. She glanced to Colleen's left and saw him. Scott was smiling like he was the happiest man in the world. She stared at him for a moment and then looked behind him where Colleen's brother stood with what seemed like a forced smile. Sandy scanned to the left of Scott, and her heart felt as if it stopped. She knew the other two men in the photo. One of them intimately. She grabbed the picture from Ian's hand and held it closer. Just to make sure she wasn't mistaken.

"I can't believe it." She said.

"Can't believe what, kiddo?" Keith was now looking over her shoulder.

"I know them." Sandy pointed to the two men.

"Who are they?" Ian asked.

"Remember the guy I told you talked to me at the club when I went back to find Dennis?" Sandy looked up at Keith. He nodded.

"That's him." She pointed to the man stood right next to Scott.

"You said you knew them?" Keith said. Sandy looked at Ian and felt ashamed for the first time in a long time.

"That's Dennis." Sandy pointed to the other man. "He wasn't dead." She walked from between Ian and Keith. She stood in front of the window trembling, and it pissed her off because she hated feeling weak.

"This is not making any fucking sense," Keith said.

It wasn't making sense to her either. How did these guys know each other and the way they all looked in the picture was as if they were friends? Lily said that the man who told Sandy Dennis was dead smelled funny and the man Sandy knew as Dennis officiated the wedding. She had everything spinning through her mind making her dizzy. Then she felt him slip his arms around her waist and pull her against him.

"We'll figure this out," Ian whispered in her ear. Sandy turned into his arms and pressed her forehead against his chest.

"I'm going to tell you something, but you can't say anything to Keith or anyone." Sandy raised her head and stared into his eyes. Keith had gone out back to meet with Gerry, and she was assuming Smash since Gerry was staying him.

"I promise." Ian crossed his finger over his chest, and she smiled.

"I'm scared." She whispered. "Not for myself but for everyone I love. Scott's crazy. He must be to do what he did."

Ian pulled her into his arms and tucked her head under his chin.

"Keith will make sure everyone is safe," Ian whispered. "And I'll make sure you're safe."

Just as she thought, Smash walked in behind Keith and Gerry through the back door. Smash looked more like a high school kid with his shaggy blonde hair and clean shaven face. He was probably the one she talked to the most besides Keith.

"Hey there Sandy, Ian" Smash gave her a half smile.

"Hi, Gage," Sandy gave him a quick smile.

"Nice to see you, Smash." Ian reached out and shook hands with him but managed to keep Sandy close. Since most of Keith's employees relocated to Hopedale, they were all familiar with Ian and the rest of the O'Connor family. The only one that wasn't living in the town at the moment was Lane.

"Gerry, I need you to look at this picture and tell me who the guys are." Keith wasn't wasting any time, and she was glad.

"This was taken after Carter married Colleen or who people thought was Carter." Sandy watched as Gerry studied the picture. His face fell a little and Sandy had no doubt it was because he was looking at his sister. “She was so happy that day.” Gerald’s voice cracked a little, but he tipped his head back and took a deep breath.

“I know this is hard, buddy but we need to know who these guys are.” Keith pointed to the two men in the picture.

“The guy next to Carter is Lefty. Like I said before I don’t know his real name. All I know the guy always stunk to high heavens of weed and body odor. The other guy was the one who performed the wedding.” Gerald shook his head. “I can’t remember what they called him but from what that cop from Manitoba told me he was the real Carter.”

“Dennis?” Sandy asked.

“Yes, Carter told me the guy went by his second name. Well, the guy I thought was Carter. This is so fucked up.” Gerald plopped down on one of the chairs and dropped his head. “I should’ve stopped the wedding, but I was so desperate to find out what happened to Luke. I know he didn’t kill himself.” He covered his face with his hand and propped his elbows on the table.

“You’re right, you should’ve made sure Colleen wasn’t mixed up in this,” Keith told him, it made Sandy want to smack him in the back of the head. Keith wasn’t known for being empathetic.

“Jesus, Keith, could you be more of an ass?” Smash shook his head and glanced over at Sandy.

“Shut up, Smash, he knew what Luke was involved in, and he was aware these guys were up to no good. What you didn’t know Gerry is, the guy you thought was Carter, is a fucking cruel bastard. He’s been raping and torturing women for years. Probably more than we know. He’s also the one that killed someone I cared deeply about and took another mother away from her little girl.” Gerald’s head slowly lifted, and he met Keith’s eyes.

“We need to know what you know, Gerry,” Ian said as Sandy felt his arm tighten around her.

“I know he’s real smart, and he’s crazy. If I knew what Colleen did with that USB, it would help. All she said was she’d hide it in her secret treasure chest.” Gerald almost tipped over the chair when Keith jumped up from the seat across the table and turned to Ian.

“You don’t think….” Ian said, and Sandy knew what they were both thinking.

“Get that box,” Keith said a little louder than he should have. Ian turned to leave the kitchen, but Sandy stepped in front of him.

“You can’t touch that box without asking Lily.” Sandy glanced back and forth between the two brothers.

“Are you fucking nuts? Everything we need could be in that box.” Keith stared at her as if she’d grown another head.

"It's also Lily's connection to her mother. A secret between them." Sandy couldn't let them do this without asking Lily.

"Sandy, for fuck's sake," Keith grumbled and threw his hands up in the air.

"Sandy, I'll explain to Lily why we had to do it and…." Ian started to step around her, but she moved in front of him again.

"No." Sandy wasn't letting them do this. "I'll ask Lily in the morning, but you two aren't invading the only thing she has that makes her feel close to her mother."

"If it's that stupid box Lily has with all the stickers and things on it, I doubt it's in there. Lily would have found it by now. She can tell you everything that's in that box. Colleen made it with her, and they treated it like it was the holy grail." Gerry sat back on the chair. "But Sandy is right, Lily would be real upset if you guys opened it."

"She's a kid, she'll get over it." Keith snapped.

"No, she won't, Keith. You've got no idea what it's like to lose a parent. It's bad enough when you're older but losing one as a child must be ten times harder. You're not touching it, and that's it." Sandy put her fists on her hips and faced off against the mountain of a man.

“We can look through it and put it back before she knows,” Ian suggested.

“Good luck finding the key.” Gerry scoffed. “Last time, Colleen used to have to ask Lily to unlock it because Lily wouldn’t tell her where the key was.”

“For fuck sake.” Keith stomped out through the back door.

“Seriously, Ian. We can wait until morning. I’m sure Lily will let me look. We have a connection.” Sandy turned to Ian.

“I know you do but if we can find out tonight…,” Ian said.

“What difference will it make? Nothing. Let me talk to Lily in the morning.” She studied his face.

“Okay, but I don’t know if Keith will agree,” Ian nodded toward where Keith had come back into the house.

“Keith, we’re waiting until tomorrow,” Sandy told him before he had a chance to open his mouth.

“Fine, but we need to do it first thing.” Keith wasn’t happy about it, that was evident. “So Gerry you come back to my place. Smash stay here.”

“I’ll move the girls into the bedroom, and you can crash in the living room,” Ian said.

Keith and Smash laughed, and Ian's expression had Sandy giggling.

"I won't be crashing, and I won't be inside," Smash told Ian.

"Ian, don't you know by now the guys don't stay in the house when they're working." Keith rolled his eyes.

Sandy stood in the doorway of the living room watching the girls sleeping. She had a connection with Evie and had since the first day she saw her, but she felt connected to Lily as well. It seemed like the two little girls had formed a bond too. One that they probably didn't understand themselves. They both lost their mothers at the hands of the same man. He was the same monster that took her baby from her too. That was the connection.

"Keith said to call as soon as Lily gets up in the morning." Ian wrapped his arms around her waist and rested his chin on her shoulder.

"How could I let myself get involved with such a monster?" Sandy whispered. The only person she ever showed her vulnerability to was Ian. Even with her sister and Stephanie, she always kept up the front that she was tough as nails.

"Don't blame yourself for this. He fooled a lot of people." Ian turned her to face him.

“He’s hurt so many people. Killed so many people.” The anger she had for Scott started to surface. “He took those little girls’ mothers from them. He took my baby from me. He even killed the father of my child, and from what we know they were friends. I don’t care how he and Dennis and that other guy are linked or what scheme they had going. Scott is a savage animal who deserves nothing but to suffer like he made everyone else suffer.”

“Churchie, let's go to bed and try and get some sleep. Tomorrow’s going to be a very long day. Keith wants the girls and me either with you or him, and he has to talk to the family to let them know why he’s got security on all of them. He also wants to get in touch with your father and Brad.” Ian took her hand and led her toward the bedroom. “Let me hold you tonight. Hopefully, that will help us both sleep.”

“You always make me feel safe in your arms.” Sandy slipped out of her clothes and slid between the sheets. Ian stood over the bed and stared down at her.

“As much as I want to have you naked in my arms all night, I think you need to at least put this on.” Ian held up a T-shirt, and at first, she was confused but when he nodded his head in the direction of the living room. Lily wasn’t used to her sleeping over.

"Good idea." She slid on the shirt and watched Ian strip down to his boxers. He lay down on the bed and pulled her into his arms.

She closed her eyes but didn't think she was going to sleep. Ian started to hum something, and at first, she didn't know what it was, but as she listened, she realized it was a country song. She'd heard him sing it before when he didn't know she could hear him.

He'd been sitting on his back deck playing the guitar. 'God Bless the Broken Road.' She remembered the name when he quietly sang the chorus. He had a beautiful voice and before she knew what was happening she was drifting off to sleep. So glad her roads led her to Ian but was it going to break and take everything she loved away because of a murderous psychopath?

Chapter 21

Ian had no issue with Sandy talking to Lily, but his little girl seemed overly protective of her little treasure chest. Sandy was probably right about it meaning more to Lily since Colleen died. Ian didn't even realize Lily had it.

Sandy walked out of the kitchen and smiled at him. He'd packed a couple of bags for himself and the girls because they were staying at Sandy's house for a while. Ian was happy that Sandy had put his things in her room without even asking. Lily and Grace were in a room right next to Evie. Ruby was in a room down the hall from them, and the room next to Ruby had been set up for her sister Kim. It looked like Sandy was going to have a houseful of people.

"I want you in the room when I ask Lily if I can look in her treasure box." Sandy rested her hands against his chest. "I know Keith wanted us to do it first thing this morning, but I wanted to make sure you guys were settled in here first. Your brother really has a colorful vocabulary when I piss him off, though."

He smiled because Keith did have a less than child-friendly way of expressing himself when he was angry. It was funny because when they were young, he was the one that cursed the least. Guess he was making up for lost time.

Sandy stood on her toes and kissed his lips softly. A throat clearing behind him had him wanting to use some unfriendly words himself. Sandy looked over his shoulder and smiled.

"Hey, John," Sandy said.

"Sorry to interrupt but Keith just filled us all in, and whatever you need we're here."

"Thanks, bro." Ian reached out and shook his brother's hand.

"You know I'm starting to think that none of us are every going to have a dull existence." Nick chuckled from behind John.

"No shit. This is why I'm staying single." Aaron stood next to them.

"Yeah, that's the reason you're single." James walked into the group of men and laughed.

"You can't keep your dick in your pants long enough to find someone to settle down with." Mike chuckled.

“If that’s not the pot calling the kettle black.” John laughed. The entire family knew the three youngest O’Connor brothers liked to play the field.

“Can you hear this?” Mike held up his fist with his middle finger pointing down to the floor. “No? Let me turn it up for you.” He turned his fist, so his finger was now pointing up at the ceiling.

“Mikey, doncha let me see dat again.” Nanny Betty slapped Mike across the arm.

“Sorry, Nan.” Yep even as adults, they didn’t cross their grandmother.

“Now, I know we got some confusion goin’ on again, but like always we’ll get it straightened out.” Nanny Betty wrapped her arms around Sandy and Ian.

“That’s right, my darling,” Tom said always backing up the O’Connor matriarch.

“Now, I’m gonna go back home and get a big scoff together.” Nanny Betty’s answer to everything was cooking enough food to feed a small army.

“Mrs. O’Connor, you don’t have to do that,” Sandy said.

“First, Mrs. O’Connor was my mother-in-law, and I'm sure I told ya 'bout dis. Call me Nan. Second, nobody can do anyting if dey don’t have lots of good food in dere bellies.” Nanny Betty held Sandy’s face between her soft hands. “Dat’s wat families do fer each udder.”

“Thanks, Nan.” Ian kissed her cheek, and she gave him a gentle pat on the chest.

“Come on Tom, we got some shoppin ta do.” Nan turned and linked into the older man.

“Who’s the lucky one to cover Nan and Tom?” Aaron chuckled.

“You and Nick.” Kurt walked into the living room with Sean behind him. “It won’t look suspicious if you two are with them. I’ve got all your shifts covered for the next few days.”

“Seriously? Nan is shopping. Do you have any idea how long that takes and how much shit she gets for her big scoffs?” Aaron whined as he put air quotes around ‘big scoffs’.

“Do have any idea what I’ll do to you if anything happens to your grandmother and Tom?” Sean growled at Aaron.

The youngest of the O’Connor brothers didn’t say another word. He followed his grandmother with Nick behind him. Nobody crossed Sean O'Connor either. He may be a doctor, but he also would still kick their asses if they were disrespectful.

Ian sat next to Sandy on the floor with Lily across from them. Her special box perched in her lap, and she looked like someone had taken her best friend but Sandy said to trust her, and that's what he was going to do.

"Lily, remember when I told you I'd make sure you got your special picture back?" Sandy asked.

"Yes." Lily nodded, but Ian could see the death grip she had on the box.

"Here you go." Sandy held the picture out to her, and Lily's face lit up.

"Thank you, Sandy." Lily took the picture and held it to her chest.

"So you know I would never do anything to make you not trust me, right?" Sandy said, and Lily nodded. "Lily, you said your mom also put things in the box that she wanted to keep as treasures, too right?"

Lily nodded again.

“Well, there’s something your mom might have put in there that we need to see. Would you mind if I looked in it to see if it’s there?” Lily glanced back and forth between Ian and Sandy as if she was about to burst into tears.

“Lily, Sandy wouldn’t ask if it wasn’t really important.” Ian needed to reassure her because it was killing him to see the look in her eyes.

“I don’t have to touch anything. I’ll just sit next to you while you take everything out and put it all back.” Sandy said.

“What do you think mommy put in here?” Lily tilted her head and stared at her.

“Do you know what a USB stick is?” Sandy asked, and Lily nodded. “Well your uncle Gerry gave her one to hold for him, and it had a lot of important information on it that we need to see.”

“Did Uncle Gerry hurt mommy and Carter?” Lily’s eyes filled with tears and Ian’s heart broke.

“No, Lily. He didn’t hurt mommy or Carter.” Ian wrapped his arm around Lily and looked down at her sad eyes.

“I heard the man tell Mrs. Anderson if she heard from Uncle Gerry to call him because he hurt mommy.” Lily sniffed.

"The man was wrong, Lily." Sandy touched Lily's knee. "Your Uncle Gerry is a good person. He's the one that told us about the USB we need. It could have something on that help us find out who did hurt your mommy."

"And Carter?" Lily asked. It made Ian tremble with anger that the guy had his little girl believing he was a nice person but at least he didn't hurt Lily or Grace.

"Yes, and Carter," Sandy murmured.

For a moment, they sat in silence as Lily gazed down. Ian glanced at Sandy. What would they do if Lily refused? Yes, she was a little girl, but he didn't want her traumatized any more than she'd already been, but if it came down to it, they would have to see inside. He had about given up that Lily was going to allow anyone to see her treasures when the little girl spoke.

"If it helps find the bad man that hurt mommy and Carter, you can look inside." Lily handed the box to Sandy.

"I promise nobody else will look inside and I won't tell anyone what you have in there." Sandy smiled and gently placed the box on the floor. "Can you unlock it for me, Lily?"

"You have to close your eyes, Daddy." Ian chuckled but did as his daughter asked. He heard her running across the room and then back again. “Okay, Daddy you can open them now.” Sandy was smiling when he opened his eyes and shaking her head.

“Don’t tell him where the key is, Sandy,” Lily opened the lock and pushed the box toward Sandy.

“I promise.” Sandy crossed her finger over her chest. Ian shook his head.

Lily observed Sandy carefully take things out one by one and place them gently on the floor. Lily seemed to relax when she saw how gently Sandy was handling her treasures. From what he could see, most of it was pictures and smaller boxes which Sandy opened and closed again. Sandy took everything out and looked at Ian. She shook her head, and his heart sank. It wasn’t there.

“That’s it. There’s nothing else in there.” Sandy sounded defeated as she started to put everything back in.

“You didn’t check the secret bottom,” Lily picked up the box.

“The secret bottom?” Ian raised his eyebrow and glanced at Sandy.

“Yeah, that’s why it’s a treasure box. Really special things are in the secret bottom.” Lily turned over the box and used the edge of the key to slide out a small door to reveal a compartment about two inches deep. Lily turned the box back over and shook it a little. Two USB sticks hit the floor along with a gold ring. Sandy picked up the sticks, and Lily grabbed the ring.

"Do you remember this ring, Daddy?" Lily held it up, and he took it from her fingers. He did remember it. It was a ring he'd given Colleen when they were about ten years old. He'd bought it out of the money he made delivering papers and gave it to her for her birthday. It was a friendship ring, and he remembered telling her that she was the best friend any guy could have.

"I remember it, Lily." Ian looked down into his daughter's eyes. It was then he realized that even though Lily had a lot of his features, she had her mother's smile.

"Mommy said when I get bigger I can have it." Lily took the ring and put it back in it's hiding place. "She said it was the most special present she ever got."

"I'm sure it was, Lily," Sandy said.

"Can I put my things back in the box now?" Lily asked.

"Thank you, Lily, for trusting me with your special things." Sandy held the box while Lily meticulously placed everything inside.

"I hope I helped." Lily closed and locked it again. "Can I go play with Evie now?" Ian nodded, and Lily put her box under her bed. She took her ratty old bunny and ran out of the room.

"What did she do with the key?" Ian stood up and held his hand out to Sandy.

"I'm not allowed to tell you." Sandy grasped his hand and stood up. "Let go see what's on these."

Keith, his Uncle Kurt, and Isaac Hunt stood behind Sandy and Smash as they searched for any information on the USB sticks. He could see Grace sitting on the floor in the living room playing with some musical toy. Lily and Evie were on the couch watching yet another princess movie.

"Gerry, these files are all password protected. What's the password?" Ian turned when he heard Keith's voice. He felt useless because there was nothing he could do except keep an eye on the girls. Standing around with nothing to do was making him anxious.

"I don't think this one has a password," Smash said.

"Gerry said the password on the stick he gave Colleen was, bring down evil. All one word and lower case." Keith said.

"Kind of appropriate if you ask me." Smash was clicking on the keys in front of him.

“I’m in,” Sandy said excitedly.

Ian asked one of the guys to keep an eye on the girls while he joined the group at the kitchen table. He was sure Sandy called the guy Hunter, but Keith said his name was Crunch.

“This one has nothing. I think it’s just personal stuff belong to Gerry’s sister. Folders are all labeled. Pictures, Income Tax, Kids Info, Letters. I think this might be just stuff she wanted to keep safe.” Smash glanced up at Keith.

“Let's just deal with the one that Gerry’s password opened.” Kurt leaned over Sandy’s shoulder. “Does that say what I think it does?”

“Dear God.” Sandy gasped.

“What the fuck is that?” Isaac asked.

“That’s a folder with a file on every one of our family and Sandy’s,” Kurt growled.

“Keith, he’s not just going after Sandy,” Isaac said.

“These are dated six months ago.” Sandy’s voice was shaky. “He was collecting information on everyone. My God he even has the birthdates of Colin and Olivia.” The sound of the names of his baby niece and nephew sent shivers down his spine.

"He must have someone here to be getting all that information." Smash closed his laptop and sat with his arm around Sandy's chair. Ian liked the kid, but at that moment he wanted to rip off his arm and beat him to death with it.

"What else is on it?" Isaac asked.

"There's tons of stuff here it's gonna take a while to go through it," Sandy said, but by the sound of her voice, she was seeing something that scared her.

"If we divide it up between both of us, we'll get through it faster." Smash opened his laptop again.

Ian's attention was distracted by Ruby waving from the kitchen door. He met her in the foyer as she was pulling on her jacket.

"My brother just texted me. He's in St. John's and wants me to pick him up. If anyone is looking for me, I'm gone to pick him up."

"Don't you think you should have one of the guys take you?" Ruby was one of the ones that could be in danger.

"My brother is one of his guys." Ruby chuckled. "I'll be okay. I just don't want to disturb them."

"Okay, but make sure you call as soon as you get to the airport." Ian figured it was what Keith would have told her.

"I'm sure Lane will call as soon as he's in the car. Maybe they'll have it figured out by then." Ruby glanced over his shoulder into the kitchen.

"With any luck," Ian said.

Ruby headed out the door. She pulled out of the driveway and turned toward the highway leading to town.

Ian joined the girls and Crash in the living room while the group in the kitchen continued sifting through all the information they'd gotten. Lily snuggled into his side, and Grace had taken up residence on the couch to have her afternoon nap. Evie sat on the other end next to Crash. Ian rested his head back against the sofa and closed his eyes. It had been a long day, and it was going to be longer.

He hadn't realized he'd fallen asleep until someone tapped him on the shoulder. He opened his eyes and looked into the beautiful brown eyes of the love of his life. Sandy was smiling down at him with her finger pressed against her lips.

"I don't want to wake the girls." She whispered. Ian lifted his head and looked down. Grace was still asleep, and Lily had her head on his leg. Ian smiled when he heard her soft snores.

"I guess we were all tired." Ian gazed up at her.

"I know the feeling. I had to wake you to ask if you'd seen Ruby. She's not in her room. Kim just got here and said she didn't see Ruby today." Sandy spoke in a whisper, but Ian could sense the concern in her voice.

"She went to the airport to get her brother. He texted her for a ride." Ian carefully eased Lily's head from his lap and replaced it with a pillow. When he turned to ask the time, Sandy was already racing out of the room.

"She went to get Lane at the airport," Sandy said, as Ian followed her into the kitchen.

"Why the hell did he call Ruby instead of one of us?" Keith snapped. His brother was exhausted. Ian hadn't seen him sleep in over twenty-four hours. Then again none of them had been sleeping very much.

"Maybe he wanted to see his sister," Ian interjected and suddenly wished he didn't because everyone's head turned to look at him.

"Lane knows that fucker is here and we're keeping everyone close. Ruby shouldn't have left without one of the team." Keith had his phone to his ear.

"She said she'd be fine because Lane was coming back with her," Ian said.

"Straight to voicemail." Keith tossed his phone on the table. "Track their phones."

Smash started to click on the laptop keys, while Keith continued to pace. Sandy wrapped her arms around Ian's waist, and he hugged her tightly as he kissed the top of her head.

"Ruby's phone is off," Smash continued to tap on the keys.

"If she went to the airport to get Lane, then we have a problem." A voice from the hallway floated it. Ian recognized it. It was Dean Nash otherwise known as Bull, another of Keith's men. He'd only recently gotten back to Hopedale. From what Ian understood, he'd been on leave dealing with some family issues.

"Why?" Keith called out.

Everyone turned as Bull walked in with a man Ian didn't know but something told him by Sandy's intake of breath the guy with his hair pulled back in a ponytail and olive color skin was Lane West.

Chapter 22

Sandy's heart jumped in her chest when Lane walked in behind Bull. She held her breath for a moment waiting for Ruby to walk in behind him but from the expression on Bull's face, Lane was alone.

"Fuck, fuck, fuck, fuck," Keith growled as he stood behind Smash. "Is there a way to turn on her phone?"

"No, she has an iPhone," Sandy said.

"What the fuck is going on?" Lane's voice thundered raspy and deep. "Where's Ruby?"

"She got a text asking her to pick you up at the airport," Keith explained.

"And you let her fucking go alone. Are you out of your mind? He's here. You remembered that, right?" Lane dropped his bag and plowed his hand through his hair.

"I didn't fucking know she was gone. We were in the middle of going through the USB Gerry had." Keith turned to face Lane. "She told my brother she'd be okay cause she was picking you up."

"How fucking stupid do you have to be to let her go alone?" Lane snapped.

"Watch it, Shadow," Bull growled.

"I thought your brothers were cops. Don't they have any training?"

"First of all Lane, not all Keith's brothers are cops, second, Ian is a doctor and not used to what we deal with, and third, I'd like you to meet the love of my life, Ian O'Connor." Sandy wasn't allowing Lane to treat Ian with disrespect. "And as much as I love Ruby, she shouldn't have left without one of the guys. She was aware of the danger."

"Look, I'm really sorry, Lane." Ian reached out his hand to shake Lane's hand only for the ass to slap it away.

"You should be." Lane snapped and lunged toward Ian but before Sandy knew what happened Bull pinned Lane against the wall.

"You don't want to do this, Shadow," Bull warned. "First, he's Rusty's brother. Second, your niece and his daughters are sleeping in the living room, and third do you remember when you challenged Keith, well, Ian was trained by the same Uncle. He'll give your ass the beating it needs."

Sandy tensed as she waited for Lane to make a choice. It pissed her off he would act so hostile toward Ian. Especially with Ruby possibly missing. Ian tensed as if he was ready to knock Lane on his ass. Sandy moved in front of him and gently placed her hands against his chest. His heart thudded, but his body did relax a little with her touch.

"Shadow, stand down, or I'll give you another shit knocking." Keith's voice rumbled from across the room.

"I've already lost one fucking sister, and you expect me to be calm about someone being so careless with her safety." Lane pushed Bull back. "You've got no fucking idea what it feels like."

Sandy heard enough. Tessa may not have been her sister, but she loved her like one, and she knew exactly how he felt.

"Just one God damn minute, Lane. We all lost Tessa, and yes she wasn't my sister, but she was my best friend and Keith's wife. You have no right to say we don't know what it's like to lose her because I still can't breathe when I think about what he did to her and how he took Evie's mother. You have no right to turn on the people who are trying to catch the bastard that did this." Sandy tipped her head all the way back so she could look up and meet his eyes. “Stop. Being. An. Ass.” With the last four words, she poked him in the chest with every word.

At first, he glared at her, but she glared right back. None of the guys she worked with scared her. She’d faced off with all of them at one point or another. The room had gone completely quiet except the sound of the television drifting in from the living room.

“It’s good to see you haven’t changed.” Lane pulled her in for a hug.

“Never.” He was like a brother to her as well, but she hadn’t seen him in a few years. He’d been spending his time trying to track Scott.

“I’d like to apologize to you, Ian. Ruby should’ve known better.” Sandy stepped back as Lane reached out his hand.

“I think we’re all wound a little tight.” Ian shook it, and Sandy stepped into his arms.

She needed to get away from the kitchen. She helped Ian tuck the girls into bed. It was getting loud with more and more of Ian’s family showing up to get news. Lane had sat with Evie for a little while until she fell back to sleep. As they walked out of the girl's room, Ian grabbed her hand and dragged her into her bedroom.

"I just need a minute with you alone." Ian closed the bedroom door and pulled her into his arms. She closed her eyes and snuggled into his warm body. With his arms wrapped around her, she just wanted to melt into him and forget everything.

"You must be exhausted." Ian's breath blew across her ear making her shiver.

"Exhausted is an understatement." She whispered.

"Maybe we should lay down for a bit. I'm sure nobody would mind." Ian started to walk her back toward the bed.

"If we lay down right now I can't guarantee I'll be sleeping." His scent filled her nose as she pressed her lips against his bare chest through the opening of his shirt. Ian moaned and slid his hands down her back and cupped her ass giving it a hard squeeze. She squeaked when she felt his hard cock against her belly.

"I'm not opposed to doing more than sleeping," Ian whispered while he nipped the outer edge of her ear.

"Ah…. I love when you do that." Ian lifted her, and she wrapped her legs around his waist.

Ian sat on the bed with her straddling his legs, and she wanted to make all their clothes disappear that very minute. Her mouth covered his, and she tangled her fingers into his hair. She loved the thick waves and the way he groaned when she pulled it.

Just as he grabbed the bottom of her shirt, her phone vibrated in her back pocket. For a moment she was going to let it go to voicemail, but Ian pulled the phone from her pocket and handed it to her.

"You know you've got to answer it." He flopped back on the bed.

"You hold that thought." Sandy glanced at her phone. Ruby's number was on her screen requesting video call. "What the hell is she doing?"

"Who?" Ian sat up and looked at her phone as she accepted the call but when the call connected it wasn't Ruby on the screen. Sandy's heart almost stopped

" Hello, Alexandra." She hated her name but coming out of his mouth made her want to vomit.

"Where's Ruby, Scott?" Sandy was on her feet and halfway down the stairs in seconds.

"Not even a how are you? When did you become so rude?." Scott sat in a huge armchair as if he didn't have a care in the world.

"Where's Ruby?" Sandy stood at the entrance to her kitchen. All eyes turned to her, and she held up her hand to keep them quiet.

"This must be the asshole's brother." Sandy felt Ian behind her, and she turned the phone so Scott couldn't see him.

"Where's Ruby?" Sandy wasn't giving into him.

"You sound like a broken record, Alexandra." Before she had a chance to say anything else Keith snatched her phone from her hand.

"Scott, I'm gonna find you, and when I do, I'll make sorry you were ever born. Now where the fuck is Ruby?"

"She's entertaining one of my friends." Sandy had to swallow down the bile that rose in her throat.

"You sick fucking bastard. Let my sister go." Lane grabbed the phone from Keith.

"Oh, we have the whole team. Fuck you, Lane." Keith cursed when Lane showed him the screen. Scott ended the call, and Keith checked to see if Smash could track the call, but from the look on his face, they were out of luck.

What the hell did he mean Ruby was entertaining his friend? She knew what that meant, and the tears flowed down her cheeks.

Ian pulled her into his arms and guided her out of the kitchen before anyone saw. Would she ever see Ruby alive again?

Chapter 23

It was almost four in the morning when Sandy finally fell asleep. Ian wasn't going to get any sleep, so he left her in the room and joined everyone in the kitchen. The only guys left were Lane, Smash and of course, his brother. Keith paced the floor looking down at a tablet in his hand. He didn't even seem to notice anything around him.

"Coffee," Lane held up the pot, and Ian nodded.

"I think Rusty's soon gonna crash," Lane whispered when he handed Ian a cup.

"I'm sorry about your sister." Ian had to say it.

"Which one?" Lane asked.

"We'll get Ruby back." Ian tried to assure Lane but what did he know? Sure they'd had some crazy shit going on over the past few years with John's and James wives but nothing like this.

“Oh dear, God.” Bull chuckled. He was peering out the window shaking his head. Ian followed Keith, Lane and Smash to the window to see something he expected but not at five in the morning.

“What the fuck is Nan doing here at this hour?” Keith groaned, but it wasn’t just his grandmother. It was Nanny Betty and Tom, and they were unloading boxes from the trunk of Tom’s car.

“Smash, come on let's go give them a hand. I’ve learned if she’s here, chances are, that trunk is full of food.” Bull chuckled as he headed out of the kitchen.

“I swear, I love that woman.” Smash sauntered out behind Bull.

Lane looked nervous as Nanny Betty scurried in and began to order everyone around. Ian was so used to his grandmother he didn’t give it a second thought when she started. It was hard for him to see it from someone else’s point of view.

“We got lots a grub here fer ya. All ya boys get somethin’ ta eat and sleep. Keithy, I don’t want to hear a'nudder word. Off ta bed wit ya.” Nanny Betty pointed her bony finger toward the stairway.

“Nan, I’ve got things to do.” Ian pressed his lips together to keep from laughing when Keith dared to defy their grandmother.

"Doncha dare say no. Now get yer arse ta bed." Nanny Betty yanked Keith's phone out of his hand. "Ya won't help anyone by droppin' down in a heap. Upstairs, before I bust yer arse."

Keith wasn't going to win, any argument with Nanny Betty. It was probably why his brother didn't say another word but held out his hand for his phone as he walked out of the kitchen.

"Ya don't need dis wakin' ya up every second." Nanny Betty held the phone tightly in her hand.

"I'm waiting for an important call." Keith should have known better.

"I'll give it ta one a da boys. Now get." Nanny Betty turned to look at Lane. He stared wide-eyed at the door where Keith had disappeared. "Here, young fella. Ya watch dis." She held up Keith's phone. "Ya know our Sandy's sister could give ya a good trim on dat mop head."

Lane's expression as he watched Nanny Betty and Tom lay out the food was how everyone looked at his grandmother when they first met her. One of confusion, shock and a little bit of fear. Bull and Smash were on the other side of the room obviously trying to keep their amusement to themselves.

“Ya know I could probably call her fer ya. I didn’t like her when she was datin’ our Johnny, but she’s grown up a lot, and she’s like part a da family now.” Nanny Betty continued to talk to Lane.

“Thanks... Um … I’ll pass.” Lane stammered as his gaze darted back and forth between Ian and Nanny Betty. It was as if he was asking for help.

“Nan, I think Lane likes his hair long.” Ian couldn’t let the guy suffer anymore even if he was kind of rude in the beginning.

“Ta each dere own.” That was her way of saying she didn’t like it.

An hour later Sandy's house was full of people. Of course, chances were they got wind of Nanny Betty’s huge feast, and it was Sunday. This meant Sandy’s house got invaded with the entire O’Connor clan.

Lane seemed annoyed by all the people and sat in the corner behind Smash. Keith had obviously needed the sleep because he hadn’t come down since Nanny Betty sent him to bed. The only thing bothering Ian was Evie kept asking where Ruby was, and everyone basically avoided her question. Sandy was the only one to give the child any answers.

“Evie, Auntie Ruby had to go somewhere for a couple of days,” Sandy told the little girl as she lifted her into her arms.

Something about seeing Sandy with the little girl made his heart hurt. Evie lost her mother and now possibly her aunt.

"Someone better have a good explanation for this." Everyone turned to see a furious Kurt O'Connor. "How could all of you be so stupid?"

"Now Kurt, watch yer tone." Nanny Betty nodded toward Evie and Sandy.

"Where's Keith?" Although his expression changed at the sight of Evie, his tone didn't.

"I sent him ta get some sleep." Nanny Betty said.

"Ian, outside." Kurt turned and left the kitchen. Ian didn't know what he wanted to talk to him about, but he followed.

The sun had come up, and although there was a chill in the air, it seemed like it was going to be a beautiful day. At least weather-wise. Ian turned to face his uncle and knew he was about to get an earful.

"What the hell is wrong with you boys?" Kurt's fists rested on his hips, and his head tilted to the side. It reminded him of the way his father would yell at them when they were misbehaving as kids.

“Uncle Kurt, I’m sure Keith was going to get in touch with you first thing this morning, but Nan sent him to bed.” Ian realized it sounded as stupid out loud as it did in his head.

“Really, that big overgrown man went to bed because his grandmother told him to?” Kurt said.

“Have you met your mother?” Ian asked sarcastically. “Would you say no to her?”

“Jesus Christ. You’ve got a point, but one of you should’ve called.” Kurt sighed. “What do they know?”

“Nothing. Scott called using Ruby’s phone last night, but they couldn’t get a lock on it, and as far as I know, it’s off now.” Kurt plowed his hands through his gray hair.

“Keith’s walking a fine line with me these days. He’s always kept me in the loop, but with this, he’s stepping over the line.”

“It’s personal to him, Uncle Kurt.” Ian realized he probably shouldn’t say anything but Kurt was pissed, and since his uncle was the Superintendent of the Hopedale Police Department it wouldn’t be a good thing to be on the wrong side of the law.

“I’m sure there’s a story there, and from the look on Keith’s face right now it’s one he hasn't told anyone but you.” Ian turned, and Keith stood behind him fists clenched at his sides.

"It's personal, and it's not something that'll help with finding Ruby. So drop it." Keith snapped.

"Watch your tone with me, young man. All I want to know is why you didn't report this or call one of your brothers or me?" Kurt asked.

"I was going to call you," his brother began.

Ian left Keith to deal with Kurt while he headed inside. Stephanie and Marina had wrangled all the kids and were playing with them in Sandy's backyard. Bull, Trunk, and Hulk were outside with them as well. The guys were around so long now they were almost like brothers. He trusted them nearly as much as he trusted his family.

For a moment he just watched the kids running around. The three babies sat on a huge blanket spread out on the grass. It filled him with joy to see his two little girls playing with their cousins. He was still worried Lily was keeping her feelings inside, but all he could do was be there for her when she was ready to talk.

"They're settling in pretty well," James said from behind him.

"Yeah," Ian said.

“They’re O’Connors, and that means they have strength.” Ian felt a familiar hand on his shoulder and turned. His father beamed at the kids.

“What are you doing here, Dad?” Ian asked before he thought about it.

“A.J. called us and let us know what was going on. I figured with all the family here; we could keep the kids occupied while they work on finding that poor girl.” It was probably a good plan, but Ian wondered if Sandy felt invaded by everyone in her place. Her house was big, but the O’Connors could fill a place pretty quickly, even one as big as hers.

“Evie seems to be enjoying herself.” Ian should have known his mother wasn’t far away. She linked her arm into Ian’s and rested her head on his shoulder.

“I think she’s formed a bond with Lily.” Ian had seen the two little girls enjoy most of the same things in the last few days.

“That’s a good thing, Ian.” His mother kissed his cheek and joined the kids and her daughter-in-laws outside.

It was an incredible thing, but if they didn’t find Ruby, it was going to be devastating. What would happen to Evie? She'd end up somewhere else, and Lily and her wouldn’t be able to see each other. That would probably kill Sandy. Ian wasn’t normally a negative person, but from everything he'd learned about Scott, Ruby was in grave danger. It sent chills through his body to think this crazy man wanted to hurt Sandy.

Another day passed without finding Ruby, and the tension was getting to a point where everyone was snapping at everyone else. Ian was doing his best to keep his irritation in check, but it wasn't easy. It also wasn't good for the girls to be around so much stress. Lily asked several times why everyone was so angry. He'd tried to make her feel more at ease, but it was hard when Keith and Lane were always snapping at someone.

"I've got an idea." Ian looked up from the game he was playing with Grace. James and John were crouched down next to them.

"It was actually mom's idea, and I agree with her," James smiled down at Grace.

"You're all ticking time bombs here and with good reason, but you know as well as I do the kids don't need to be around this," John said.

"I know it's not a weekend or anything. Keith's going to send two of the guys with them and you know that means they'll be safe."

"With Steph and Marina still on maternity leave, it would be easy for them to take off. I'd feel better with them and the kids somewhere safe." John continued.

"Will you get to the point." Ian groaned.

"The cabin," John said, and Ian didn't need him to explain. It was the family's summer home. It was once where his grandmother and grandfather lived before Granda Jack passed away.

"Steph and Marina are going to take all the kids to the cabin by themselves?" Ian was a little surprised that his brothers would agree to their wives being so far away when they could be possible targets for a psychopath.

"No, Dad, Mom, Kristy, Jess, Tom and Nanny Betty are going with them," James said.

"I don't know." Ian wasn't sure how the girls would handle being away since they'd only been with him a few weeks.

"I know you're worried about being separated from them but don't you think it's better for them to be away from all this shit? The girls will be safe, and we can all concentrate on catching this bastard." John was right, and Ian knew it.

“Let me ask Lily and gauge her reaction.” Ian picked up Grace and stood up. When he glanced at his brothers, he knew someone had already asked Lily.

“I’m sorry, bro. Danny and Mason were so excited they blurted it out to Lily and Evie when we got here.” James shrugged his shoulders.

“So they’re taking Evie too.” Ian knew the answer when he glanced out in the back yard. Evie and Lily were jumping up and down with James’ two boys.

“Marina figured it would be better for Lily,” James said.

“I guess it’s all been taken care of then.” Ian looked down at Grace. She was chewing on her fingers and staring out at the kids in the yard. “Do you want to go spend the weekend with Nanny and Poppy O’Connor?” Ian asked the baby. She stared at him, and it made him smile. Her big blue eyes sparkled as she babbled something that he wished he could understand.

“I think that settles it. Gracie’s on board with it.” John laughed.

“Oh, so you understand baby talk now.” Ian chuckled.

“I’m an expert in all babbling. Olivia’s a good teacher,” John said.

He stood in the driveway as the four SUV's drive off with his daughters and their cousins. Bull, Hulk, and Crunch were with them as well. Although, his cousin Kristy wasn't too happy about Bull driving the SUV with her in it and Bull didn't seem too happy either.

He'd had a shouting match with Keith over it and only gave in when Nanny Betty intervened. For some reason, Bull had become Nanny Betty's favorite. She convinced him to go since she was also riding with Kristy.

"I get the feeling something is going on between those two." Sandy chuckled as she wrapped her arms around his waist and watched the vehicles disappear onto the highway.

"If there is, Bull, needs all the luck he can get." Ian kissed the top of her head as he tucked her under his arm.

"They'll be alright," Sandy said. She must have sensed his apprehension.

"I miss them already," The girls had moved into the corner of his heart and taken it over.

"Maybe by the time they get back, this will all be over," Sandy said. "They aren't coming back until Sunday. Which means we have five and a half days to catch Scott and get Ruby back."

"Let's do this." Ian turned her around, and they walked into her house.

Chapter 24

Sandy jolted up in the bed. Another nightmare of the night Scott had shot her, but this time Ruby stood in front of her full of blood and blaming her for everything. She glanced over to the other side of the bed. Ian was staring up at her. For the last two nights, he'd been waking her up from nightmares and holding her after.

"Do you want to talk about this one?" Ian sat up and pulled her into his arms.

"Ruby was there blaming me for everything." Sandy swallowed hard. She didn't have time to be emotional about all this.

"Just so you know, none of this is your fault," Ian whispered.

Sandy nodded, but she wasn't sure he was right. If she hadn't asked Scott about Tessa that night, he never would have gone after her. Evie would have her mother and Sandy would have her little girl.

A couple of deep breaths and she managed to keep the tears from starting again. She glanced out through the window. The sun was just coming over the horizon. It was time to get up and face the day.

"Why don't you try and get a little more sleep? I'm gonna jump in the shower and head downstairs. Maybe there were some developments overnight." Ian kissed her cheek and got out of bed. She watched him saunter into the bathroom. The man's ass made her want to squeeze and bite every inch of it. She was about to jump out of bed and join him, but her phone buzzed.

She snatched it off the side table and looked at the screen. She didn't recognize the number, and her heart began to pound. She tapped the screen and put the phone to her ear. The first thing she heard was Ruby's cries for help.

"No, please no," Ruby begged. "Stop, please." Then there was a long scream.

"Ruby," Sandy yelled into the phone.

"Ruby can't come to the phone right now. She's entertaining." She knew that voice.

"Scott, let her go. She didn't do anything to you. It's me you want." Sandy knew it was a stupid thing to say.

"Yes, I do. I want to hear you scream just like this." Ruby screamed again, and Sandy started to shake. "You really like that don't you, Rubes?"

"Please, stop." Ruby sounded weak, but she was alive.

"Tell Sandy you want her to make this stop." Scott was so sadistic it made Sandy want to vomit.

"Sandy, help me, please." Ruby cried into the phone. Then another scream.

"Scott, what do you want?" She really should be letting someone know he was on the phone but she wasn't taking a chance he would hang up before he gave her something.

"I want to make you suffer. I've been on the run for nearly nine years because of you and that fucking prick. I'm going to make you both suffer." He growled into the phone.

"Then come get me. Hurting Ruby isn't going to make you feel any better. I'm the one you want to make scream. Come get me, Scott." Sandy taunted.

"Do you think I'm really that stupid? I come get you and one of those fuckers come out and kill me." He was right. Nobody was going to let him near the house.

"Then I'll come to you, but you have to let Ruby go." Sandy was playing with fire.

"You'd trade yourself for her?" Another scream from Ruby.

"I'll trade myself for Ruby." What was she saying? Ian was going to be furious, and Keith was going to kick her in the ass, but she didn't know what else to do. It was her fault Ruby was in this situation.

"Yeah, and then your boys come charging in. I told you I'm not stupid."

"No, I won't let them know. Scott, I'll even leave my phone here and my weapon." What the hell was she saying? She was going completely against her training as a police officer and the training she received from Newfoundland Security Services.

"You're really going to trade your life for Ruby?" Scott seemed shocked, but then he laughed. "Now I get it. You feel guilty for Tessa's death."

"Just tell me where to meet you and when. I'll be there. Then you let Ruby go. She has nothing to do with this." While she waited for him to respond, she ran scenarios of how to pull it off through her head. Scott was quiet for what seemed like forever, and Sandy kept glancing at the bathroom door to make sure Ian didn't hear her conversation. She could hear the water shutting off, and she started to pace. “Scott, do we have a deal?”

“Keep your phone close. I’ll text you the directions, but if you betray me, Alexandra, I will kill Ruby, and I can assure you it will be slow and painful.”

“I won’t betray you.” Sandy ended the call just as Ian walked out of the bathroom.

“I figured you’d be sleeping.” He rubbed a towel vigorously around his hair.

“I couldn’t go back to sleep. I’m going to grab a shower, and I’ll meet you downstairs.” Sandy hurried around Ian and into the bathroom grasping her phone tightly in her hand. She closed the bathroom door and pressed her back against it. She took a couple of deep breaths to calm her pounding heart. After a few minutes, she’d finally stopped shaking, but her phone buzzed in her hand making her almost drop it.

“I told you to let me know when and where.” Sandy didn’t look at the screen when she answered.

“I’m not sure what you mean, Sandy.” Her father’s voice. Damn it. This was something she really didn’t need.

“Dad, I’m kind of in the middle of something right now…” Sandy started, but her father cut her off with a tone she’d never heard from him since she’d first spoke to him.

“I know what you’re in the middle of my dear. Do you know one of the biggest men I've ever seen in my life has become my shadow? I’m worried about you, Sandy. Why didn’t you ever tell me about this?” He sounded hurt.

“It’s not something I like to talk about, but I promise I’ll make the time to tell you when this is all over,” Sandy said, but then an idea hit her. “You know what dad. I need to get out of here. I’ll come by, and I’ll tell you everything.”

“You will?” The shock in his voice made her feel guilty, but this was probably the only way she was going to be able to sneak off without someone asking questions.

“Yes, I’ll be there in an hour.” Sandy ended the call and held the phone to her chest. Now all she had to do was be able to convince Ian, and Keith let her go by herself or with someone besides either of them. This wasn’t going to be easy.

“You’re not fucking going,” Keith growled.

“I’m going, and I really don’t give a shit what you say. He’s my father, and he’s in the dark about all this.” Sandy snapped.

"Keith, I'll be with her," Ian said.

"No," Sandy said a little louder than she meant to.

"I'm going with you, Sandy." Ian's eyes narrowed.

"I want to talk to my dad alone." Sandy glanced down at her phone. Scott still hadn't messaged her.

"Listen to me, kiddo. If you go and I'm not saying you are, Either Ian or myself will be going along with Hulk."

"Yeah, cause the huge guy you have at dad's place now is not enough," Sandy said sarcastically. "Who is it anyway?"

"He's a guy I hired from the United States. He used to be in the military. His name is Caden Dixon, but he goes by Rex." Keith shook his head. "Don't try to change the subject."

"Keith, I'm going." Sandy grabbed her purse from the counter. When she turned toward the door, Ian was opening the front door and jiggling the keys. Fuck.

"Me or Keith. Which would you rather take a drive with?" Ian smiled, and she wanted to punch him. Of course, she would pick Ian but the fewer people she had to shake the better.

"Fine," Sandy sighed.

Hulk, aka Bruce Steel, followed behind Ian's truck in a black car. She kept glancing at her phone and checking her purse. Her weapon was inside because Keith wanted to make sure she had it. Was she really going to see Scott without it? Of course not, she wasn't an idiot. She just had to hide it when she came face to face with the man.

"What's wrong, besides the obvious?" Ian must have noticed her distraction.

"I'm just trying to figure out a way to explain all this to him." Sandy lied, and it hit her in the gut like a punch. She didn't want to lie to the man she loved, but she had to make sure Ruby was safe.

"Sandy, don't hand me that bullshit." Ian didn't look at her.

"What are you talking about?"

"There is no bloody way the only reason you're going to see your father is to explain all this. I'm not stupid, and I'm pretty sure Keith isn't." He stopped at a red light and glanced at her. "What are you doing?"

"I'm just going to tell dad about all this and then I'm going back home. That's it." Sandy wouldn't look at him because he'd know she was being dishonest.

"For the record. I don't believe that." Ian snapped, and her heart felt like it was going to break. It was evident he knew she was lying and he was pissed.

The rest of the drive to her father's house was quiet. The only time Ian spoke was when he called Keith to let him know they'd made it to town and were pulling onto her father's property. She had no problem finding the guy Keith had sent to watch over her father. Rex stood outside the front door his hand clasped in front of him as if frozen in place. He was definitely military.

"You must be Caden." Sandy forced a smile as she walked up the front steps to her father's house.

"Call me Rex." His deep voice boomed, and she could hear the slight Georgia accent he was trying to hide.

"Sorry, I don't usually call the guys by their nicknames," Sandy said.

"I don't answer to anything but Rex." He replied.

"Well, Okay then. Rex this is Ian O'Connor, and that's Bruce standing next to the truck." Sandy pointed down to the end of the driveway.

"I already know Hulk, and Rusty sent me photos of both of you," Rex said.

"I'm gonna go see my dad," Sandy shook her head and walked by Rex. "Thanks for the enjoyable conversation." Ian probably didn't miss the sarcasm because he chuckled.

"He's waiting in the study," Rex said.

Sandy could count on her hands how often she'd been inside her father's huge house. She should feel a little guilty using his huge home to sneak away from everyone, but it was necessary. There was just one small problem. She still hadn't heard from Scott, and it made her worry he wasn't going to take the bait.

Ian followed her into her father's study. At first, she didn't see her dad until she turned to see him crouched down on the floor in front of a huge cat. She didn't even know her father had a pet.

"Dad, I'm here." When her father turned to see her, Sandy gasped. He looked like he'd aged ten years since the last time she saw him, that day in the hospital when Ian kicked him out.

"I see you're not alone either." Her father nodded at Ian.

"Mr. Michaels, it's good to see you again." Ian reached out his hand.

"You too Dr. O'Connor." Her father shook Ian's hand.

"Ian, please." Ian always seemed to be uncomfortable with anyone calling him Doctor.

"I do want to apologize for that day in the hospital. I've recently come to realize that I haven't been the nicest person for most of my life." Her father reached out and touched her shoulder hesitantly. "I haven't been a very good father either."

"It's not too late Mr. Michaels." Leave it to Ian to see the positive in things.

"I'm afraid sometimes it's hard to repair all the damage you've done." Something about the way her father's eyes studied her face made her blood run cold.

"Dad, is something wrong?" Sandy glanced at Ian. He seemed to know something was up as well.

"That's a story for another day. Now tell me how all this got started." He motioned to the large leather sofa. She felt Ian's hand on the small of her back as he guided her toward the couch.

Sandy managed to explain everything to her father just before she felt the vibration of her phone in her pocket. She didn't pull it out because Ian was next to her and would be able to read the screen.

"Dad, I need to use your washroom." Sandy stood up and headed toward the door to the study.

"Sandy, there's a bathroom right there." He pointed to a door in the study.

"I'll use the one down the hall." Sandy was out the door of the room before her father could say anything else. It probably looked suspicious to Ian but she needed to be able to sneak out through the back, and she couldn't do that from the bathroom in the study.

She reached the bathroom at the end of the hallway next to the kitchen. She hurried inside and pulled out her phone. There was a text from Scott.

I know you've arrived in St. John's. Never mind how I know, but I'm assuming the reason you're at your father's house is so you can give that boyfriend of yours the slip. It's going to be interesting to see how you get free of those muscle bound idiots.

How the hell did he know where she was? There was no way he could trace her phone. Smash made sure of that with a program he wrote to block unwanted tracking. The only problem was Smash could still trace her. Scott had to have someone watching her. Her phone buzzed again.

Wondering how I know where you are, Alexandra? Come meet me, and I'll tell you.

She started and stopped typing a message to him at least four or five times before she came up with the perfect response.

Give me the place, and I'll be there. You don't have to worry about anyone following me.

She waited for a response, and at first, it didn't seem like she was going to get one. Then she saw the text pop up on her screen. Her heart raced as she stared at the address on the screen. How was this even possible. Her father's house was directly behind the address on her screen. She opened the blind of the small bathroom window and gasped.

The back of her father's property was not an easy escape. Completely enclosed by trees on the back she didn't know how thick the trees were. She knew there was a subdivision on the other side of the greenbelt because her father recently gotten into the real estate market and had several subdivisions going up around his neighborhood. The address Scott texted was one of those subdivisions. As far as she knew, nobody lived in any of the homes yet. She remembered Kim saying her father was having issues selling the lots. Was it possible Scott was hidden in one of them?

Sandy didn't have time to figure that out because she needed to get out of the house before Ian or her father came looking for her. She pushed up the window, glanced outside, and took a deep breath. As she propped her foot on the toilet seat and shoved the pocket-sized semi-automatic Derringer into her boot, Sandy kept taking deep breaths. With her purse and cell phone on the back of the toilet, Sandy blessed herself and lifted herself onto the window ledge. She'd set her phone to send a message to Keith in twenty minutes. That would give her enough time to trick Scott into believing she was at his mercy. She looked outside and made sure nobody was doing a check on the back of the house.

"Mom, I hope you're keeping an eye down here. I really need you to watch over me right now." Sandy whispered. She jumped out through the window and crouched down. She took another scan of the back.

"God help me." Sandy blessed herself and ran as fast as she could into the line of trees. "Please, God. Give me a hand here.

Chapter 25

Ian glanced down at his watch. Sandy seemed to be taking forever in the bathroom, and he wasn't the only one to notice. Her father had frequently been glancing at his watch as well. Something was off with the way she'd been acting the whole day. Keith warned him to keep a close eye on her because he was sure she was trying to shake the protection detail.

"Ian, I know you and my daughter are involved. Kim told me." Stewart started.

"I love her, Mr. Michaels, in case that's what concerns you."

"I don't doubt that. I can see it in the way you look at her." Stewart bent forward in the chair, rested his elbows on his knees and clasped his fingers together. He was staring at the floor.

"Mr. Michaels, I'm a doctor, and I can see you aren't well." Ian noticed it as soon as he looked at Stewart.

"I've been keeping it from my kids because I'm not sure any of them would really care." His voice cracked.

"I don't believe that." Ian couldn't believe Sandy or her siblings would want to see anything happen to Stewart.

"Maybe not with my daughters, but it sure as hell's true with my sons." Stewart sighed and squeezed his hands together.

"Sons?" As far as Ian knew Sandy only had one brother and Ian had seen first hand the hatred Brad had for his father.

"Yes, and another daughter." Stewart looked up and met Ian's eyes.

"Sandy never mentioned them."

"That's because Sandy, Kim, and Brad don't know about them, but they do know them." Stewart sighed.

"Mr. Michaels, I know it's none of my business, but I don't think you should be keeping this hidden from your kids." Ian could see the struggle written all over the man's face.

"It didn't start out that way. When Sandy went to Yellowknife all those years ago, I'd asked my son to keep an eye on her but didn't tell him who she was. You see their mother had passed away and it seemed I was the only family besides another sister, they had left. I took care of them and the other sister. I used that to guilt him into keeping Sandy safe. Then when she got hurt and lost the baby, I blamed him and my daughter." Stewart stood up and walked to the window. "My son only recently started speaking to me again. My daughter is troubled, and I'm afraid she's going to do something to hurt my other children. Sandy especially."

"Don't you think this is something Sandy should know. Jesus Christ, she's already got a nut case out to get her and now this." Ian stood up and started to pace the floor.

"I know, and I'm…." Stewart stopped speaking as he stared out through the window. "What the hell is she doing?" He spun around and almost knocked Ian over as he hurried out of the room. Ian ran to the window just in time to see Sandy disappear through the line of trees on behind the house.

"Fuck." Ian pulled his phone from his pocket as he ran down the hallway to find the bathroom where Sandy was supposed to have gone. He found the door closed and locked. Ian stepped back and kicked it hard. The door frame split as the door flew open. The first thing he saw was her purse and phone sitting on the back of the toilet. The blind was pulled all the way up, and the window was wide open.

"Ian, what's going on?" Ian turned. Hulk was behind him looking over his shoulder into the bathroom. "I'm going to kick her fucking ass." Hulk spun around and ran down the hallway toward the front door. The last thing Ian heard was him telling Keith he'd have to get in line too.

Ian walked into the bathroom and grabbed Sandy's phone from the back of the toilet. He glanced down on the screen. She'd left it open to the last thing she'd been reading. Luckily, she didn't set her phone to shut off after a certain amount of time. Ian's blood ran cold when he read the texts from Scott. He was so pissed he was trembling. She was trading herself for Ruby. What the hell was wrong with her? Did she not trust Keith and the rest of the team to handle this? His phone vibrated, and he glanced at the screen.

"She's gone to meet that bastard," Keith yelled into the phone when Ian answered.

"I know. I just found Sandy's phone in the bathroom." Ian was headed out of the house when Stewart met him in the doorway. His eyes were wide with fear.

"Smash got the address. We're on the way there now. Tell Hulk and Rex to get over there now. Ian, are you carrying?" Keith asked.

"Yeah," Ian pulled his weapon out of the holster.

“Don’t ask questions just shoot the bastard the first chance you get.” The call ended, and for a moment Ian wasn’t sure he heard his brother correctly. Then a text flashed on his screen.

I mean it.

Ian didn’t know if he could take a life, he was a doctor, and his whole career was about saving lives. Then he thought about Scott hurting Sandy the way he hurt the other women. Ian knew if it came down to it. He could kill the monster without a second thought.

Chapter 26

Sandy slowly made her way up the long driveway leading to the address where Scott said he wanted her to go. The house was only one of two sitting on the small cul-de-sac. It was dark and seemed deserted. She scanned the road behind her as well as the sides of the house, but it was as if she was the only one there. Had Scott lied to her or was he watching to make sure she hadn't set him up? She knew it wouldn't be long before Keith got the message she sent him.

"Scott, I'm here," Sandy shouted as she approached the house, but nobody answered. The front door did open with a quiet creak. Sandy's heart was beating so hard she was sure anyone within a hundred miles could hear it. She pushed the door all the way open with her foot and scanned the inside of the foyer. She stepped inside making sure to keep her back to the wall just inside the door.

"Scott, can we stop playing games. I'm here. Alone. Now let Ruby go." Sandy yelled.

"Come down the hall to the room at the end." Sandy heard his voice echo through the empty house. Sandy slowly made her way toward his voice careful to check behind her as she inched forward.

"Scott, send her out," Sandy yelled from just outside the room.

"Come into the room, and I'll send her out." He sounded amused. It took every ounce of restraint she had not to grab her weapon and shoot him as soon as she walked into the room.

She kicked open the slightly ajar door with the toe of her boot and peeked around the corner of the door before she attempted to enter. For all, she knew Scott would kill her the minute she walked into the room.

The scene in front of her took her breath away. Ruby was sat on a chair her head hung down and her hands behind her. Her hair draped over her face, and she wasn't moving. Sandy wasn't even sure if the woman was even breathing.

She stepped into the room with every intent to run to Ruby, but someone grabbed her from behind. From the pungent smell of body order, she knew who it was.

"I see you've kept in touch with the rest of the low lives." Sandy pulled at Lefty's arm and gagged from the smell. "Have you ever thought about getting a wash?"

“Still such a smart mouth. I bet I’d shut it pretty quick if I stuck my dick down your throat.” His foul breath blew across her face making her want to throw up.

“I tell you what, let me get a magnifying glass and a pair of tweezers, and when you sneeze, I’ll grab it.” Sandy choked out as she tried to hold her breath to keep from smelling him.

“You fucking bitch. It’ll be such a pleasure to see you beg me to stop when I fuck you.” Lefty pushed her so hard she flew across the room and landed in a heap against the wall. When she looked up, he was unzipping his pants and grinning down at her. She started to reach for her boot to pull out her gun but Scott walked into the room.

“Lefty, you’ll have plenty of time to do that later. Put it away for now.” Scott walked around him and crouched down in front of Sandy. If someone didn’t know him, people would probably say the man was handsome. He’d aged since the last time she’d seen him, but she could understand how he could fool women.

“I would’ve thought you found better friends by now, Scott.” Sandy knew she was walking on thin ice, but she had to stall for time.

“Sorry, babe. Lefty and I grew up in the same group home. We’re like brothers.” Scott rested his elbows on his knees.

"What about Dennis?" Sandy asked without thinking.

"He was like a brother too, but I still look out for number one." Scott was so casual about it that she wasn't sure if he even felt bad.

"You don't even feel bad about killing your friend?" Sandy shook her head.

"I didn't kill him." Scott chuckled, and Lefty scoffed.

"Scott, let Ruby go." Sandy glared at him.

"I'll let you be the one to release her." Scott held out his hand to her, and for a moment she was going to slap it away, but she realized she had to be civil until Ruby was safe. She took his hand, and he helped her to her feet. When he pulled her against him, she froze.

"Still so beautiful, Alexandra." Scott gazed into her eyes. She was so tempted to knee him in the balls that she'd actually lifted one foot off the floor but heard Ruby moan from the other side of the room.

"Let me get her out of here, and we can discuss my looks," Sandy said. At first, he didn't move, but when Ruby moaned again, he stepped back. Sandy hurried over to Ruby and crouched down in front of her. She pressed her fingers against Ruby's neck even though she'd heard Ruby moan a couple of times.

Ruby's pulse was strong making Sandy breathe a sigh of relief. She stood up and walked behind her but when she reached to untie Ruby's hands, but they weren't bound. Sandy glanced up at Scott. He propped himself against the wall with an amused grin on his face. Sandy moved in front of Ruby again.

"Ruby, can you lift your head," Sandy reached under Ruby's chin, but before she could lift her friend's face, Ruby grabbed her wrist. Ruby was smiling as she stood up and squeezed Sandy's wrist hard.

"I really should have been an actress." She sneered. "I can't believe you fell for all this."

"Ruby, what…" Sandy stammered as she tried to pull away. This couldn't be the same woman she'd called a friend for so many years. The same woman who had custody of Tessa's daughter.

"What am I doing?" Ruby released her arm with a shove and tilted her head. "I'm getting the attention I deserve."

"What's going on, Scott?" Sandy didn't dare take her attention away from the crazed look in Ruby's eyes.

“Why don’t you tell her, baby?” Scott wrapped his arm around Ruby’s shoulder. Sandy glanced back and forth between them.

“You see, I’ve known Scott a long time. Longer than you, actually. You see we both have a common goal. We want to destroy the people who ruined our lives. One of which is my dear sister.” Ruby smiled.

“What does Tessa have to do with this?” Sandy started to back away but stopped when she backed into Lefty.

“Tell her. I want to see her face when she finds out.” Lefty chuckled.

“I’m not talking about Tessa. I’m talking about my other sister or should I say half sister.” Ruby crossed her arms over her chest. Sandy wasn’t aware of Ruby, Tessa and Lane having another sibling. She knew that Ruby and Lane had a different father than Tessa.

“I didn’t realize you had another sister.” Sandy stepped forward to move away from Lefty, but he moved right behind her again.

“I know you didn’t. You also didn’t know that I not only have one half-sister but two and a half brother.” Ruby said.

"Tell her." Lefty pressed his body against her back, and Sandy had to swallow down the vomit rising in her throat when she felt his erection against her ass.

"Do you know who my father is, Alexandra?" Ruby narrowed her eyes and the saying, if looks could kill, came to mind.

"Tessa told me your father left just after Lane was born and your mom met Tessa's dad." Tessa had told her Ruby, and Lane hadn't seen their father since. Tessa's father raised them until he died. Her mother died a few years later, and Ruby took care of Lane and Tessa.

"That wasn't exactly correct. He left when our mom got pregnant by another man. Of course, that didn't stop him from going back to his home province and knocking up three other women." Ruby snarled.

"I'm sorry he did that." Sandy knew what it was like to have a father that was absent.

"Ask me his name." Ruby snapped.

"What's his name?" Sandy whispered.

"Stewart Elliot Michaels," Ruby said slowly, and all the air whooshed out of Sandy's lungs. For a moment, she thought someone had punched her.

"Wha… What are you talking about?" Sandy stammered, not sure if she even said it loud enough for them to hear.

"Haven't you figured it out? I'm your half-sister." Ruby stalked closer to her, and Sandy stared at her in disbelief.

How was that even possible? Her father never mentioned ever being in Yellowknife or having more children. Not that it was a surprise she had more siblings because she and Kim always figured with her father's history, there were more somewhere. It also made sense he never mentioned it because when had she ever sat down and had a real conversation with him. She'd even used the ruse of a serious conversation to put herself in her current situation.

"Look, honey, she's so happy about having another sister she's speechless." Ruby laughed.

"Wait until you tell her the rest." Lefty cackled behind her.

"How long have you known?" Sandy finally found her voice again.

"Since our dad called Lane and made him look out for you when you came to Yellowknife to whore around." Ruby snapped. "He didn't believe me when I told him and called me a liar. He said you were too smart to be bed hopping but then again like father like daughter."

"He called Lane?" Sandy couldn't believe Lane knew and hadn't told her. Was he involved in all this too? "Lane knows he's my brother?"

"Not until I told him, but he was warned to keep it to himself by daddy." Ruby's eyes looked wild. "It seems our father favored his Newfoundland children. Not his half-breed kids."

"I'm sure that's not true." Sandy couldn't believe her father was that cruel. "He wasn't a real father to any of us." Even though it was true, it was hard for Sandy to say the words at that moment.

"Tell her the rest." Lefty was pressing his groin against her ass again, and she wanted to turn and punch him.

"Ruby, tell her." Scott kissed Ruby's temple.

"You see Tessa thought you were a stranger that needed a friend. She wasn't the smartest girl in the world, as you know." Ruby rolled her eyes. "The little bitch was so easy to manipulate and so easy to kill." When Ruby laughed, Sandy's legs started to shake, but she managed to keep herself from falling.

"You were there when Scott killed her?" Tears burned her eyes, but she refused to let them fall and blinked them back.

"I thought you were so smart." Ruby laughed. "He didn't kill her, I did but not before I let Lefty have some fun with her. Scott just helped me get rid of the baby. That child was nothing but a bastard that should have never been born."

"But you took custody of her, and she loves you." Sandy couldn't believe what she was hearing. How could she not see how crazy Ruby was?

"If you mean Evie, of course, she loves me. I've given her everything she could ever want. Thanks to her father, that idiot O'Connor and you of course. Now we did have to get rid of her father. He thought I was going to marry him and raise Evie together. He wanted to tell her mother who Evie was."

Sandy's head was spinning. Ruby had completely snapped. One second she said she killed Tessa and got rid of the baby. The next minute she was going to marry the baby's father and tell the mother.

"Ruby, you hated Evie's father, and you let him see her?" Sandy studied her former friend. She didn't even look like the same person. Her eyes were crazed, and her face was tight with anger.

"I never hated him. I was in love with him before he knocked up that whore." Ruby growled. "Dennis was mine first."

Dennis? There was no way it could be the same, Dennis.

"Is it sinking in yet?" Scott smiled. Sandy glanced at him and then back to Ruby.

"Dennis got Tessa pregnant too?" Tessa had told Sandy her baby's father was a married man.

"You really are as dumb as Tessa. Come in here, Ted." Scott called out. A figure appeared in the doorway. At first, she didn't recognize him until he walked into the room.

"Dr. Butler?" The doctor that held her hand when he gave her the news her baby didn't make it shuffled into the room. The same man who told her it wasn't a good idea for her to see the baby because of the damage the bullet had done.

"I'm so sorry Ms. Churchill. I had no choice." He wouldn't look her in the eyes.

"Shut up, you coward," Lefty yelled.

"Now do you understand, Alexandra?" Ruby grinned.

"He told me my baby didn't make it, but he lied didn't he?" Sandy couldn't hold the tears back anymore and lunged at the doctor. "You bastard. You lied to me. You made me think my baby was dead." Sandy pinned him against the wall as she slammed her fists against his chest.

“I didn’t have a choice.” He didn’t make a move to stop her.

“You didn’t have a choice? You didn’t have a fucking choice?” Sandy pulled back her fist and punched him right in the face. The man crumpled to the floor and curled into a ball.

“They weren’t going to let me have my daughter if I didn’t. They were going to kill her.” He sobbed on the floor. “She was just a baby, and they’d already killed Tessa.”

“You’re Evie’s father? I thought Dennis was.” She was confused.

“Evie is not Tessa’s daughter, Alexandra.” Ruby snarled. “She’s yours.”

The statement had Sandy’s head spinning. She stepped back until her back was against the wall and wrapped her arms around herself. Before she could stop it, she bent over, and her stomach lurched emptying its contents all over the floor.

“Oh, and you shouldn’t have any trouble having children either. That was just something we made him say, for fun.” Scott laughed.

“How could all of you be so cruel?” Sandy stood up and wiped her mouth with her sleeve. “Ruby, how could you be so cruel?”

"Cruel is when you've got a father who abandons you to go make more children he cares about more than the ones he had with his wife. Just because she got pregnant with another man's baby by mistake."

It all made sense. Sandy's father slept around because of a broken heart. Maybe she was like her father more than she knew.

"So, Ted we no longer need you now." Ruby pulled a gun out of her pocket and pointed it at the man. He sat against the wall with blood running from his nose where Sandy had hit him.

"You said I only had to tell her the truth and I'd be free from my debt to you." The man held up his hands as if it would stop a bullet.

"Yeah, we can't take the chance of you going to the police. Your daughter will be fine. She has her step-mother to care for her." The next thing Sandy heard was the loud crack of the gun and Ted falling over. Sandy dropped to her knees and rolled him over. The bullet hit him right in the middle of his forehead. He was dead.

"Ruby. For God's sake. You just killed him." Sandy yelled.

"He's not the first, and he won't be the last." Ruby laughed as she slowly turned the gun and pointed it at Sandy. "Do you have any idea how long I've wanted to put a bullet in your head? I even had Scott bring women to me for practice."

"Sweet, Jesus." Sandy gasped. Scott didn't kill those women in Halifax. Ruby did. She was insane.

"Not yet, baby. We promised Lefty he could play with her for a while. The man's had a tent in his pants since Sandy got here." Scott pointed to the obvious erection that Lefty was sporting.

"It would serve her right that the last face she sees is his." Ruby laughed.

"Tell me something before you kill me." Sandy needed to stall. Keith and Ian had to know what was going on by now and where she was.

"Sure, it's not as if you'll live long enough for anyone else to tell you," Ruby said.

"What did Ian's ex-girlfriend have to do with all this?" Sandy couldn't figure out how they were involved.

"Had to get rid of her because she was asking too many questions. Her stupid brother gave her a USB stick that he stole from Lefty's computer. It had everything on it. She started asking questions about Keith's family. That's when Scott realized that you were screwing her ex. What a small world, huh?" Ruby paced the floor and rested the gun on her shoulder. We got rid of one of her brothers, but the other one slipped through our fingers." Ruby crouched down in front of her. "Everyone thought you were the smart one of the family. I'm the genius. I had you and Keith believing that Scott was the monster. He is I guess. He does like to have his way with women. Guess it's why he and Lefty are such good friends, but the truth is I'm the brains of this operation." She whispered. Probably because she didn't want Scott to hear what she was saying. Sandy glanced over Ruby's shoulder. Scott had his back to them talking to Lefty.

"You're a monster." Sandy spat at Ruby.

Ruby pulled back her hand and slapped Sandy across the cheek. Her head snapped to the side her ears rang. Nobody ever hit her in the face before.

"Don't ever speak to me like that," Ruby screamed. "I'm going to enjoy killing you, but first Lefty will make you suffer. Just so you know, he likes to play with his toys." Ruby stood up and turned. "Come on Scott. Let's go get a bite to eat while Lefty has his fun."

Sandy slowly reached down in her boot and clasped her hand around the handle of her weapon. As she slid it out, she kicked out her foot hard against the side of Ruby's leg. Ruby hit the ground screaming, and her gun skittered across the floor. Sandy raised her gun and aimed it at Lefty. One shot to the head, and he hit the ground. With Ruby rolling around on the floor Sandy stood up and aimed at Scott.

"Don't move a fucking muscle," Sandy yelled as she slowly made her way toward the doorway. She prayed to God someone was close. She was in such shock that her hand trembled. Ruby rolled around the floor shrieking in pain, and for the first time in her life, Sandy didn't care what happened to Ruby.

"You fucking bitch. I'll kill you." Ruby screeched.

"The only thing you're going to do is spend the rest of your life in jail," Sandy yelled, but she kept her gaze trained on Scott. His eyes darted to where Ruby's gun. "I'll put a bullet in your head before you move an inch," Sandy warned him.

"Sandy." Ian's voice echoed through the house.

"I'm here," Sandy called and turned as Ian, Keith and Lane hurried toward her. Before they got to her, something yanked her into the room. Scott wrapped his arm tightly around her neck and held Ruby's gun to her head.

"Kill her," Ruby screamed. "Kill her now."

"Ruby." Lane's voice boomed when he entered the room behind Keith and Ian. All of them held their weapons on Scott.

"Lane, he made me do it." Ruby wailed. "He threatened to kill me like he killed Tessa."

"Don't say a fucking word," Scott growled in Sandy's ear.

"Ruby, don't lie. That USB Gerry gave us had everything. Thanks to Scott's little habit of keeping a journal, we know everything." Lane's voice was cold as he glared down at his sister. "I don't know how I never saw what kind of a monster you were. You've killed so many people Ruby. Doesn't that bother you at all?"

"What do you care? The only ones you ever cared about were Tessa and Alexandra. When did you ever ask me if I needed anything?" Ruby wailed at Lane.

"Shut up all of you," Scott shouted, and it echoed in Sandy's ears painfully. The room became eerily quiet. "Now, I'm leaving here, and none of you will stop me. I'm taking Alexandra with me."

"Like fuck you are, Coates." Keith hadn't lowered his weapon since he walked into the room. Ian hadn't either nor had his gaze left Sandy. "The only thing you're going to do is drop that gun and let Sandy go because if you don't, I will put a bullet right between those two fucking beady eyes." Sandy didn't need to look at Keith to know her boss had his weapon aimed right where he said.

"Go ahead, and I'll put a bullet in her head before I hit the ground." Scott pressed the barrel of the gun against her temple and squeezed his arm tighter around her neck.

"Don't count on it, asshole," Ian growled. For some reason, Ian kept meeting her eyes and then quickly looking at the floor. "Sandy will drop you like a bag of shit," Ian emphasized the word drop, and at first, she didn't understand.

"If you don't want Alexandra's pretty little brain splattered all over this room, I suggest you put your guns down in front of you and kick them over to me." Scott pressed the gun harder against her head and not only did it hurt it pissed her off.

"You watch way too much television, Scott." Sandy laughed. "Nobody trained in law enforcement would ever do that. It's a stupid move."

"Shut the fuck up." Scott pushed her head with the gun.

"None of us will drop our weapons," Ian said slowly and again emphasizing the word drop.

"Doc, do you really think you worry me. You're a fucking doctor. What are you going to do, give me a tetanus shot?" Scott cackled.

"I'm just as precise with my shooting as I am with giving shots. Do you want me to prove it?" Ian snarled. "I can drop you in a second." This time when Ian emphasized the word drop, Sandy remembered. They'd watched a movie one night where the hostage let her body go completely limp and dropped to the floor letting the hero take out the villain. She remembered Ian saying it would probably work because the villain wouldn't expect it and dead weight would be hard for him to hold up with one arm.

"Kill her, you fucking idiot, before they kill you," Ruby screamed.

"Ruby, if you say one more word I will shoot you myself. Sister or not." Lane turned his gun on Ruby, and for the first time since the whole situation started, she saw fear in Ruby's eyes.

"You'd kill your own sister?" Ruby sobbed.

"You didn't have any problem doing it," Lane growled.

"Sandy, I'm going to count to three," Ian said, and Sandy nodded.

"Count all you want." Scott snapped.

"One," Ian said, and Scott backed up.

"I don't know what you think you're doing but it's not going to work," Scott yelled.

"Two," Ian continued.

"Shut the fuck up." Sandy could feel Scott trembling.

“Three, now,” Ian yelled, and Sandy let her body go completely limp. Scott wasn’t expecting it and lost his grip on her. Sandy didn’t see what happened after that because she covered her head and closed her eyes. The only thing she heard was three gunshots, and then someone fell on top of her. When she opened her eyes, Scott’s hand was hanging over her shoulder, and something warm and wet started to run down her neck.

“Get this asshole off me,” Sandy yelled.

Seconds later the weight disappeared and warm arms wrapped around her. She didn’t need to see to know it was Ian. She didn’t know when it started or how long she sat curled up in his arms sobbing, but she did.

“It’s over, kiddo,” Keith touched her head.

“She’s dead.” Sandy opened her eyes and looked up. Rex was crouched down over Ruby.

“Wha… what…happened?” Sandy stared at Ruby’s lifeless body.

“Scott shot her before we had a chance to stop him,” Ian whispered with his lips pressed against the top of her head.

“Sandy, who are the other two bodies?” Kurt and her father were in the doorway.

"That's Lefty." She pointed to where he dropped when Sandy shot him. "That's Dr. Butler." Sandy sat up straight. "Oh my God. Ian. My baby didn't die." She screamed.

"What?" Ian and Keith said together.

"Ruby and Scott blackmailed him. He was Tessa's baby's father." Sandy was shaking. "Evie's my daughter."

The room went completely quiet, and all eyes were on her as she explained everything in between broken sobs. As she was talking, she could tell that none of them believed what she was saying.

"Come on, kiddo. That's a little out there." Keith said.

"I'm kind of with Keith on this, Sandy." Ian looked down at her.

"I don't care what either of you believe. Evie's my daughter. It makes sense. I've always had a connection with her, and the doctor confirmed what they said." Sandy was on her feet.

"We can do a DNA test to make sure, but I wouldn't get your hopes up, sweetheart." Ian stood up and took her hands in his.

"I don't need a test to tell me the truth." Sandy yanked her hands out of his and ran out of the house.

“Sandy, get back here.” Keith’s voice echoed through the night. She didn’t stop and ran into the woods toward her father’s house. She didn’t care what any of them thought. She knew deep in her heart Evie was her daughter and test or not nothing was going to change her mind.

A police cruiser was sitting in her father’s driveway with the lights flashing and the engine running. What did it matter if Kurt fired her or worse charged her with stealing a cruiser? She was getting back to Hopedale and her daughter. Before she had a chance to sit in the car, strong arms wrapped around her waist and pulled her back against a body she knew well.

“Sandy. Stop.” Ian yelled as she struggled to get away from him.

“I’m going home and telling Evie the truth,” Sandy yelled.

“Sandy, Evie’s at the cabin with my parents.” Ian reminded her. She stopped struggling and let Ian turn her around. “I know you want this to be true, and I hope it is, but you can’t just blurt this out to Evie without being sure.”

“I can still have children.” Sandy cupped his face in her hands. “They made the doctor tell me I couldn’t. Should I not believe that either because I want that to be true.”

“There are ways to check that, too.” Ian held her head between his hands and used his thumbs to wipe the tears streaming down her face.

“I want Evie to be my daughter. I want to be able to have children. I want to have your babies.” Sandy sobbed as Ian pulled her into his arms.

“We’ll figure all this out.” Ian sat down on the grass and cradled her in his arms. Could they figure all this out? She wanted so much for Evie to be her daughter but she had to be realistic and look at where she'd gotten the information. She had to have proof before she could let herself believe any of it is true.

Chapter 27

Two weeks, and four days. That's how long they'd been waiting for the results for Sandy's and Evie's DNA results. Even with her father's connections, they weren't able to get them any faster. Ian held the envelope in his hand and waited for Sandy to get back from her appointment with the Gynecologist. Ian and his father had called in some favors to get her in with one of the best, and ten minutes after she left, the mailman showed up.

He paced back and forth between the living room and kitchen. When they returned from that horrible night, Ian never went back to his house. Sandy didn't want him to. He looked out the window for what seemed like the thousandth time.

"Daddy, what's wrong?" Lily stopped her coloring and looked up from the floor.

"I'm just waiting for Sandy to get home." Ian smiled at his daughter. Evie gazed up at him with the same curious eyes. He'd been studying her a lot over the last couple of weeks, and he could see the resemblance between the little girl and Sandy. The dark eyes, curly hair and the smile. Then he would convince himself he just wanted to see those things for Sandy's sake.

They hadn't told Evie about Ruby up to that point. They just told her that Ruby had to go away and wanted her to stay with Sandy. Evie was upset of course. It was Lane's suggestion not to tell the little girl. He'd decided to stay in Hopedale and get to know his new siblings as well as his father.

"I'm worried about her," Evie murmured.

"Why honey?" Ian crouched down.

"She said she had to go see a special doctor. Uncle Lane told me that grandpa was sick and had to see special doctors." They'd introduced Sandy's father to Evie as grandpa. Stewart finally admitted he was dealing with diabetes, he started to see a specialist to help regulate his insulin, but thanks to Ian's father, he was much better.

"Sandy's fine, sometimes we have to see special doctors for things to make sure we don't get sick." Ian smiled at her.

"Are you a special doctor?" Evie asked.

"I'm just a regular old doctor." Ian chuckled.

“You’re not just regular.” Ian looked up. Sandy was standing in the doorway of the living room with her cheek pressed against the doorframe.

“You’re very special, daddy.” Lily stood up and hugged him.

“Thanks, Lily.” Ian kissed her cheek. “Sandy and I have some things we need to figure out. So can you girls watch the baby monitor and let us know when Gracie wakes from her nap?” Both little girls nodded and went back to their princess coloring books.

Ian took Sandy’s hand as they walked upstairs to the bedroom. He didn’t want to take a chance of Evie and Lily overhearing the conversation. He closed the bedroom door and pulled the envelope from his back pocket.

“Is that what I think it is?” Sandy seemed afraid to touch it when he held it out to her.

“It's from the DNA lab in Ontario.” Ian shook the envelope, and Sandy stepped back.

“You open it.” Sandy wrapped her arms around herself and stared at the envelope as if it was about to bite her.

“Are you sure you don’t want to be the one to open it?” Ian wanted to make sure she didn’t want to be the first to read it.

“Ian, open the damn thing.” Sandy groaned and held her hands against her stomach.

He tore open the envelope and pulled out the papers inside. Sandy started to pace back and forth while he read the papers. He flipped through them until he found the page giving the results. He read it and then read it a second time to make sure.

“Ian, what does it say?” Sandy stood in front of him, and nobody could deny the hope in her eyes.

“Evie’s your daughter.” Ian grinned. Sandy covered her mouth with her hands and backed up toward the bed. When her legs hit the bed, she slowly sat down.

“Really?” Ian kneeled down in front of her and showed the paper.

“There’s no doubt.” He waited for her to jump up and down and scream but she just sat there staring at him.

“Really?” She asked again.

“Really.” Ian pulled her hands down from her mouth and squeezed them gently. “So even if you can’t have any more children. You have your daughter.”

“Oh, Ian.” She wrapped her arms around his neck and at first, he thought she was crying, and his heart sank.

“It’s okay, baby.” He tried to soothe her the best way he could.

“How could I forget?” She started jumping, and he realized she wasn’t crying she was laughing.

“What did you forget?” Ian pulled back and smiled at the look on her face.

“I forgot to tell you what the doctor said.” She started laughing again and fell back on the bed. The next thing he knew they were both rolling around laughing but Ian had no idea why he was laughing.

“What’s so funny?” Ian looked toward the door. Lily and Evie stood there staring at them like they were crazy.

“I’m not sure.” Ian sat up on the bed and tried to pull himself together.

“Gracie is throwing things out of her crib again. I think she’s finished with napping.” Lily jumped on the bed next to Sandy who was still giggling. “Sandy, are you okay?”

"I've never been better in my life, sweetie pie." Sandy sat up and the minute she saw Evie she burst into tears.

"You're sick. Oh, Sandy please don't leave me too." Evie wrapped her arms around Sandy's neck.

"I'm not sick, Evie. I'm just really, really happy." Sandy pulled back and held Evie's little face in her hands. Ian wanted to give Sandy time alone to tell Evie the news.

"Lily, I think Gracie is about to toss her mattress out. Why don't we go get her?" Ian held out his hand, but Lily didn't move.

"I want to know what is making Sandy so happy," Lily said.

"Ian, it's okay. You check on Gracie. I'm okay with Lily here." Sandy smiled at him, and all the air whooshed out of his lungs. Her smile left him breathless, but for some reason, it was even more beautiful at that moment.

The pungent aroma greeted him when he opened the door to Gracie's bedroom. It amazed him how someone so small and cute could make such a terrible smell.

"Little girl, you're way too sweet to be smelling like a sewer." Ian lifted her out of the crib and put her down on the changing table. He wrestled to get the dirty diaper off and clean her bottom before she could get her little hands into the mess. Gracie gurgled and said her first word.

"Dada," Ian stared down at her.

"Do you know you're not supposed to make your daddy cry while he's changing a poopy diaper?" Ian cleared his throat and blinked back the tears forming in his eyes. His two little girls had turned him into a big ball of mush.

"Dada," Gracie repeated, and Ian shook his head.

"I just realized. I'm outnumbered. Four women. Now I know how Nanny Kathleen felt with all us boys." Ian picked the baby up and tickled her belly. "Please tell me you're not going to put me through what my parents went through?"

"Maybe the next one will be a boy," Ian glanced toward the open door. Sandy stood with her hands clasped in front of her.

"Yeah, maybe," Ian said, but then he realized what she'd said. "Wait, the doctor told you everything's okay."

"Not only is everything okay but you may get your boy in about eight months." Sandy smiled. Ian realized his mouth hung open when Grace stuck her fingers inside.

"You're… pregnant?" Ian pulled Grace's fingers from his mouth. Sandy nodded as Evie and Lily ran in behind her with huge grins.

"I'm gonna be a big sister," Evie informed him.

"I'm already a big sister, but I don't mind having another brother or sister," Lily said. "It's fun being a big sister."

Ian placed Grace on the floor with Lily and Evie and slowly stepped toward Sandy. She smiled for a moment and then it disappeared.

"You're not happy about this are you?" Sandy tried to turn, but Ian grabbed her hand and tugged her into his arms.

"Are you kidding me? I've never been happier." Ian gazed into her glistening eyes.

"Four kids is a lot," Sandy whispered.

"My parents raised seven, and they're still alive." Ian placed a quick kiss on her lips.

"Your mom is a superhero." Sandy sighed.

"You're Superwoman." Ian placed soft kisses across her cheek to her ear.

"I'm a terrified, Superwoman." She said softly.

"You wouldn't be a Superwoman if you weren't a little scared," Ian whispered into her ear. "I'm sure when everyone finds out we'll have all the help we need but you've got to promise me something."

"What's that?" She smiled.

"No more secrets."

"No more secrets." She wrapped her arms around his neck and pulled his head down until they were eye to eye. "I love you."

"I love you too." Ian brushed his lips against her in a soft tender kiss. He wanted to spend the rest of his life with this woman.

Chapter 28

Sandy did not enjoy kneeling on the floor in the bathroom with her head over the toilet. Ian told her this would pass, but at sixteen weeks it was a little less than in the beginning, but she still didn't have to like it. It certainly wasn't as frequent with her first pregnancy either.

She closed her eyes and sat back on her heels. Hopefully, the wave of nausea eased. She hadn't heard anyone come in the bathroom, but a cold cloth pressed against her head.

"Thank you, whoever you are, you're my best friend right now." She sighed.

"You're a tough cookie, kiddo." Sandy opened her eyes. Lane was smiling down at her. Besides Keith, he was the only one that called her that.

"I know, but this sucks." She grabbed his hand, and he pulled her to her feet.

“I hate to add to your sucky day, but I need to talk to you.” His face looked serious. She didn’t want to hear anything bad, but he was her brother. It still seemed weird to think of Lane as her brother.

“Do I need to sit down for this?” Sandy walked out of the bathroom and plopped down on her bed.

“I probably should’ve told you, but I didn’t want to upset you. Especially with what Ruby put you through.” Lane hung his head and took a deep breath.

“Ruby.” Even saying the name made her chest hurt. It was still surreal that a woman she called a friend was responsible for so many deaths and such horrible things.

“Yes.” He sat next to her, and they both stared out through the window. The view still calmed her. “I had her cremated, and I’m taking her remains to Yellowknife. I’m going to put her down with my mom. I know what she did was unspeakable, but I need to give her a proper burial so she can rest in peace.”

“I agree.” Sandy didn’t believe in grudges or holding onto hatred. Especially, for someone who spent their lives doing hateful things. It only gave them more power. She wanted to move on with her life and be happy with Ian and the kids.

“The doctor’s remains were sent back to his wife,” Lane said. “I don’t know what they did with Scott and Lefty.”

"Me either and I really don't want to know," Sandy admitted.

"I'll be back in a couple of weeks." Lane stood up. "Rusty suggested I take some time off, but I don't think it was as much a suggestion, as it was an order." Lane rolled his eyes, and Sandy laughed.

"We all need a little down time right now," Sandy said.

"That cop Issac went to explain everything to the doctor's wife. She's going to keep Tessa's little girl. Would you believe they called her Teresa? It was Tessa's full name." Lane pulled his long hair back into an elastic and let out a long huff. "The doctor's wife called me. She said Issac gave her my number. Guess he must have gotten it from Rusty. She said if I ever want to come and visit with my niece, I'd be welcome anytime. I think I might do that."

No matter how strong Lane appeared, he was still a man who lost two sisters. It had to be incredibly difficult knowing one had killed the other.

"I think it's an excellent idea. I'm taking a little me time until after the baby is born. Plus, I want to make up for lost time with Evie." She'd never get the time back she lost with her daughter.

"Have you found out what you're having?" He asked.

"No, we want to be surprised." Again, there was a comfortable silence.

"I'll see you in a couple of weeks, kiddo. Call if you need me." Lane bent down and kissed her cheek. "I'm sorry I never told you about being your brother, and I'm so sorry I didn't see how crazy Ruby was. I knew she hated our father for leaving, but I never knew she'd go so far to hurt him or you."

"Let's just forget that and go from here." Sandy stood up and wrapped her arms around Lane's waist. Things were different now. When she first met Lane, she was at a point in her life when she had nobody. Now she had so many people that she loved and a budding relationship with her father.

"You deserve all the happiness you have, Alexandra." Lane hugged her and stepped back. "I guess I should stop using that name."

"I'd rather you call me Sandy."

"I'll see you soon, Sandy."

Sandy watched him leave the room and slowly lowered herself to sit on the bed. She picked up a drawing Evie placed on her night table and smiled. She'd drawn a picture of their family. With names above each stick figure on the page. Sandy glided her finger over the letters above one of the stick figures. It said, mommy. How could a word make someone so happy?

Sandy had been so nervous to tell Evie the truth that when Lily asked to stay in the room, Sandy felt a wave of relief.

Ian left the room, and Sandy suddenly felt a wave of panic run through her. She turned around and stared at the two little girls kneeling in the middle of her bed. They were such complete opposites. Lily with her strawberry blonde hair, bright blue eyes, and porcelain skin. Evie with her deep brown eyes, dark hair and olive skin.

"Sandy, are you sick?" Evie asked, and Sandy could see the concern on the little girls face.

"No, honey. I'm not sick, but there is something I need to tell you." Sandy knelt on the bed facing the girls.

"Is it bad?" Lily looked about ready to cry.

"I don't think it is. I believe that it's perfect." Sandy took Evie's hands.

"What is it?" Evie asked.

"Evie, do you remember when I told you about how I had a little girl who was in heaven?" Evie nodded, and Sandy took a deep breath. “Well, it turns out that she isn’t really in heaven. Some awful people took her away from me and lied about her going with the angels.”

“So she’s still alive?” Evie asked.

“Yes, they gave her to someone and made everyone think she belonged to someone else.” Sandy was so afraid to say the actual words because she was terrified of how Evie was going to react.

“Was it the bad people that hurt my mommy?” Lily asked.

“Yes, Lily but you don’t have to worry about them anymore,” Sandy reassured Ian’s daughter.

“I know, daddy told me.” Lily smiled.

“Where is your little girl?” Evie asked and Sandy’s eyes filled with tears.

“Evie, weren’t you listening? You’re her little girl.” Lily said excitedly.

“I am?” Evie’s eyes were as big as saucers, and for a moment it looked like she was about to cry.

“Yes, Evie. I didn’t know they’d taken you. They wanted me to believe my little girl died.” Sandy squeezed Evie’s little hands and pulled them up to her lips. “I love you with all my heart, and I promise you nobody will ever take you away again.”

“You’re my mommy?” Evie seemed to be finding it hard to get her head around it.

“Yes.” Sandy gazed into the little girl's sweet face.

“Is Ian my daddy?” Evie asked.

“No, honey. Your dad’s in heaven.” Sandy prayed she didn’t ask too many questions about Dennis. She’d tell her someday, but she was really too young to hear about all the terrible things that happened.

“It’s okay, Evie. I’ll share my daddy with you, and if Sandy marries him, he’ll be your daddy.” Lily started to bounce on the bed.

“It’s gonna be hard to remember to call you mommy,” Evie said.

“You can call me whatever you want, Evie.” Sandy hugged her and kissed the top of her head. “I just wanted you to know the truth.”

“I’m glad you’re my mommy.” Evie tipped her head back and stared up at Sandy.

"I'm glad too." Sandy smiled. "I also have a big surprise for both of you."

"What is it?" Evie and Lily were jumping on the bed excitedly.

"I probably should tell Ian first, but maybe it would be more fun to tell him together." Sandy took both little girls hands.

"Tell us." They squealed.

"I'm going to have another baby," Sandy whispered.

The next week Sandy lay in bed wrapped in the arms of a man she loved more than she ever thought she could love anyone. He'd been really quiet most of the day, but he'd been back and forth to his father's office putting the finishing touches on his own office. He said he was looking forward to working with his dad.

"Sandy, I love you." Ian kissed the top of her head.

"I love you too." She kissed his bare chest.

She was ready to close her eyes and get some sleep, but light flashed across the ceiling. She watched as it shot back and forth.

"Did you see that?" Sandy asked.

"Umm.... Yeah.... Hey, I've got something for you." Sandy lifted her head and looked into his beautiful blue eyes.

"What?"

"Get up and get dressed." He jumped out of bed and pulled on a t-shirt and lounge pants.

"Ian, it's after midnight." Sandy groaned.

"Just meet me in the backyard." Before she could argue, he was gone.

"Ian O'Connor, this better be good." She pulled on a tank top and pajama pants.

Sandy walked out into her yard and gasped. Lanterns covered the garden in the shape of a large heart, and Ian stood in the middle holding a bouquet of flowers.

"Come here." He held out his hand.

"What did you do?" Sandy moved toward him. When she was next to him, he took her hand. He held the flowers in front of her and started to speak.

"I'm holding a bouquet of roses and as you can see they are all different colors. The reason I picked roses because they mean something to you. You wear them on your body for the people you love."

"I do," Sandy admitted.

"First, you need to know the roses are thornless. It means love at first sight because I fell in love with you the moment I saw you." When he dropped her hand, she was confused. Then he continued.

"This rose is red, and it means, love, beauty, courage, and respect." He handed her the red rose. "I give this to you because I respect you so much for your courage and I love you more than I could even tell you." Sandy took the rose and listened as he continued.

"This white rose means many things one of them being, beauty. Sandy, you're the most beautiful woman in the world to me both inside and out. A beauty that no rose could ever compare to." He gave her the white rose and continued.

"These three pink roses each represent the three little girls sleeping inside but as you can see each is a different shade of pink. The dark pink is for gratitude because you've accepted my little girls and treat them as if they were your own. The pale pink is for joy, it's how I feel every day knowing you love me. The plain pink is the perfect happiness I feel when I see my life with you." He gave her the three pink roses.

"This yellow rose with the red tip means two things, falling in love and friendship. I give this to you because I've truly fallen in love with my best friend."

"Ian," Sandy whispered.

"Let me finish, this red and white rose signifies unity. The red and yellow means happy feelings. Again they show how happy I am that we're together. The color of this rose is coral I'm told, and it signifies desire. I've never desired anything more than this." He held out two red roses wound around each other. She looked at them and then at him. She had no idea what it meant.

"Ian, this is beautiful, but I don't understand." He chuckled and slowly dropped down to one knee.

"Two roses intertwined means this, Sandy, will you marry me?" In his hand, he held a gold ring with a diamond in the center of a golden rose. It was the most beautiful ring she'd ever seen. "Make me the happiest man in the world and say yes."

Sandy couldn't speak. The only thing she could do was nod and hold out her hand. Ian slipped the ring onto her finger and rose to his feet. He slid his hand around the back of her neck and lowered his head until his lips hovered above hers.

"I'm assuming that the nod meant yes." Ian smiled.

"Yes." She finally managed to squeak.

"Did you notice that there were only eleven roses?" He still hadn't kissed her, but she lost herself in his eyes.

"Not really but okay." She smiled.

"Aren't you curious why?" He seemed very anxious to tell her.

"Would it make you feel better if I said I was very curious?" She laughed.

"Yes." He gave her a quick kiss on the nose. "Eleven roses means the person that receives them is truly and deeply loved."

"You must have done an awful lot of research to find out all this." Sandy stood up on her toes and gave him a quick kiss on the lips.

"I did, and Jess helped me get the roses." He turned her around so she could see the yard of the house next door. Stephanie, Marina, Jess, and Kim were all crying on the other side of the fence.

"I'm guessing those lovely ladies were causing the light flashing on the ceiling in our room." She waved to them as they were leaving.

“Yes, they were very excited about helping.” He took her hand and led her into the house.

“Remind me to thank them tomorrow.” Sandy smiled.

“Right now I want to take my fiancée upstairs and make love to her.” Sandy giggled as Ian scooped her up into his arms and carried her upstairs. Her future husband was going to make love to her, and she couldn’t wait.

Epilogue

"Another one bites the dust." Aaron laughed.

"Feeling a little jealous, little brother?" Keith knew his youngest brother was not even thinking about following in the footsteps of the latest of the O'Connor brothers.

"Not in the fucking least." He laughed. "You better watch out, though. The way things are going, you could be next."

"I don't see that happening anytime soon." Keith rolled his eyes not because he never thought about settling down but because he married once and that ended tragically. He didn't love Tessa the way his brothers loved their wives. It was evident when he glanced around the room at John and Stephanie, James and Marina, and Ian and Sandy. Even his parents looked at each other with nothing but pure love.

"Doncha worry Keithy, she's out there. Closer than you think." This was all he needed. Dear Aunt Cora and her freaky cupid power.

"Seeing the future now are you, Aunt Cora?" Keith chuckled.

"I've seen her, Keithy." With that statement, she walked away, and he glanced at Aaron.

"Don't laugh, A.J. She's working on all of us." Keith chuckled when Aaron started to choke on the beer he was drinking.

He stood in the back of the hall watching his cousin Kristy try to make Bull jealous. It was working whether his friend wanted to admit it or not. He understood Bull's reluctance to date anyone. Until the man figured out who was screwing with his family and hurting them, he wasn't going to let anyone get close. Especially, someone he loved, and there was no doubting Bull in love with Kristy.

Sandy tossed her bouquet, and Jess caught it. Ian threw the garter and low and behold, Jason snatched it out of the air. Jason was of Nick's closest friends and one of the guys that played in his brother's band. Also, the same guy Jess dated and ended it. She avoided the man ever since. Watching as he slid the garter onto her leg was like watching a sinking ship. Especially when he stood up and leaned in to kiss Jess's cheek, and she pushed him away.

Once the bride and groom were carried out to the car with his grandmother ordering everyone to be careful with Sandy. At eight months pregnant, she looked about ready to burst, but in all the years he'd known her, Keith had never seen her happier. It was good to see her that way.

Then there was Ian. He'd started working with their father, and according to him, he was enjoying it. He loved being home in the evening with the kids and Sandy. If he was honest, Keith was a little jealous, but that wasn't something he was going to admit to anyone. He also still felt a little uneasy around Lily, but he'd come to figure out it was because she reminded him so much of himself. She was intense and didn't miss anything.

Once Ian and Sandy were gone, Keith could finally head home. It wouldn't have looked great for the best man to leave before the bride and groom. He was ready for a glass of wine and some soft mellow music. Nobody would ever believe by the gruff persona he portrayed that he ended his night like that. Especially, when they saw him drive down the road on a Harley with a leather jacket and biker boots.

Keith was glad his brother and Sandy decided to get married at the Hopedale country club. He could have a few drinks and walk home. It was a beautiful night, for March. A little brisk but nice for a walk. He loved Hopedale and living in the small town he grew up in gave him peace. Even with all the shit that had gone down over the last few years with his brother's wives.

He walked up to the security gate of his property or as his brothers called it, the compound. Keith bought the property when he was still living in Yellowknife. When he returned home, he had his construction company build his house. He'd also put up bunk houses for his employees to stay when they were in Newfoundland. Although, most of them seemed to be relocating to the quaint town.

He unlocked the gate and was headed inside when his phone buzzed. He pulled it out of his jacket and saw a number he didn't recognize. It was after midnight which meant it was probably a job and an urgent one.

"Keith O'Connor." He closed the gate.

"Mr. O'Connor, I need your help. Someone is threatening my family. I want to hire you to protect my daughter."

About the Author

Dreams can come true

First of all, I'm a wife and mother. I'm also a grandmother. That alone would fulfill any woman's life. To be honest, it does. But ...

I'm also a writer. Someone who loves to tell stories of love, suspense, heartache and of course happily ever after. For most of my life, I've written those stories for myself. A type of therapy, I suppose. I love the characters I create. They become part of who I am because there's part of me in them.

So... Now that you know this about me. I hope when you read my books; you fall in love with them.

You should also know that I'm a Newfoundlander. What is that you ask? Well, we're a proud people who live on an island, off the east coast of Canada. Some people believe Canada ends with Nova Scotia. It doesn't. If you keep going east, there is a beautiful island full of amazing people and magnificent scenery. That is where my stories are set because let's face it. The best stories always come from the places you know and love.

If there is anything else, you would like to know about me

Coming Soon

O'CONNOR BROTHERS

Book 4

Available May 20, 2017

He's hired to protect her,

But it may kill him.

O'Connor Brother Series

Book 1 & 2

Available on

Amazon and

Kindle Unlimited.

Also Available

Dangerous Therapy

Book 1

Officer John O'Connor is giving up on life after a terrible accident. His family are at their wits end when he refuses any kind of therapy. The only thing keeping him sane is his dreams of a beautiful woman he pulled in for a traffic violation months before.

Physical Therapist Stephanie Kelly is healing from a broken heart. When she is hired by Nightingale's personal care and physical therapy, she's ecstatic, but she's shocked when her boss asks her to take on a new patient. Shocked because the patient is her boss's nephew and he's not exactly keen on therapy. He's also the cop who's been heating up her dreams.

As Stephanie helps John get back on his feet, they grow closer, but someone is out to hurt Stephanie, or worse. After multiple attempts on her life, John's family tries to figure out who's after the woman he loves and stop them before it's too late.

Dangerous Abduction

Book 2

Widower James O'Connor has been fighting his growing attraction to his brother's sister-in-law for four long years, but when someone breaks into her home, destroying everything she owns, James takes her and her young son into his home. The break-in wasn't random. Marina and her son are in danger, and James swears to protect them, but can he keep them safe?

Marina Kelly dedicates her life to caring for her sweet little boy, Danny. Since she broke free from her abusive husband, she's sworn off men, but when James O'Connor keeps entering her thoughts and her dreams, it takes everything she has to keep her feelings hidden. Now, her sister and parents are out of the province, and she's in danger, Marina has no choice but to accept James's help and try to hide her attraction and growing feelings.

The attraction between them impossible to resist. Only her ex's family secret may tear it all apart. Can Marina and James unravel the family's hidden mystery without losing each other?

Rhonda Brewer

Keep up to date on all things new.

Follow me on

Facebook

Twitter

Instagram

Sign up for my newsletter and never miss another release!

http://www.rhondabrewerauthor.com/talk-to-me

Made in the USA
Columbia, SC
25 March 2020